ALREADY

MISSING

(A Laura Frost Suspense Thriller —Book Four)

BLAKE PIERCE

Blake Pierce

Blake Pierce is the USA Today bestselling author of the RILEY PAGE mystery series, which includes seventeen books. Blake Pierce is also the author of the MACKENZIE WHITE mystery series, comprising fourteen books; of the AVERY BLACK mystery series, comprising six books; of the KERI LOCKE mystery series, comprising five books; of the MAKING OF RILEY PAIGE mystery series, comprising six books; of the KATE WISE mystery series, comprising seven books; of the CHLOE FINE psychological suspense mystery, comprising six books; of the JESSE HUNT psychological suspense thriller series, comprising nineteen books; of the AU PAIR psychological suspense thriller series, comprising three books; of the ZOE PRIME mystery series, comprising six books; of the ADELE SHARP mystery series, comprising thirteen books, of the EUROPEAN VOYAGE cozy mystery series, comprising six books (and counting); of the new LAURA FROST FBI suspense thriller, comprising four books (and counting); of the new ELLA DARK FBI suspense thriller, comprising six books (and counting); of the A YEAR IN EUROPE cozy mystery series, comprising nine books, of the AVA GOLD mystery series, comprising three books (and counting); and of the RACHEL GIFT mystery series, comprising three books (and counting).

An avid reader and lifelong fan of the mystery and thriller genres, Blake loves to hear from you, so please feel free to visit www.blakepierceauthor.com to learn more and stay in touch.

BOOKS BY BLAKE PIERCE

RACHEL GIFT MYSTERY SERIES
HER LAST WISH (Book #1)
HER LAST CHANCE (Book #2)
HER LAST HOPE (Book #3)

AVA GOLD MYSTERY SERIES
CITY OF PREY (Book #1)
CITY OF FEAR (Book #2)
CITY OF BONES (Book #3)

A YEAR IN EUROPE
A MURDER IN PARIS (Book #1)
DEATH IN FLORENCE (Book #2)
VENGEANCE IN VIENNA (Book #3)
A FATALITY IN SPAIN (Book #4)
SCANDAL IN LONDON (Book #5)
AN IMPOSTOR IN DUBLIN (Book #6)
SEDUCTION IN BORDEAUX (Book #7)
JEALOUSY IN SWITZERLAND (Book #8)
A DEBACLE IN PRAGUE (Book #9)

ELLA DARK FBI SUSPENSE THRILLER
GIRL, ALONE (Book #1)
GIRL, TAKEN (Book #2)
GIRL, HUNTED (Book #3)
GIRL, SILENCED (Book #4)
GIRL, VANISHED (Book 5)
GIRL ERASED (Book #6)

LAURA FROST FBI SUSPENSE THRILLER
ALREADY GONE (Book #1)
ALREADY SEEN (Book #2)
ALREADY TRAPPED (Book #3)
ALREADY MISSING (Book #4)
ALREADY DEAD (Book #5)

EUROPEAN VOYAGE COZY MYSTERY SERIES

MURDER (AND BAKLAVA) (Book #1)
DEATH (AND APPLE STRUDEL) (Book #2)
CRIME (AND LAGER) (Book #3)
MISFORTUNE (AND GOUDA) (Book #4)
CALAMITY (AND A DANISH) (Book #5)
MAYHEM (AND HERRING) (Book #6)

ADELE SHARP MYSTERY SERIES
LEFT TO DIE (Book #1)
LEFT TO RUN (Book #2)
LEFT TO HIDE (Book #3)
LEFT TO KILL (Book #4)
LEFT TO MURDER (Book #5)
LEFT TO ENVY (Book #6)
LEFT TO LAPSE (Book #7)
LEFT TO VANISH (Book #8)
LEFT TO HUNT (Book #9)
LEFT TO FEAR (Book #10)
LEFT TO PREY (Book #11)
LEFT TO LURE (Book #12)
LEFT TO CRAVE (Book #13)

THE AU PAIR SERIES
ALMOST GONE (Book#1)
ALMOST LOST (Book #2)
ALMOST DEAD (Book #3)

ZOE PRIME MYSTERY SERIES
FACE OF DEATH (Book#1)
FACE OF MURDER (Book #2)
FACE OF FEAR (Book #3)
FACE OF MADNESS (Book #4)
FACE OF FURY (Book #5)
FACE OF DARKNESS (Book #6)

A JESSIE HUNT PSYCHOLOGICAL SUSPENSE SERIES
THE PERFECT WIFE (Book #1)
THE PERFECT BLOCK (Book #2)
THE PERFECT HOUSE (Book #3)
THE PERFECT SMILE (Book #4)
THE PERFECT LIE (Book #5)

THE PERFECT LOOK (Book #6)
THE PERFECT AFFAIR (Book #7)
THE PERFECT ALIBI (Book #8)
THE PERFECT NEIGHBOR (Book #9)
THE PERFECT DISGUISE (Book #10)
THE PERFECT SECRET (Book #11)
THE PERFECT FAÇADE (Book #12)
THE PERFECT IMPRESSION (Book #13)
THE PERFECT DECEIT (Book #14)
THE PERFECT MISTRESS (Book #15)
THE PERFECT IMAGE (Book #16)
THE PERFECT VEIL (Book #17)
THE PERFECT INDISCRETION (Book #18)
THE PERFECT RUMOR (Book #19)

CHLOE FINE PSYCHOLOGICAL SUSPENSE SERIES
NEXT DOOR (Book #1)
A NEIGHBOR'S LIE (Book #2)
CUL DE SAC (Book #3)
SILENT NEIGHBOR (Book #4)
HOMECOMING (Book #5)
TINTED WINDOWS (Book #6)

KATE WISE MYSTERY SERIES
IF SHE KNEW (Book #1)
IF SHE SAW (Book #2)
IF SHE RAN (Book #3)
IF SHE HID (Book #4)
IF SHE FLED (Book #5)
IF SHE FEARED (Book #6)
IF SHE HEARD (Book #7)

THE MAKING OF RILEY PAIGE SERIES
WATCHING (Book #1)
WAITING (Book #2)
LURING (Book #3)
TAKING (Book #4)
STALKING (Book #5)
KILLING (Book #6)

RILEY PAIGE MYSTERY SERIES

ONCE GONE (Book #1)
ONCE TAKEN (Book #2)
ONCE CRAVED (Book #3)
ONCE LURED (Book #4)
ONCE HUNTED (Book #5)
ONCE PINED (Book #6)
ONCE FORSAKEN (Book #7)
ONCE COLD (Book #8)
ONCE STALKED (Book #9)
ONCE LOST (Book #10)
ONCE BURIED (Book #11)
ONCE BOUND (Book #12)
ONCE TRAPPED (Book #13)
ONCE DORMANT (Book #14)
ONCE SHUNNED (Book #15)
ONCE MISSED (Book #16)
ONCE CHOSEN (Book #17)

MACKENZIE WHITE MYSTERY SERIES
BEFORE HE KILLS (Book #1)
BEFORE HE SEES (Book #2)
BEFORE HE COVETS (Book #3)
BEFORE HE TAKES (Book #4)
BEFORE HE NEEDS (Book #5)
BEFORE HE FEELS (Book #6)
BEFORE HE SINS (Book #7)
BEFORE HE HUNTS (Book #8)
BEFORE HE PREYS (Book #9)
BEFORE HE LONGS (Book #10)
BEFORE HE LAPSES (Book #11)
BEFORE HE ENVIES (Book #12)
BEFORE HE STALKS (Book #13)
BEFORE HE HARMS (Book #14)

AVERY BLACK MYSTERY SERIES
CAUSE TO KILL (Book #1)
CAUSE TO RUN (Book #2)
CAUSE TO HIDE (Book #3)
CAUSE TO FEAR (Book #4)
CAUSE TO SAVE (Book #5)
CAUSE TO DREAD (Book #6)

CHAPTER ONE

Veronica fought desperately, determined not to give up. She wasn't going to die here. Not like this. Not today.

It was hard to move, even a little bit. Whoever did this to her had made sure of that. It started with her hands, bound behind her back so tightly that she was losing feeling in her fingers. Her ankles, too, were bound, preventing her from doing much more than shuffle around on the tiny platform she had been placed on. The gag in her mouth prevented her from crying out, from calling for help. Even if she could, she doubted very much that anyone would be able to hear her.

She had no idea where she was. She had never been anywhere like this before. It looked like an abandoned warehouse, with a few broken windows letting in light that danced through the dust. That was the only thing that allowed her to see. Besides that, the room was dim, so dark that she couldn't see to the far sides. She was sure the person who had put her here was gone, but it was so dark there could be anything out there in the shadows. It had taken her eyes a long time to adjust to the darkness, to show her the immediate surroundings and the danger she was really in.

Not that she had been under any impression she was safe. The ropes and the gag, they would have been a dead giveaway. But even if they hadn't, the third rope, the one that was around her neck, would have given her the clue.

Her last memory was simply walking to her car at home before she'd woken up here hours ago and found herself hauled to her feet. Before she could even react, before she had enough awareness of what was going on to begin to struggle, the rope was around her neck, a noose tightened until it was resting against the place where her skull met her spine. She could still feel it now, brushing against her hair every single time she moved, making her terrified gasps for breath shorter and shorter.

She knew exactly how many hours it had been that she had stood here, trying to fight the ropes, trying desperately to figure out a way out of this. She knew exactly how long, because the ticking clock around her neck told her.

That was one of the first things she had made out, as her eyes adjusted. It had been terrifying, the feeling of something clunking against her chest, not knowing what it was. She thought it might be a bomb. But that would have been unnecessary because the noose was threat enough. Instead, there was only the clock.

It was digital, more of a timer than a traditional clock. When she had finally been able to read it, moving her head and tossing the clock against her own chest until it turned the right way, she saw that eleven hours and fifty minutes had passed. Out of a total of twelve, she supposed.

She had spent over eleven hours trying to free herself.

She was finding it hard to breathe now, not because the rope was getting tighter but simply because she was so afraid for her life. There was nothing around her but the small and fragile-seeming wooden platform on which she stood. It was flimsy enough to bounce slightly when she tried to move around, and more than once she had almost stepped off the edge with her shuffling feet only to scramble backwards in horror. She knew the rope was tight enough around her neck that she would not simply slip through if she fell.

She would hang.

She would die.

There were only ten minutes left. No one had spoken to her, no one had told her what would happen when the timer was over. But Veronica wasn't stupid. She could work this out herself. The platform, it was going to drop. She was sure of that. She had been sure of it since the moment she had turned around enough, taking tiny shuffling steps and trying not to strangle herself on the rope, to see that it was hinged at one end.

It was going to drop, and she couldn't get out of the ropes.

She breathed raggedly, through sobs, barely able to see anymore. She could not reach up to wipe the dust and tears and the sweat out of her eyes. She had tried for so long to get out of the ropes that it felt like her shoulder was dislocated, her arms strained, the skin on her wrists and thumbs and fingertips red raw. There was nothing around her she could use. No sharp hooks, no nails sticking out of the wood, not even a splinter. The rope was tight enough that she could not even walk all the way to the far edge of the platform, try to hook the rope around the hinge and use that somehow. Even if she could, she wouldn't dare. She could end up triggering the mechanism that way, hanging herself before the timer even went off.

2

When she had had twelve hours left to go, it had seemed like she might manage it. But now she had nine minutes, and it was beginning to feel more and more like she had nothing else to risk.

She was desperate. She had to get out of here. She couldn't die, not like this. Not today. She had so much to live for: her friends, her family, her boyfriend. Her job, which she loved. There were people who relied on her. She wasn't going to give up.

She'd been afraid. This whole time, she'd been terrified. Of falling. Of the rope around her neck getting tighter. Of so many things. But there was on fear in her mind now and one only: the fear of not getting off here before the platform dropped.

And all her other fears came secondary to that. Even the fear of great pain. Of mutilation. There were eight minutes to go. This was survival. This was it. She had to do this now.

She cried out through the gag, screaming with the force it took to push her shoulders apart one more time. She counted seconds in her head, keeping track of the time she had left. Trying to push herself to strive for longer. It felt like every muscle, every bone in her upper torso was going to pop, to snap open. And her skin - the skin on her wrists - it felt like it was tearing, coming off, ripping away from her. Seven minutes. She had to keep going. It didn't matter about the pain anymore. It didn't matter about what happened to her hands. She could lose a hand. She could do this. She could lose a hand instead of her life.

Six minutes to go. She pushed, straining, her eyes squeezed tightly closed against the pain and the dust in the air and the tears that streamed from them, still screaming raw and horse, her throat scrubbed until it was a mess of broken glass. Something was happening. Something was moving. She could almost...

She gasped for breath, panting, having to stop the exertion for a moment. Five minutes. She didn't have time for this. There was no time to regain her strength. She could feel something hot and wet on her hand, dripping from the edge of her finger, just at the edge of where her sensation still remained. Blood. She knew it was blood. It didn't matter. Only one thing mattered.

She had to get off this platform. Four and a half minutes. She took a breath and pushed again, leveraging one arm down and then the other one up, trying with all her might to just squeeze one hand out. Just one hand was all she needed. The ropes could remain on the other hand, and it wouldn't matter. She could use it still to rip the noose from her neck, to lunge for the end of the platform, to scramble over the hinge and out of the line of danger.

3

Four minutes. She pulled, screaming, feeling more pain than she'd ever felt in her life. All the exertion of the previous hours had taken it out of her, all the pushing, all the raw edges of her skin. All the attempts to twist her fingers so that she could untie the ropes, searching for a loose end. All the attempts to force the ropes apart, both with her hands and with her feet. The attempts to duck her head, to push back so that the noose just slipped right over her head, which had only tightened it. They had all led to this moment. Three minutes to go.

She was so weak, so tired. She couldn't bear the idea of carrying on. But she couldn't stop. She couldn't give up. This was it, the moment that her life hinged on. It was now or nothing. She pushed, squeezing and crying through the pain, a raw scream ripping its way from her throat when she thought she'd had no sound left to give.

And her wrist came free.

Her eyes flew open, gasping for breath and panic, the pain now beginning to set in even more. She couldn't look at her hand. She didn't dare. She kept it behind her back, ducking her head to look at the clock -

No. No, she had miscounted! She had been weak, almost delirious with the pain, unable to hold on -

Seconds remained, only seconds, and she had to get off, she had to reach out and yank the noose from her neck -

Her hands were still on it when the platform fell, and all she could do was to scramble helplessly, one hand bloodied and useless, the other not strong enough even if it had a partner. She scrambled, trying to dig her fingers under the rope to relieve the pressure crushing her windpipe, but she was not strong enough. She felt her legs kicking in the air, a terrible pressure in her head, the edges of her vision turning black as she groped desperately for a breath.

The black filled everything, and Veronica stopped kicking, her hands falling limply at her sides for the final time.

CHAPTER TWO

Laura didn't stop moving until she reached Nate's front door. She stood in front of his neat little house – the kind of house she could have been living in, if it wasn't for the whole messy divorce and the alcohol and all the rest of the last few years of spiraling – and hesitated for the first time.

She literally froze with her hand up in the air, about to knock on the door but not quite getting there. For a brief and ridiculous moment, she felt a bit like a cartoon character, a larger-than-life movie moment that didn't seem real. Imagine, getting all the way here and then losing your nerve.

But that's what was happening. She had been fueled during the whole drive from her apartment to here by a fierce determination that had pushed her onwards. She had decided she was going to tell him everything. He was her partner, after all, and he deserved to know the truth. If he didn't, things were never going to be the same between them again. He had already figured out that she was lying to him, and there was no way she could brush it off any longer.

Nathaniel Lavoie was a great FBI agent, and he wasn't going to be fooled by any more excuses she could give him.

The only option she had was to come clean, if she wanted to keep him as her partner. And she did. Getting back partial custody of her daughter, coming off another brutal case, knowing that staying on the wagon had the power to bring her back to the life she really wanted - all of that put together was showing her the things that she really cared about. The things that really mattered. Lacey, her daughter. Her job. And her personal relationships with the people she cared about.

Nate was one of them, and even though she had been scared for such a very long time about admitting to anyone that she had psychic abilities, Laura recognized that it was now or never.

Except...

Well, it would be a lot easier for her if it was never.

There were so many arguments for telling him, and so many arguments against it. When she'd been sitting at home, she had realized beyond any shadow of a doubt that she had to tell him right now. But here, standing right in front of his door, those arguments seemed to disappear into the void. She could barely even remember what they were. Instead, all she could picture was the way he would look at her. That way he might reject her.

Laura dropped her hand back down to her side and turned to move away.

Which was exactly when the door opened.

"Laura?" Nate asked, his deep voice a rumble in the quiet street. She could not exactly ignore it. He was right behind her. Laura froze, for a moment wishing she could just simply disappear.

But unfortunately, her powers did not seem to extend that far. She turned, looking up at him guiltily.

He was leaning casually in his own door frame, but even so, Nate still towered above her. In casual clothing, just a tight t-shirt and a pair of loose jeans, Nate somehow seemed even more intimidating than he did when he wore his FBI standard suit. The thick muscles of his arms rippled under his Black skin as he moved, and the heavy frown above his eyes did nothing to help Laura's nerves.

"Hi, Nate," she said, trying to inject a bit of false brightness into her voice and absolutely failing. "I was just in the neighborhood..."

She trailed off, unable to think of a way to end the sentence. She was just in the neighborhood, and decided to stop by and see the person who demonstrably was not talking to her and had not been for days? She should have been able to come up with a better excuse than that, surely.

"How did it go with your custody hearing?" Nate asked, making Laura hang her head. Of course, he would remember to ask. Of course, despite everything that had happened between them lately, he was never going to be angry enough with her to forget the most important things in her life. He was just that good of a guy.

"It went great," Laura said, allowing herself to smile just slightly. "I got weekends."

"That's amazing," Nate said. The smile that crossed over his face was just as brief as hers, but it was genuine. The tension behind it wasn't going anywhere. "Why are you here?"

Cutting right to the chase. Damn. Laura took a breath. She had a feeling that anything less than the truth was not going to convince him, not right now.

"I came here to talk," she said. "About... well. You know."

"I hope I do," Nate said, raising an eyebrow. He looked her up and down, assessing. Trying to gauge whether this was going to be one more let-down, no doubt. "You're ready to tell me the truth?"

6

Laura tucked a strand of her blonde hair behind her ear and nodded, swallowing nervously at the same time. She didn't trust herself to answer him. She had a feeling her vocal chords were going to say *no*, all on their own.

"You'd better come in," Nate said, moving aside to allow her through the doorway.

Laura moved through the house into a comfortable yet minimalist living room, perfectly suited to Nate's style. Everything was dark wood, the furniture outfitted in brown leather, only a few framed photographs up on a bookcase to the side of the room. Laura passed by them, catching a glimpse of Nate in his dress uniform from the day he had joined the police force. She knew he'd been a serving officer before he joined the FBI. Then there was an image of him with his parents, looking much younger, clearly a family photograph.

There was no photograph of a woman anywhere in the house, not one that he wasn't related to. Laura knew that his last relationship had ended somewhat badly, and he hadn't settled down with anybody else yet. Still, the bachelor life seemed to suit him. His home was clean and tidy, the shelves stacked with well-thumbed books. She actually envied him. He seemed so comfortable here. Her own apartment was full of second-hand, rickety furniture and bad memories. It was ironic, she thought, that she was only coming here for the first time now that their relationship was so rocky. Years of friendship, and she'd never found a reason to visit.

She took a seat on the sofa, more to keep delaying the inevitable moment than because she needed to sit. Nate settled into an armchair, set at a slight angle to the sofa, both of them facing towards a large screen television. Beside him on the coffee table was a steaming mug of coffee, and Laura found herself wishing for one. Maybe if she asked him to fix her one, that could delay the conversation even more as well...

"Well, then?" Nate asked. "Are you going to tell me?"

So much for that.

Laura took a breath. She reminded herself that she had come over here for this purpose. No matter what happened now, this had to be the right thing to do. She had already decided that so many times. She wasn't going to change her mind again, not this time. She wasn't going to get a choice. Nate was looking at her expectantly, and she needed to say something, needed to find some way to deliver the news that would soften the blow. That would make it sound more believable. That would...

"I'm psychic," she blurted out.

Nate stared at her.

"Laura," he said, his voice serious and full of rebuke. "I've already told you I'm not going to take any more of these lies. You need to tell me the truth, right now. Or this is it, I'm not going to take any more. I'm going to go right to Rondelle and get a transfer and tell him that I have serious doubt in your abilities. Or at least, where they come from."

"No," Laura said, deep panic setting in already. This wasn't how it was supposed to go. She should have thought this through ahead of time, come up with some kind of speech. Prepared herself. Just blurting it out was the worst possible thing she could have done. She needed to backtrack, explain, make him see. "Nate, I'm being serious. It's not a lie this time. That's how I know things. I get these... these visions. I see what's going to happen."

Nate stared at her again for a long period of time, or so it felt to her. It must realistically have only been a few seconds, but every moment was dragging on into eternity. At the same time, it was all moving far too quickly. She felt out of control. Like she was scrambling to keep up.

"I mean," she said, trying to make this better, any way that she could. Trying to make up for the mistakes her mouth had already made, only by piling on more. "It makes sense, if you think about it. I mean, if you really think about it. All the things that I know. How else could I know them? I just see them before they happen. I see these visions of possible futures. They don't always come true, because we can prevent them. Sometimes they're completely wrong. But that's okay, because it means that we made a difference. Do you see what I mean?"

"Not really," Nate said, with a slow blink. He narrowed his eyes now, looking at her closely. She was beginning to feel like a specimen under glass. "Laura... you've been under a lot of stress lately."

It was her turn to blink.

Stress?

"I... yes," she admitted, nodding. "I have. There's been a lot going on. The custody hearing for Lacey. All the cases we've been working. Having to keep this all a secret, even though I knew you suspected something. And Amy, of course – getting her away from her abusive father, making sure it would stick this time. And..."

She almost said, *and knowing that you were going to die soon, but not knowing how* – but she stopped herself. That would be too far, right now. Too much for him to know. She would tell him, but... not yet. Not until he was comfortable with the concept as a whole.

8

If he got comfortable with it.

"Right," Nate said. "And I know that is a heavy burden to bear. All that stress. I'm sure you haven't been sleeping properly. You've been fighting not to take a drink, too, and I know that's been hard for you. It's been a lot, hasn't it?"

"Of course," Laura said, staring at him in a way that she was sure made her look stupid. Where was he going with this? It was like he hadn't reacted at all to the news that she was psychic, not after first declaring it a lie. Was he convinced it was true, now? Did he believe her? Or...

"And in our line of work?" Nate shook his head. "Law enforcement people like us need therapy at the best of times, Laura. The things that we have to deal with on a daily basis, I don't need to tell you. They can be overwhelming. There's a reason that they encourage us to go for counseling, you know."

"I know," Laura said, tilting her head slowly as she looked at him. Was he saying...?

"The thing is," Nate said, steepling his hands together in front of himself, leaning in and looking at her intently. "There's no shame in it, no shame at all. The most important thing is that you get the help you need. And if you've been seeing things, especially things that disturb you, you should talk to someone about it."

"I'm telling you right now," Laura said, holding on desperately to the slim sliver of hope that he actually did believe her for just a second longer, even though she knew she was only being dense.

"No, not me," Nate said, rubbing the light stubble around his chin with one hand before looking at her intently again. "Laura, I think you need to go and see a professional. Someone who can really help you out with all of this. Like I said, there's no shame in it. I saw the counselor for a few sessions after my first shot fired in the line of duty. It's never easy, dealing with something like that. And you've had your share of it. We probably should have seen this sooner, made sure that you had someone to talk to earlier on."

"I…" Laura paused, staring at him. She felt like a fish in a tank. Her eyes as wide open as her mouth was. And him, staring back at her like she was a freak.

No, not like that, she realized. If he believed her, that was when he would probably look at her like a freak.

He was looking at her with pity. Like she needed help.

She couldn't believe it. She'd finally come clean, told him the truth like he wanted. And now…

9

It would have been one thing for him to yell at her. To tell her to quit lying. To stop trying to pull the wool over his eyes. But he was just sitting there, looking at her like she was someone damaged, someone broken, who needed help getting put back together.

He believed her. At least, he believed that she thought she was telling the truth. He'd just skipped right on to believing she was delusional.

"Nate," Laura said, taking a breath, trying to measure her words more. Maybe if she sounded less panicked. Maybe if she talked him through it, step by step. "I'm not... seeing things. Not like *that*. It's real. I see what's going to happen, and then it happens. Or, it doesn't – so long as we step in and change it. It's an ability I have."

"You have damn good intuition, Laura," Nate said, shaking his head. "I'm sorry you've been struggling with this. Let's talk to Rondelle when we're next at HQ, alright? There are free sessions you can take up as part of the Bureau. He'll want to make sure you're being looked after; I know he will. Just hang in there until then. We'll get you through this."

Laura opened her mouth to try again, but then closed it. What was the point? He'd already made up his mind. He didn't believe it was true.

Who would?

No one would ever think it was possible for her to see the future like that. It sounded like something out of a movie. A fairy tale. A complete myth. In all the years she'd been searching, Laura had never even been able to find someone else with the same abilities that she had. And now, she was expecting Nate to believe her?

He was an FBI agent. A man who dealt in facts, proof, evidence. And she had none. She couldn't prove what was inside her own head. Couldn't show it to him.

Laura got up from her seat.

"Are we... okay now?" she asked. She didn't need to put on the way her voice shook or add doubt to her eyes. She had come here to fix their relationship. If she hadn't even managed to do that...

"We're okay," Nate promised her, getting up to walk her to the door. His voice was gentle. It made her want to scream. "Just so long as you get the help you need, this is all going to work out. See? It wasn't so bad in the end, telling me."

"No," Laura said, distantly. "I guess not."

But as she turned to walk back to the door, back to her car, there was almost a numbness settling over her.

He hadn't believed a single word she'd said.

Was she ever going to be able to find someone who would help her with this burden she had to carry? Someone who would understand?

Right at that moment, it didn't feel as though she was ever going to be anything but lost and alone and haunted by demons that no one else in the world had to see. But tomorrow, she reminded herself, she was going to see someone who really needed her – and that was one very strong reason to keep going.

CHAPTER THREE

The next day was a new day. It had to be.

Laura sat in her car at the steering wheel, her hands still resting in the ten and two positions. She had to get last night out of her mind. The way Nate had reacted. She had to forget about it, at least for a short while.

She needed a clear mind for this. No distractions. And definitely no inner monologue telling her that this was going to go just as badly as that had.

This was important, and Laura couldn't let whatever was going on in her personal life bleed into it. Even if it was becoming increasingly difficult to distinguish between her personal life and work these days.

Laura took her hands off the wheel with a deep breath and used that same momentum to reach for the door of the car and open it. She had to get moving. It was already the time that she'd said she'd be here.

She looked up at the house as she left the car, trying to gain a clear first impression. It was a big house, for sure. Not quite as big as Amy's old house. Governor Fallow, her father, had purchased an impressive colonial-style manse for his family. This one was a little more modest.

But the yard out front was neatly mowed, the brickwork was clean, and the windows shone in the sun. it was bigger than any house Laura had ever lived in, in her life. It was nice. A good neighborhood. Quiet, except for a couple of young children playing in a yard down the street.

Everything looked good. So, why did Laura have a pit in the bottom of her stomach when she looked at it?

It wasn't hard to self-psycho-analyze. She was probably overreacting, projecting. When she'd responded to a report of a kidnapping earlier in the year and rescued six-year-old Amy, the child had seemed safe at last. Until a vision in the hospital room showed her Amy being beaten by her own father, the Governor who put on a family-friendly face to the world but was privately dealing with serious anger issues.

And if that hadn't been enough, then what followed would definitely have made anyone paranoid about the girl's safety. Wading into the family home herself and forcibly removing Amy from the situation, and even retrieving videotaped proof of the beatings, should have been the end of it. But instead of staying in care, Amy had ended up going back with her father after he pulled strings behind the scenes.

And then she'd been in the house when her father went on one of his rampages, took things too far, and beat his own wife to death. If Laura hadn't had another vision warning her, she'd have ended up another victim.

Laura walked up the short path to the front door, flanked by a white-painted portico that added a suitable amount of stately drama to the property. She was going to get the chance to touch Amy again today, and she was already mentally bracing herself for another vision. Another sign of calamity.

Amy had been taken in by her uncle, a certain Dr. Christopher Fallow. A man of whom Laura had absolutely no experience. The fact that he'd agreed to let her see the child again had to be a good sign, but how much of one she wasn't sure. Was it just going to be a smokescreen? An attempt to fob her off with a family-friendly face, the same way that John Fallow had always operated?

She needed to know for sure.

Laura knocked, loudly, feeling the power of that knock reverberate through her hand even as it shook. She was nervous, badly so. Afraid. Not for herself, but of what she was going to find. Of the fight not yet being over.

She knew she was going to do whatever it took to make sure that Amy was safe. But that, in itself, was the scary part. Putting everything on the line. Never quite knowing whether it would be enough.

"Hello?"

The door opened with a rush, and Laura found herself standing there agog, somehow not ready for it to happen even though she'd been the one to knock. She took in the man who stood in the doorframe immediately, her brain marking comparison points to John Fallow.

He had the same dark hair as his brother, the same kind of build. Tall. But he was slimmer, actually, as she looked at him, and his beige slacks paired with a white button-down shirt seemed somehow more casual than anything John Fallow would ever wear. He was never not in a suit. Even the day Laura had watched him carted off by the local police, covered in his wife's blood, he had seemed somehow stiff and formal.

Christopher's eyes, too, were softer. The same dark shade of brown, but softer somehow. There were more fine laughter lines around them. He was in his late thirties, Laura estimated, not yet showing any signs of gray in his hair. Fit, slightly tanned, and with a wide smile that showed straight white teeth, almost dazzlingly so.

"You must be Laura," he said, his initial doubt cleared up.

Laura found her voice, checked herself, cleared her throat. "Hello," she replied. "And you're Christopher Fallow."

"That I am," he said, with another wide grin. His mouth was still open, like he was about to say something else, but whatever it was, it was cut off immediately. There was a kind of screeching sound from somewhere inside the house, and before Laura had time to process it, she was being tackled around the legs by a streak of pink.

A streak of pink that turned out, once she'd managed to stop herself from falling over, to be Amy Fallow.

The blonde-haired, blue-eyed child looked up at Laura with an expression of absolute joy and excitement, hugging her tight around her legs. "You came to see me," she said, making Laura blink her eyes quickly twice to clear any moisture from them as she looked down at her. With the instinct of a mother, she found herself reaching for Amy in return, laying her hand on top of one of her tiny arms and using the other to stroke her hair out of her face.

"Of course, I did," Laura said, waiting for the vision to come. Her skin was in contact with Amy's. She tried to concentrate, to will something to come. She took a deep breath, honed in on her senses. "I said I would, didn't I?"

Nothing was coming. No single hint of anything. If there was something bad coming in Amy's future, then Laura was none the wiser to it.

Of course, the frustrating thing was that a lack of vision didn't mean she was safe. It just meant that, for whatever reason, Laura wasn't having a vision.

But Amy was smiling, and she was clean and well-dressed and looked healthy, and that was a good start. It just wasn't a vision that Laura was going to trust entirely, not until she had more evidence to support it.

"Would you like to come inside?" Christopher asked, his face hovering behind a kind of pleased look at Amy's happiness and something else, something Laura found it hard to put her finger on. Almost like he was put out.

"Sure," Laura said. "Amy, why don't you show me your new room?"

14

"Yeah!" Amy cheered, disengaging from her legs and immediately dashing back inside with the kind of enthusiasm only a six-year-old could muster.

Behind her, Christopher stepped back uncertainly, hesitating. Laura zeroed in on that immediately. He didn't look happy about her request. But a moment later he stepped fully aside, gesturing her in. "It's upstairs, first door on the left," he said – a necessary instruction, given that Amy had already shot away out of sight.

Laura's mind was in full FBI mode, searching every corner as she moved through the house and up an impressively wide staircase towards the upper floor. She was looking for small signs that might give something away: a smudge of blood in a corner that hadn't been properly cleaned up, anything that was broken or looked newly repaired since that could be a sign of violence. Everything seemed so neat and proper. Wasn't that in itself a red flag? He'd known she was coming over.

Laura stepped into Amy's room – and into a little girl's dream. The walls were painted a light pink, and all the furniture looked brand new. She didn't recognize any of it from the Governor's house. She supposed the whole place was still locked down, almost everything saved as evidence. The bed was heaped high with plush toys, and there was a dollhouse resting on a side table with so many dolls accompanying it they couldn't all fit inside.

It was impressive, for sure. And as Amy rushed through showing Laura all of her new toys, along with their names and a description of their life stories, Laura tried to analyze whether that was a good or a bad thing.

Amy had never wanted for anything at her father's home, after all. She'd had anything money could buy. Anything but stable and loving parents.

"Can I get you something?" Christopher asked from the doorway. Laura turned around to see him standing there, shuffling his feet, his hands in his pockets like he couldn't figure out what to do with them. "A cup of coffee?"

"Thanks," Laura said. "That would be great."

"Actually, maybe we could drink it downstairs?" Christopher suggested, raising an eyebrow slightly.

That thing she hadn't been able to put her finger on: Laura saw it now. He was nervous. Unsure of himself.

A new parent, thrown into a situation headfirst. She could see how that might build the nerves. Still, it was something to keep an eye on.

15

"Of course," Laura said, though she wished she could stay with Amy. She'd like to take the girl aside, talk to her alone. Make sure that nothing was going on. But she wasn't going to come out and say that in front of Christopher. She didn't want to give him the opportunity to send Amy some kind of signal about behaving herself and staying quiet.

The three of them moved back downstairs, into an airy kitchen complete with a breakfast bar. Amy scrambled up onto one of the stools beside Laura as Christopher poured the coffee, with a juice for the girl.

"So, how long have you lived in this neighborhood?" Laura asked, for the sake of making conversation as well as to dig up a little more information on his background.

"Oh, a few years," Christopher said, glancing at her in apparent surprise at the question. "I just got back to the US – let's see... yes, a little under three years ago."

"Back?" Laura asked, her interest piqued. "Where were you before then?"

"Around," Christopher shrugged, with a self-effacing smile. "I'd been with Doctors Without Borders for about ten years. Since not long after I finished my residency. I moved around West Africa a bit during the Ebola crisis and stayed on a little after that to provide healthcare for HIV and AIDs patients. I came back when my mom got sick."

"Amy's grandmother?" Laura said. Obviously, his mother would be Amy's grandmother. But this was the first she was hearing about any sick relative. And she didn't want to react to the fact that he seemed to have dedicated a decade of his life to serving others, rather than making money as a doctor at home. It almost seemed too good to be true. Like he was leaving her a trail of breadcrumbs to why she should go away and stop worrying about Amy.

And she was never going to do that.

"Yeah," Christopher sighed, setting down the mug of coffee in front of Laura. "She only hung on a few months, but it was worth it to be with her at the end. Anyway, coming back here reminded me about what I was missing, and I ended up taking a job at a hospital around here and staying."

"What were you missing?" Laura asked. It didn't escape that this felt a little like interrogating a suspect. Only in a much more comfortable setting.

"Family," Christopher said, looking at Amy and smiling a sad kind of smile. "And good coffee." He let his face brighten with the joke, raising his mug in the air and taking a sip.

16

Laura wasn't going to let him fool her with that kind of routine. Anyone could be charming and pleasant and yet turn out to be a psycho. Even selfless doctors who gave ten years of their lives to looking after the most unfortunate and needy in another country. And then came home to look after a dying parent. And then volunteered to take in a small child after a relative was no longer able to look after her.

Though even she had to admit, he was looking pretty good on paper.

"Can I go play outside?" Amy asked, interrupting the conversation and making the adults both turn in her direction.

"No!" Christopher said sharply – and Laura knew that she was right.

Something here was very, very wrong.

CHAPTER FOUR

Laura's hand formed into a fist on the countertop, her mind ready to reach for her gun. Not that it was necessary, not right now – and besides, she was off duty, not even wearing it. But she was angry. She'd almost been fooled. She'd really started to think that Christopher Fallow could be genuine.

He sighed, the sharpness going out of his face. "Sorry, sweetie, but we talked about this," he said, focusing on Amy. "Not until the fence has been put in around the pool, okay? I don't want anything to happen to you. You've got to stay inside unless I'm with you."

"Then let's all go outside," Amy said. She seemed to have recovered a little. Laura noticed how she'd shrunk down at his sharp word, like she was bracing for the hit. Her voice still trembled slightly, pleading rather than suggesting.

The only thing was, she couldn't tell whether that was a learned reflex because of her father, or whether the girl had come to expect it from Christopher as well.

"In a little bit," Christopher said, glancing at Laura. "Actually, I wanted to talk to Laura about some... some grown-up stuff. Why don't you play in your room for a little bit? You can take your juice with you."

"Okay," Amy said, getting down from her stool. She was obedient, not even sulking. It was like she'd learned to accept being told to go away, rather than getting hit or shouted at, as the best option. It still made Laura's heart break every time she saw a new sign of the damage that had been done to the beautiful, sweet little child. She shouldn't have had to go through any of that.

It wasn't until Amy was out of the room completely, her tiny footsteps disappearing up the stairs, that Christopher seemed to sag.

In front of Laura's eyes, he dropped the charming and friendly smile, the almost fatherly look – the one that just seemed to need a little more practice – and leaned against the counter as if he needed the support. When he looked up at her again, he seemed tired, drained. Barely holding it together.

"Christopher?" Laura asked, prompting him, but also with some concern. The man looked like he was about to fall down.

18

"Sorry," he said, running a hand over his face. "God, I'm just... I'm so scared something's going to happen to her."

Laura found herself blinking. "What?"

He gestured around, presumably at the house in general. "It's just... not child-proof. At all. The whole place. After I agreed to take her on, at first, I was just thinking about making sure she would be happy again. Getting her to school, making sure I had childcare covered while I was at work, that kind of stuff. But then I found this article about child-proofing your home and I just... do you know how many things there are that could hurt a child in a kitchen alone?"

Laura felt like she was on the back foot. This wasn't what she had been expecting him to say after sending Amy upstairs. Maybe some polite but thinly veiled threat about leaving them alone. An attempt to reassure her that he was going to look after her and she didn't need to check up on them again. Even an outright charm offensive.

But not this.

"Yes, I do," Laura said, as evenly as she could. "I have a daughter around Amy's age, myself."

"You do?" Christopher's eyes seemed to light up with hope. "Oh, God, please help me. I don't know if I'm doing anything right. Will you just... will you take a look around with me? Just see if anything stands out to you? And... her toys and her clothes and all that stuff. I went to the store and just asked them to give me everything a six-year-old girl might need, no expense spared. I have no idea if they gave me everything or just ripped me off."

Laura held up a hand, trying to slow his rapid babbling. "Christopher?" she said, hoping it would get his attention and make him focus.

"Chris," he said, like it was an automatic reflex. "Sorry. I hate my full name. Always makes me feel like I'm being summoned by my dad."

"Chris," Laura said, keeping her tone the same. "Just slow down. Making a child happy is not about buying them everything under the sun."

"I know that," he said, nodding glumly into his coffee cup. "I just... I don't know what else to do. She's been through so much. How am I supposed to make her feel safe, now? After what my brother did... I just can't even stomach the thought of it."

"You make her feel safe by showing her that she *is* safe," Laura said. She glanced down at the counter for a minute, considering her next words, before looking up at him again frankly. "And by showing me. Because if I get even a hint of concern that things aren't right here, I'm not going to hesitate."

"No," Chris said, seemingly in full agreement. "No, you shouldn't. But I'm not going to... I mean... I'm not John." He said the last words with what seemed like some difficulty, having to swallow around a lump in his throat.

"I will hold you to that," Laura said, making sure he kept eye contact, that he saw how serious she was.

And, totally unexpectedly, he smiled.

He wasn't a bad-looking man, Chris Fallow. And when he smiled like that, it transformed him. Made him charming and handsome and erudite. It was the kind of smile you'd want to take home to meet your parents. But Laura wasn't going to let her guard down just because of a smile like that.

"I'm glad," he said. "Because I was going to ask you for your help."

"My help?" Laura frowned.

"Well, I know you have kind of a bond with Amy," Chris said. He gestured helplessly in the direction of where Amy had gone. "Actually, you're kind of all she talks about. Christ, I think she likes you a lot more than she likes me. It's kind of intimidating. And now I know you have a young daughter, too, it's perfect. Isn't it?"

"What is?" Laura asked guardedly.

"I mean, you must know... everything," Chris said. "Everything she'll need, how to look after her, even what she's like. I wasn't around much before the last few years, and lately I've been busy at the hospital. I didn't even know what kind of toys she would like. But you can help me. Can't you?"

Laura must have been looking at him somewhat askance because Chris laid his hands down on top of the counter and stared at her, like he was trying to stare into her very soul.

"Please?"

Laura sighed, shaking her head. "You don't even have to ask. Of course, I'll help out. Anything to make sure Amy is safe and happy from now on." And, she added privately in her own head, anything to make sure that she could keep an eye on him.

Even if he was putting his best foot forward now, that might not last. And Amy was too important, too vulnerable, for Laura to leave that to chance.

"Thank you," Chris said, breaking out into another grin. He genuinely looked relieved. "Thank you, so much. Can I take your number, so I can annoy you with stupid questions and call you if I need emergency help?"

Laura dug her cell phone out. "Not just in emergencies," she said. "You can call me about this any time. I'll answer. I might not be in the state, but I'll answer."

"That's good enough," Chris beamed, typing on his screen as she pulled up her own contact book. They exchanged numbers quickly, and Laura was about to set the phone back into her pocket when she felt it buzzing.

For a second, she assumed it was just Chris testing her number by calling it. But then she saw the caller ID and frowned.

"Hang on," she said. "I've got to take this. It's work."

"Oh, sure," Chris said, gesturing for her to step out and lifting his coffee mug in a kind of salute. "Please."

Laura moved only as far as the hall before she answered, knowing whose voice she would hear on the other end of the line.

"Agent Frost, I hope you're enjoying your day off," Chief Rondelle said, his familiar tone carrying just the lightest edge of humor.

Which meant only one thing.

It wasn't her day off anymore.

CHAPTER FIVE

When Laura arrived at the J. Edgar Hoover Building, the FBI headquarters, Nate was already there. She pulled up next to his car in the parking lot and rushed to the elevators, knowing she was behind. She'd been further out than usual, in the suburbs where Chris and Amy now lived. From what Rondelle said on the phone, this was urgent.

She'd wanted to get some time alone with Nate before they went inside. A chance to meet him in the corridor, ask him not to start mentioning therapy to their boss. But now she was just going to have to hope that he'd stayed quiet on his own.

She half-ran down the hall, her blonde hair flying in a ponytail behind her, arriving at Rondelle's door and then pausing for only a moment. It was closed. She could hear them talking on the other side.

She knocked and then opened the door and went in without waiting to be told, hoping she would catch them in the act if they were talking about her. But though both of them looked up at her with a startled expression, neither of them looked guilty.

"Agent Frost," Rondelle said, from behind his desk. He was seated casually, behind a stack of paperwork as he always seemed to be. He watched her with inquisition in his sharp eyes, like he was reading more than she would have liked into her quick entrance. "We were just about to discuss the case. Do come in."

Laura closed the door behind her, having to pretend not to hear the quiet rebuke in that statement. The fact that she hadn't been invited in *before* entering. "It sounded urgent, sir. I rushed over as quick as I could."

She glanced at Nate, standing in front of the desk in an easy, relaxed pose. He, too, was still wearing street clothes, probably not having come from home either. He met her glance, no longer avoiding it, but he didn't give anything away either.

"That it is," Rondelle said, leaning back in his chair and looking at both of them. The light by his desk highlighted the grays in his dark hair – or the dark in his gray hair, since the gray seemed now to be winning. "We have a very interesting case unfolding in Atlanta, Georgia. After you tackled the twins' case so easily, I figured you'd need something more of a challenge."

Nate snorted. "Thanks for that, Chief."

He was playing around with them, and all of them knew it. The last case hadn't come easy at all. It had been hard. They all were. That's what it was like, being an FBI agent. Taking on the cases that were too complex for the locals to figure out. It was never going to be easy.

Chief Rondelle smiled. At least he seemed to be in good spirits, for whatever reason. Maybe because he could see that his two favorite agents were talking to each other again, if nothing else. "We had a report a couple of hours ago about a murder victim discovered in very unusual circumstances. She had a clock placed around her neck and was bound and gagged, hanging from the ceiling in an abandoned warehouse. She's the second such victim found in two days. It looks like we have a pattern on our hands, and it's a very specific one. Both women, both with the clock, both hung by the neck as a method of death. As for the clocks themselves, they appear to not only tell the time, but count it down."

"Count it down?" Nate frowned, picking up on that immediately. "This is some kind of sick game or something? He lets them know how long it will be until they die?"

"You appear to have it already," Rondelle nodded. "The setup includes a kind of mechanism which allows a platform to drop at the time marked on the clock. When it falls, the woman is hung."

"We'd better get there as soon as possible," Laura said, glancing at Nate. "Someone like this, they're not going to take two victims and stop. This is someone having the worst kind of fun. They're playing a game, and they'll keep playing it until we stop them."

"Agent Frost has it," Rondelle nodded, with a sly look in his eyes. "I've got the pair of you on flights that leave in less than an hour. You'd better get moving as soon as possible."

"Yes, sir," Laura said. She stepped forward, holding out a hand to take the briefing documents, which he handed over readily. She turned, only sparing one glance to make sure that Nate was following her as she left the room. To her relief, he did.

Laura had found in her time in law enforcement that sometimes, if you just walked quickly and purposefully enough in one direction, people would end up following you.

"Laura," Nate said, his voice low as they made their way down the hall.

"What?" she asked, throwing the word over her shoulder on her way to the elevators. "We need to keep moving."

"Yeah, but…" Nate sighed, breaking into a light jog to catch up with her just as she stepped inside the elevator and turned to face the hall. "Wait, just for a second. Are you up for this?"

"Am I up for what?" Laura asked, blinking. "Doing my job?"

The doors closed, leaving them in privacy at least for the moment. "Yes," Nate said, ducking his head to look her in the face on her level. "After last night – are you sure you want to take this on right away? I'm guessing you didn't speak to Rondelle about starting therapy, given he didn't mention it."

"Neither did you," Laura said. Not an accusation or a question. More of an assessment.

"I thought you should have the chance to do it yourself," he said. "But, honestly, I still think you need to do it. And I'm more than happy to do this one solo, or take someone else. Jones, maybe. He hasn't done a lot of out of state cases since his partner retired. I'm sure he'd jump at the chance."

"Nate, I'm fine," Laura said. She passed a hand across her brow, then looked up at him. "You know what? What you said… It got through to me. I started thinking. A lot. That's why I took today off. To process everything."

"And?" Nate said, expectantly.

"You're right. I haven't been in the right frame of mind," Laura said. "I've been letting the pressure get to me, the stress. But that's not a problem anymore. Amy Fallow is settled somewhere safe. I've got custody of Lacey back, if only partially. I mean, I get to actually see my daughter again. And I'm sober. And staying that way. These crazy ideas I've been holding onto… I don't need that crutch anymore. I've been lying to myself, trying to find a way to keep going. But now – I actually have something to keep going for. It's all going to be fine. No more stupid stuff. I can see clearly now."

Nate studied her carefully. The doors slid open on the parking lot. "You're sure?"

"I'm sure," she said, offering him a tired smile. "I am. I just hope we get this case done quick. It's Tuesday now, and I've got Lacey's first court-mandated visit this weekend. I don't want to risk missing it."

Nate blinked, following her towards their parked cars as she strode out. "Are you sure, then?" he said. "You don't want to sit this one out? There will be other cases."

"But I'm fine," Laura said, looking at him with a smile as she reached for her car door. "I really am fine, now. And I love my job. I still want to keep doing it. Lacey coming around – it's every weekend, now. So, I'd better get used to this new normal."

Nate nodded slowly. "Alright," he said, looking her over one more time. "Meet you at the airport?"

Laura smiled, a full smile, the kind that would set off a dimple in one side of her cheek. "Race you there."

It was only after he'd peeled out of the parking lot, and she followed him before diverging onto a different road, that she allowed herself to relax. Privately, she thought she'd just performed some of the best acting in her life. It was a shame that no one else was ever going to appreciate it.

Nate had made it clear that he wasn't going to believe her. That was fine. She couldn't keep trying to get him to. Not with something like this. At least she had tried it once, tried to tell him the truth. What more could she be expected to do now?

It was too damaging, too difficult. Humiliating, even, to keep trying to convince him of something that even she would have admitted sounded absurd in any other circumstance.

If this was how it had to be in order to get him to work with her again, to trust her and not push things anymore, then this was how it could be. Laura could live with that.

They had people to save. A case to solve. A killer to catch.

And Laura was going to keep her head down this week, get it done, and be back in time for her weekend with Lacey in three days.

As far as she was concerned, there were no other options.

CHAPTER SIX

Laura got out of the car and shaded her eyes, though with the gray winter sky above them it was hardly necessary. Still, she surveyed the whole scene first before stepping forwards. An abandoned warehouse, part of an industrial area that had clearly seen better days. There wasn't a lot of activity anywhere behind or around them, but in front, local police cars filled the parking lot and blue-uniformed men and women swarmed in and out of the doors.

She checked her watch. It was just after two in the afternoon. Not a whole day's start, but at least they would be able to get a good amount of work done before needing to get some rest. No one had met them at the airport given the short notice, so Nate had seconded her plan to drive straight to the most recent crime scene and see what they could see.

"Hey," Laura called out, snagging the first person to go anywhere near to them. "Who's the commanding officer here?"

The young woman she had chosen gave her a wide-eyed and somewhat startled glance. "That would be Captain Blackford," she said.

"Where is he?" Laura asked.

The young woman hesitated. Her eyes went to the doors of the warehouse, which was all the information Laura needed.

She'd been a little brusque, probably. But she had a mission in mind, here. Get in, solve it, get out, go home. See Lacey. Pleasantries were something you could spend time on when you didn't have a ticking clock above your head.

Quite literally, Laura thought, as she walked into the warehouse, ignoring the protests of the young officer that the crime scene was supposed to be closed. Because this was where it had happened: the young woman hung with the clock around her neck. There was no sign of her now, but Laura saw the rope dangling from the roof beams and the busy activity below it.

"Um, ma'am," the officer protested again, but Laura drew out her badge and showed it to her, barely looking. "Oh. Um. Right. Captain Blackford is over there, by the platform."

Now Laura did look, to see where the woman was pointing. Up above, there was a rickety-looking metal staircase leading to a gangway. The platform, or so Laura guessed it had to be, was hanging down now, a flat vertical line against the side of the gangway. A couple of uniformed men were standing up there, looking down.

"Thank you," Nate said, warmly, taking over where Laura's social graces had apparently failed her. "We'll go have a chat with him now."

His words effectively released the young woman from her duty of making sure they got where they needed to, and she rushed away gratefully. Laura didn't spare her a second glance. She was almost captivated by the platform, the rope. The cruel juxtaposition they made. A story: a fall, then an arrest of that fall.

Death, even if one of them didn't work. The rope breaking would have caused anyone up there a fall from a great height, enough to damage a body beyond repair.

"After you," Nate said, seemingly with a note of humor.

Laura glanced at him, and saw he was eyeing the metal staircase with significant distrust. "So gentlemanly of you," she said, glad they could go back to this: the idle banter. Winding each other up.

She wasn't afraid of the staircase, given that someone else had already climbed up there. As Nate snorted in response to her comment, she moved towards the stairs with purpose, trying not to wince when the metal step creaked as she put her foot on it.

It was rusted, old, no doubt completely forgotten and out of repair. But it held. She had an eerie feeling, climbing up and feeling it sway underneath her feet. Like she was moving through something other than air. Swimming, maybe. Or floating. Like the ground was no longer a guaranteed concept.

Looking back, she saw that Nate had stayed on the floor below her. He had a slightly green look about him, now.

"You're doing great," he called up. "Keep going. I'll stay down here and take in the forensics situation."

Laura laughed, shaking her head at him. Nate wasn't afraid of much, but from time to time, her big, strong, masculine partner did show a little weakness. Fear of heights was one of them, and while she'd seen him push himself when he needed to, going up a rickety ladder like this was apparently a step too far for him. "I'll fill you in later," she called down.

The exchange had lifted her spirits a little. The climb, somehow, did too. Like it was a thrill. Taking a risk, doing something that could be dangerous. On the other hand, she had no doubt that the locals would already have assessed the stairs, deemed them fine for people to climb, at least in the service of investigation. If they hadn't, the local Captain wouldn't be standing up there so casually.

Laura finally reached the top of the stairs, looking down at the sickening distance to the ground and trying not to imagine what it would be like to smash down onto it. In front of her, the two men she had seen were facing her curiously, no doubt having been unable to avoid hearing her climb up towards them on the clanking, creaking metal frame.

"You must be the FBI," one of them said in a strong Georgia accent, moving towards her a couple of steps. He was younger than Laura had expected from below, maybe around her own age or a little older. He had a blunt, kind of slab-shaped face, a wide nose and square jaw like he'd been punched so hard once it stuck like that. Dark hair was visible just under his cap; he wore a full Captain's uniform, making him out undeniably as the man in charge.

"Special Agent Laura Frost," she said, showing him her badge. "My partner down below is Special Agent Nathaniel Lavoie. You mind filling me in on what you have so far? The briefing notes didn't give much away."

The Captain nodded sharply. Behind him, the man who was dressed in a Sergeant's jacket folded his arms over his chest, listening and waiting. "The victim would have been brought up here by the killer," the Captain said. "From the first glance, it looks as though there's no sign of a struggle, so we're thinking she was unconscious or tightly restrained at that time."

"Some work, bringing a second person up those stairs," Laura said, looking back down the way she had come. The way the stairs had swayed with her weight had hardly been encouraging. The killer would have had to climb without holding onto the handrails to steady themselves, hauling another body at the same time. They wouldn't have needed to be gentle, but it still wouldn't have been easy.

"Whoever this bastard is, he's a strong one," Captain Blackford agreed. "Over here, there's a kind of mechanism attached to the platform. Looks like he brought the whole kit and caboodle with him. Attached the platform himself, since it wasn't here before. Rigged up the hinges to fall at a certain trigger, controlled by a timer. Then he must have hung the rope, right there."

Laura tilted her head up. Another impressive feat. The rope was high up, too high to reach from the gangway itself. He would have had to erect the platform first, and even then...

28

"Any machinery brought in here over the last weeks?" Laura asked, trying to picture if there was any other way he could have done it.

Captain Blackford shook his head, but then turned to point into a dusty corner of the warehouse. It was dark in here, even with the light streaming through the windows and the lights the police had set up. The shadows behind the light rigs were thick. "There's a crane truck with a basket that was left here by the previous owners," he said. "Gassed up, even though it shouldn't have been. Wires have been damaged, got it running again. He used that, we think. Lifted himself up there. Could have used it to move her, too, but we don't think so. The dust on the floor has already covered some of the truck's tracks."

Laura followed his pointing finger down to the ground, to an area that looked somewhat scuffed compared to the rest. But he was right. It wasn't totally clear. Dust had fallen again since the rope and platform had been set up.

There wasn't much more to see here. But Laura was curious about one thing: what the physical evidence left behind on the victims would tell them.

"Where's the body?" Laura asked.

"Coroner," Captain Blackford grunted.

Laura held back on the urge to roll her eyes. "I mean, where is that?" she asked. "We've only just got into town, came here straight from the airport. We'll need directions, or at least an address."

"I'll take you there myself," Blackford said, straightening up slightly. "You two got a car yet?"

Laura nodded. "Rental. You can drive with us. I'd like to ask some questions about the first victim as we go." She turned towards the stairs, expecting him to follow her. It was only when she looked back with a raised eyebrow that he started to.

Laura was already starting to get a certain feeling from Captain Blackford, one she'd felt before. Although many officials on the ground were glad to get the help of the FBI, sometimes they would come into a case where it was felt as if they were stepping on toes. Taking over in an area where the locals already felt they would have been capable alone.

Though he'd been ostensibly polite enough, answering all her questions, Laura could sense that Captain Blackford was not happy with their presence here. That he resented being told what to do by someone who was outside of his own agency. Someone who, for all intents and purposes, outranked him in this case.

Being a Captain, he probably wasn't used to being pushed around so much anymore. But it must have been his superiors who'd decided to call in the FBI.

And now he was going to take that out on Laura and Nate.

Fabulous.

So long as he cooperated fully, Laura could take a little attitude, though.

Nate pulled away from conversing with a forensic photographer as Laura approached, nodding his goodbye. He held out a hand towards Captain Blackford, who only gave a moment of sullen hesitation before shaking it.

"Agent Lavoie, I'm given to understand," Blackford said.

"Call me Nate," Nate said, giving him that wide-toothed grin he often used when he needed to disarm someone. So, it wasn't just Laura who had picked up on the mood.

"Alright, then," Blackford said, gesturing towards the door, but declining the obvious move of using Nate's first name right away. "We're to head out to the coroner in your car, so I'm told."

Nate did a good job of not batting an eyelid. Laura let her fingers curl tightly into a fist by her side, where she was turned slightly away from the Captain, so he couldn't see it. Letting him bother them, and letting him know he'd bothered them, right out of the gate was not a good way to keep control of this relationship. It would give him a license to print money, as far as antagonizing them went.

"Let's go," Laura said, cocking her head towards the door. She led the way without hesitation, knowing as she always did that Nate had her back.

Well, usually always. The last couple of weeks had been tough.

But he was back on her side now, she knew.

They headed into the car, Blackford pointedly taking the passenger seat so that he at least wasn't relegated to sitting in the back. He stretched out long legs in front of him, setting the seat back a couple of notches. Nate got into the back seat behind Laura without any comment, taking it mildly. He was good at that. Choosing his battles.

"So, what can you tell us about the first victim?" Laura asked, starting up the car and beginning to pull out of the weed-strewn lot.

"Another woman," he said. "You got the victim profile in your briefing notes?"

Laura nodded, and Nate spoke up from the backseat where he had the notes beside him. "We looked them over on the journey here. From what we understand, we're dealing with a couple of women, both in

30

their mid-thirties and local to the Atlanta area. Beyond that, the similarities seem to end – one blonde, one brunette, no correlation in height or weight, working in different industries. Have you found any connections between them?"

"Not yet," Blackford grunted. "It's early days."

"And the crime scene?" Laura prompted. She wanted to hear it from him. If he was determined to make it difficult, that was fine. She still had a job to do. She still needed to know.

"It was a boarded-up old gas station out on the outskirts of the city," Blackford said. He was reclining almost lazily in his seat, one hand tilted up against the window, almost like he was pointing to the roof. A casual position, as if to tell them that he wasn't at all intimidated by their presence. "No one around. It's a whole abandoned area, just like this one. There's supposedly a security guard, but they don't patrol, and it turns out the cameras weren't working on the stretch covering the road and the gas station itself."

"Convenient," Laura remarked. "Is this a recent development?"

Blackford shook his head. "Hard to say," he replied. "The files aren't preserved for long. Overwritten. Time we got to check them, everything was just blank. No way of knowing when that happened. Course, the security firm are claiming they knew nothing about it."

"No backups, no records?" Laura asked.

"Nope." Blackford tapped his knuckles against the glass of the window in a short, staccato pattern. "Ask me, the firm's been ripping off the landowners. Not doing their jobs. What it boils down to for us is a whole lack of evidence when there could have been plenty available."

"What about the victim?" Nate asked. "Our notes say she was found in pretty similar circumstances to the scene we've just left."

"That's right," Blackford nodded. Laura noted that he seemed to hold the same level of disdain for both of them, from the tone of his voice and the way every word seemed forced. At least it was good to know he wasn't just a misogynist, though it wasn't much of an improvement. "She was strung up on a platform, same mechanism as the one you just saw. She had the clock round her neck and the ropes, all the rest of it. Looks as though the timer was set for twelve hours again, and went off at midnight."

"How do you know the exact time of death?" Laura asked.

"The clocks stop when the timer hits zero," Blackford said. After a brief pause, he shrugged. "Well, it could be the clocks weren't accurate. But the coroner says the window for the time of death is around midnight. It stacks up. From what we can gather, the clock starts at exactly twelve noon and gives them twelve hours before they drop."

"Why?" Laura said. It was the obvious question. More of a rhetorical one right now, but one they were going to have to answer if they were ever going to get to the bottom of this case. It was a huge part of the MO, and therefore clearly very important to the killer.

"Who knows?" Blackford shrugged. "Maybe the sick bastard just wants them to suffer. To know they're going to die."

"There's no way for them to escape, you don't think?" Nate asked. "It's not some kind of sick test? Like those movies that were going around a few years back – trying to force them to do what it takes to survive?"

Blackford made a noise in the back of his throat. "You'll see in a minute," he says. "Pull in on the left here. This is the coroner's office."

His ominous words hung in Laura's ears as she parked the car, feeling that crawling sensation on her skin that came with the knowledge she was about to go and purposefully look at a dead body.

There hadn't been any photographs of this scene in their briefing notes. And she wondered, given Blackford's hint, what exactly they were about to find.

CHAPTER SEVEN

Laura walked into the cold underground room first. It was like diving into the deep end of a pool. If you knew you were going to have to get wet, sometimes it was better to just get it over with and do it all at once. Not to linger back, dipping a toe first, letting others go ahead of you.

You had to take charge of your fear, put your head forwards, and just go.

The coroner turned out to be a middle-aged little man in a white coat with wiry hair, and a half-stooped back, no doubt from years of bending over corpses without proper posture correction. He turned as they entered, frowning at Laura but then brightening as soon as he saw Blackford.

"Ah," he said, nodding. "You must be here to see the Marchall and Rowse bodies. I heard the FBI were being drafted in."

Blackford had stepped forward, keeping level with Laura after passing through the doorway. She saw his jawline tense out of the corner of her eye. He really wasn't happy with this, was he?

"Just show them the bodies, if you could, Jerry."

Jerry did so, nodding rapidly like one of those nodding figurines people put in their cars. He led them over to the far side of the concrete and metal room, towards two steel tables which were covered with foreboding sheets.

It didn't matter how many times you had to go into one of these chilled rooms, filled with bodies and silence. It was always creepy, every time. Sometimes even more so, when the coroner was weirdly cheerful and friendly – which, in Laura's experience, a lot of them were.

But approaching those covered bodies, knowing you were going to have to take a very thorough look at what was under the sheets – there was nothing quite like it.

"This is our first victim," Jerry was saying, gesturing to the furthest table. They all filed around it dutifully. Blackford held back a little, down by the feet, having clearly already seen what was to be seen. Jerry took up a position by the head, leaving Nate and Laura to gather side by side along the torso. "The cause of death was definitely hanging

33

by the neck." He flipped back the sheet with little ceremony, revealing the body of the woman who'd been listed in their briefing as Stephanie Marchall.

She was naked, already bearing the signs of several incisions that had been sewn back together. Her skin was sallow, almost a gray color, and her hair hung limp from the back of her head. Her eyes, thankfully, were closed.

Laura tried to flip that switch in her mind, going from looking at the woman as a dead human to seeing her as an object to be studied. It wasn't always possible to do it completely, but keeping evidence at the forefront of her mind helped. She needed to gather as much information as possible from what she could see here, rather than letting emotion enter the picture. The dead faces would haunt her later, when she tried to sleep – but no more than her visions of the living ones already did.

There was no wonder she'd turned to drink in the past. No wonder that many law enforcement officials ended up going down that path. But someone had to look – because this woman, and all the others like her, deserved justice. And all the living ones – they deserved to be safe. Which meant looking at this body and finding the clues which would catch her killer.

"Looks like rope burns around the wrist and mouth," Laura said. Her eyes traced the familiar patterns of bruising, red raw burns, and raised welts on the skin. It was clear that not only had the victim been tied up, but she had fought. Tried to free her wrists. It would have been immensely painful, judging by the raw skin left behind. In a few spots, it had even given way, leaving behind scratch-like cuts across the surface of the skin that would have been terribly painful if the victim had survived.

"Yes," Jerry said, with the kind of methodical and professional tone that coroners often slipped into when describing all kinds of bodily injuries. As if he, too, knew how to flip off that switch and look at the body as an object instead of a person. "Judging by the impressions around the mouth in particular, I would suggest that the ropes were bound in place for a longer period of time before death took place. Hours, certainly."

"How long?" Laura asked, glancing at him.

"Difficult to say exactly," Jerry replied. "Though Captain Blackford here tells me that there was a stopped clock and a timer found at the scene. Twelve hours, wasn't that correct?"

"That's right," Blackford replied laconically. "Techs have managed to take the clock apart, confirmed it was a twelve-hour timer."

"So, in my professional opinion," Jerry concluded. "The victim was bound and gagged on the platform for the full twelve hours before the hanging occurred. As for death, it would have been fairly instant. Her neck was snapped by the fall, which is exactly what you usually prefer when it comes to a hanging. She didn't even have time for strangulation."

"Anything else to note, with this particular body?" Nate asked. Laura glanced at him and saw that he was keeping his eyes to certain spots on the body. Only looking at the hands, the neck and mouth, the legs. As if, even in death, he wanted to be respectful to the woman who had lost her life.

"Nothing affecting the case," the coroner shrugged. "I can tell you that she ate a fruit salad for her last meal. Again, quite some time before her death. There were a few existing injuries, though nothing serious - a couple of minor bruises and a scratch across one knuckle. Upon examination, it does not appear to be connected to the case. I would say it happened a couple of days before."

"What about the second victim?" Laura asked, turning a full one eighty degrees to look at the table behind them. Jerry took her cue, replacing the sheet over Stephanie Marchall's body before removing the one from over Veronica Rowse.

"We have a very similar story here," he said. "I'm not seeing anything pre-existing that would have any bearing on the case, except for a small bruise to the back of the neck which could have taken place in the time before she was brought to the platform. Perhaps the day before, perhaps earlier that morning. It's a little difficult to say, because of the burns left by the rope – they partially cover it, I'm afraid."

Laura ran her eyes over the second body, trying to convince herself that it was easier the second time. It wasn't. But she could at least pretend. "You're thinking he may have knocked them unconscious before bringing them to the platform?" she asked.

"It would certainly make sense." Jerry paused, cocking his head. "But I don't want to give too many assumptions, here. It's also possible that the women were tied up *before* being put into place. Perhaps threatened with a weapon if they didn't comply, which would explain the lack of defensive wounds. He might have walked them right up there himself. I can't say that I have the evidence present in the bodies before us to be able to tell you exactly how they arrived where they did."

Laura nodded again. She appreciated the way Jerry spoke. He was very clear about what he did and did not know. That was helpful, as an investigator. It was good to discuss theories and whether they might be plausible, but equally good to know which ones were confirmed and which were just theories.

"What happened to her hand?" Nate asked.

Laura lifted her eyes to the other side of the body. She hadn't even noticed it, until he'd said something. She'd been looking at the wrist closest to them, but the other one...

It was mangled. Beyond repair, certainly. Even if Veronica Rowse had been alive and breathing, she'd have needed a huge amount of medical help. Her skin was all but ripped away, leaving behind gouge marks over the surface of her thumb, wrist, and the back of her hand. Her fingers were clean but oddly bloodless, no doubt as a result of Jerry having cleaned away all of the blood that must have issued from such a wound.

"Well, I'm afraid it wasn't a pretty end for her," Jerry said, with a note of sympathy in his voice. "While Marchall fell and broke her neck immediately, Rowse did not. She appears to have managed to get a hand free before her death, though I don't think it was very long before. If it had been a long while, she may well have suffered enough blood loss to die from that alone – or to tip herself off the edge of the platform when she fainted. Either way, we'd be looking at a different result. And the platform itself, while it did contain some significant blood spatter, was not bloodied enough to suggest that she was bleeding down onto it for long."

"So, she was strangled to death by the rope?" Nate asked. His tone was low, sickened.

"Yes, I'm afraid so," Jerry said. "It would have been a slow death by asphyxiation. She does appear to have emptied her bowels at the moment of death, and before we cut away her clothes and the rope, there was blood on the noose consistent with the shape of her fingers. My guess would be that she made a last-ditch, desperate attempt to get her hand free as the timer ticked down, partially degloving herself in the process. She then fumbled to get the rope from her neck but wasn't able to make any significant impact before dropping. Unfortunately, her angle or perhaps the way her arms were braced prevented her neck from snapping, and there we have it."

Laura suppressed a shudder. It was a gruesome way to go. In terrible pain, panicking, knowing that it was almost over and not being able to stop it. But at least she'd been able to fight until the end.

She reached for the sheet, as if she wanted to be respectful and cover up the suffering this woman had endured. But she had an ulterior motive, as Jerry reached to help her: she let her hand brush just lightly over Veronica Rowse's wrist, the less injured one, right across the rope burn. A spot the killer must surely have touched while tying her up. She concentrated on the feel of the cool skin, and as a faint headache spiked in her forehead. she knew she'd managed it. She let the sheet drop quickly into place, not wanting to interrupt her own movement when she came back to –

She was looking ahead, but there was blackness all around her. It was like looking through a tunnel. Not being able to see anything beyond this small circular window onto the world, this tiny glimpse…

And the window – it was almost entirely filled by a clock.

Immediately, viscerally, Laura recognized it. It was the same kind of clock that had been used in both of the other crime scenes. She'd seen it in the photographs. An old-fashioned, circular, pale white clock face with black hands and Roman numerals, the kind that might have been a kitchen clock. Below it, a timer that was built into the same frame, allowing you to time your dishes and ensure you never forgot to take anything out of the oven.

And yet, the timer itself was changed, updated, modified somehow. She'd seen those clocks, remembered one hanging on her grandmother's wall, a place that filled her memory with the scent of freshly baked cherry pie. The timers on those clocks went up to an hour, no more. This one had obviously been removed and replaced with a more modern timer, something with a digital display.

There were hands in her vision, two of them. One steadied the clock, turned it as it caught a glint of the sun across the face. She saw a reflection of a window, a real window, with a blue sky beyond. There wasn't much detail, though she strained to make it out – and then the clock shifted slightly, and the reflection was gone. Instead, she saw the other hand covering the timer. Tapping it.

The clock showed almost three. Three in the afternoon – it had to be. The sunshine precluded three in the morning.

And the hands holding the clock were shaking. Laura couldn't see the timer properly, not the whole display, but she could see a second counter ticking downwards rapidly. Ticking someone's life away.

They were already on a deadline.

Laura snapped out of the vision and back to herself, staring down at the freshly covered body on the table. She moved to cover her momentary lapse, as she always did, instinctively able to return to what she had been doing so as not to give away that anything was wrong.

"I think we've seen enough here," Nate said, his voice a low rumble in the cold room, echoing slightly from the metal shelves that surrounded them. "Laura?"

"Yes, absolutely," Laura nodded, her mind elsewhere. Twelve. That was what she had been unable to see. The timer must have been set for a certain hour, and twelve had come up four times now in the crime scenes. Both women were set on their respective platforms for twelve hours, it seemed, and both of them were on timers for twelve hours. From twelve noon to twelve midnight.

Laura was no numerologist, but that was a lot of twelves. Surely more twelves than was usually expected to be a coincidence.

If the latest victim – who she hadn't seen, not in the slightest, not even to get a glimpse of them – was already set up on a platform at twelve noon, then she would die at twelve midnight. Over seven hours after the vision Laura had seen. Tonight? Laura checked her watch. It was almost three, now.

Almost three – and that was odd. It had been only a couple of minutes past the hour, according to the clock. Normally, when Laura's visions struck, they caused a corresponding pain in her head. The more severe the headache, the sooner the thing was going to happen.

So…

Not three, today?

Three, tomorrow?

"We should get going to the victims' families," Nate said, and Laura realized with a start that he and Blackford were already striding out of the morgue. She hurried after them, attempting to keep up and pass off her hesitation as a moment of thought and nothing more. "We need to talk to them, find out if there's any possibly link between the two of them. Laura, you good to drive again?"

"Of course," Laura nodded, managing to fall back into stride with them as they moved to leave the room and go out to the parking lot.

Three, today, she decided. Her visions had seemed to change in the past. She didn't truly know what rules governed them, or what things might affect them. Maybe she had a weaker headache because there was a lower possibility that she could do anything about the vision's outcome, given that it was happening so soon, and she was so far off from knowing anything about the killer yet. Maybe it was because she'd had a nutritious breakfast, or because she was in a good place with Lacey and Nate and her outlook was happier. She had no idea how it all worked.

38

It wasn't as though she'd been born with an instruction manual, as much as she wished she had.

So, she had to assume it was happening now. That the victim was already out there, waiting to be found. She had to. She couldn't risk assuming otherwise, in case someone was going to die, and it was all her fault for not feeling rushed enough.

"I'll give you the addresses," Blackford said, dismissively, as they emerged into the cold winter sun again. It did little to dispel the chill from Laura's bones. "I'm needed back at the station."

"Fine," Nate said. "Let's go see Veronica Rowse's family first. Right, Laura?"

"Sure," Laura said, because it was as good a place as any to start. The locals must have already spoken to the Marchall family, given that Stephanie Marchall was found a few days ago. Might as well go over new ground before ground that was already covered. They needed to find a clue, and it was going to be easier to find one there.

And they needed to find a connection to the number twelve – because if they didn't, the chances of the person on that platform dying would increase as the day wore on.

CHAPTER EIGHT

Nate glanced at Laura from the side of his eye as they drove, the GPS showing that they were pretty close to the Rowse household. She looked calm. A little tense, but that was normal for a case.

Normal – that was how she looked, Nate decided. Like nothing had happened. As if the last two cases, and all the arguments they'd had, had disappeared into the ether.

It should have reassured him, but if anything, it worried him even more.

"You feeling okay?" he asked, casually, keep his gaze ahead as if it was just small talk. He caught the way she darted a glance at him, though, the surprised and uncertain movement of her head.

"Yeah," she said. "Why wouldn't I be?"

Because last night, you told me you were seeing psychic visions.

Nate didn't say it out loud. He was trying to tread carefully. This whole thing was so strange, and he wasn't sure he had his head wrapped around all the intricacies of it, yet.

"I don't know," he said. "Guess we just saw some dead bodies. That's not usually a very nice thing to experience."

"Oh, yeah," Laura said, shrugging. "I'm fine. You? You looked a little peaky, in there."

Nate grunted a little, low in his throat. He'd been trying to keep that a little more under wraps. "I just don't like the feeling of it, sometimes. Like we're looking at these people's bodies. I don't think they would have enjoyed it, if they knew."

"It's good that they don't," Laura said, softly, pulling up outside a small family home with two cars parked outside already. It was clear that everyone had gathered around, having only just heard the news of Veronica's passing themselves. Which was both a good thing, and a bad thing, in Nate's experience.

Good, because they could talk to everyone at once. Bad, because everyone was going to want to stick their oar in – even the people who weren't relevant.

"Let's go in, then," Laura said, with a sigh, opening the driver's side door. Nate nodded, moving to get out of his own side. He couldn't help his mind drifting back to the whole psychic thing.

It was so weird. It was like she'd come up with the most unbelievable explanation, and yet the one that fit all the facts the most neatly.

She did know things, he thought, watching the back of her head as she walked up the path in front of him, her blonde ponytail swinging from side to side. She did seem to figure things out before other people could, to know what was going to happen and where the killers or victims in their cases would be. But that was…

Well, it was one thing to say that someone had expert knowledge. That they had a lot of experience in this kind of investigation combined with a natural talent allowing them to figure things out. Or even that they had people to talk to, shady underworld people who could give them tip-offs and inform on their colleagues in crime. Claiming that they were psychic was another thing altogether. It was ridiculous. Psychics, mediums, clairvoyants – they didn't exist. It was all old wives' tales and con artistry, wrapped together in a nice, neat package to take financial advantage of anyone who was grieving enough to believe them. He'd come across psychics before – most cops or law enforcement officers involved in big cases had. They'd come out of the woodwork when someone was missing or a body couldn't be found, trying to claim that they knew where to find them.

Almost all the time, it was a load of bunk. Sometimes someone would make a lucky guess, and then on interrogation it would turn out they actually knew a lot more about the case than they'd let on. Cold reading and investigative journalism, combined with a healthy knowledge of your given city's underworld, could bring you all kinds of hints.

But actual psychic powers? No. There was no way Nate believed in that. Just like he didn't believe Laura now, and for all the same reasons.

Laura knocked on the front door of the property decisively, the kind of loud knock that couldn't be ignored by the people inside. She seemed fine. She had seemed fine for the whole case so far, actually. If anything, she was in slightly better spirits – probably, he thought, because she had that visit with Lacey to look forward to. She was racing ahead every time they had to get somewhere, like she wanted this solved so she could get home. He didn't blame her for that.

But if she really believed what she'd told him last night…

Of course, she'd said this morning that she was over it. That she'd come to her senses. But you would say that, wouldn't you? If someone greeted you with skepticism and told you that you needed help?

41

Especially if you were an FBI agent like Laura, who knew what could happen to people with mental health issues.

The kind of powers that could be brought to bear until they were healthy again.

If she was sectioned, she'd be taken away from her daughter.

It was an unsettling thought, and one that Nate was grateful not to have to consider any longer when the front door opened.

The person behind it was a balding man in perhaps his sixties, mostly gray-haired in what little remained and bulging a little at the waist. He had a downcast, grim look to his face, like he was trying to come to grips with a terrible truth.

"Mr. Rowse?" Nate guessed. He had to be the father.

"Yes?" the man replied, his gaze sweeping across them expectantly. He didn't seem terribly surprised to see a pair of strangers on his doorstep. After the first visit from the police early this morning, he was probably just waiting for more news to come.

"I'm Special Agent Laura Frost," she said, holding up her badge. Nate followed her lead. "This is my partner, Special Agent Nathaniel Lavoie. We'd like to speak to you for a few moments, if we can. We're investigating what happened to your daughter."

"Her death," Mr. Rowse said, a sadness spreading through the words that seemed to soak through him like water through a sponge. "You can say it."

"Yes, sir," Laura replied, softly.

"Come in, then," he said, with a certain amount of resignation.

There was a living room inside the first door in the hall, though Nate could barely make out anything more than the fact that there were a couple of battered sofas and a television in one corner. The room was filled with far too many people, particularly after Mr. Rowse had walked in to join them. He sat down heavily on the one vacant spot.

Beside him was a similarly-aged woman who must have been Veronica's mother – even in death, he could recall the shape of the lips and nose of the body and compare them exactly against this woman's features. There were also two brothers, judging by the resemblance to their father, and a couple of women who might have been their wives. Two small children, too, who were playing on the floor, seemingly totally unaware of what was going on around them.

"Hello," Nate said, which seemed to be about the most appropriate thing he could think of at that moment.

Everyone looked at him, and no one said a thing.

Laura cleared her throat awkwardly, which prompted Mr. Rowse to speak up on their behalf.

"These are the FBI agents they were sending," he said, glumly.

His wife patted his hand, silently.

"That's right," Laura said, glancing sideways at Nate before seemingly taking charge of the situation. "We have a few questions to ask. It could be a little complicated if we have everyone chipping in – can we ask that just those who knew Veronica the best stay? We'll need to ask about her day-to-day life, her background, and so on."

There was some general shifting in the room. One of the brothers, the older one by the look of him, spoke up first. "I'll take the kids to the backyard," he said. "I haven't been around much the last few years, anyway."

"Right, same here. I'll go with you, honey," one of the women said – and after a few moments of awkward shuffling to let people out of the room, Laura and Nate were down to just the parents and one brother.

"Okay," Laura said, taking out a notebook and standing at the front of the room, facing them. It was awkward not to be able to sit, but it was going to have to do. Nate stood beside her, resisting the urge to put his hands in his pockets or cross his arms over his chest. He wasn't sure what else to do with them, so he dug his own notebook out of his inner jacket pocket, just for something to hold. "First of all, let us just express how very sorry we are for your loss."

"Absolutely," Nate added. "We understand that the circumstances of our meeting today couldn't be worse. But your cooperation is very much appreciated. We're doing whatever we can to bring whoever did this to justice."

"You don't know who it was, yet?" the brother asked, lifting his eyes. He looked angry. That was a fairly common reaction among grieving relatives.

"I'm sorry, I didn't catch your name?" Nate asked.

"Stephen," he said. "Steve."

"Steve, we're still chasing down leads at the moment. How much have the local police told you?"

"Just that she was found dead in an abandoned warehouse," Mr. Rowse said. There was a hitch in his voice as he continued. "Hung," he said. "But she wasn't... she didn't do it to herself. Someone did it to her. That's what he said."

"That's correct," Laura said softly. "I'm sorry to have to tell you this, but we're also investigating another death which happened in similar circumstances. We have reason to believe that the two killings are related."

"There's some kind of murderer out there?" Stephen asked furiously. "Someone's murdering people, and they got my sister?"

"It looks that way at the present moment," Nate said, putting as much respectful regret into his voice as he could. "But at this time, we're not yet sure whether the two deaths are connected in more ways than that. What we need to do is to establish whether there was any link between your Veronica and our other victim, or whether there was anyone in Veronica's life who might have had reason to want to hurt her."

"We already told the other officer," Mrs. Rowse spoke up, her voice wavering and sniffy. "She didn't have any problems. She was just a normal person. She didn't have enemies or anything like that."

"She was unmarried?" Laura asked, waiting with her pen poised above the empty page of her notebook. She seemed so in control. Like she was handling everything just fine. Nate had to wonder, though, what signs he'd missed before.

"Yes, that's right," Mr. Rowse said, staring at an indeterminant point in the carpet. Nate could see how the man was probably picturing his daughter, the life she could have had. The life that had been cut short so cruelly. It wasn't a feeling he could completely relate to, not being a father himself – but he knew how bad it would feel to lose a sister. Sometimes, he wondered if his inability to keep a relationship with a woman going was something to do with all the death he'd seen. The fear of losing someone that you loved so much. "Never did quite get round to finding her Mr. Right, did she, love?"

Out in the hallway, a door opened and closed. "No," Mrs. Rowse said, dabbing at her eyes with a tissue again. "Though we thought that Bradley had a bit of potential, didn't we? She didn't let us meet him, before."

"Why not?" Nate asked, his interest piqued. This could be a potential lead. The statistics of the number of murders carried out by people who knew the victim, and particularly by romantic partners, spoke for themselves.

"It was all a bit new," said a new voice from the hallway.

Laura and Nate both turned at the same time, relying on their whip fast reaction speeds to assess the direction of the newcomer, and whether or not they were a threat. The man framed in the doorway, holding a plastic carrier bag in his hand, looked to be in his early to mid-thirties. He was dressed casually, in a dark sweatshirt over jeans, and he had the same tired, haggard look that the rest of the family wore.

"That's Bradley," Stephen said, with a hint of animosity.

Nate took this in, weighed it carefully. He thought about his own sister, who he was always very protective of. When she brought home new boyfriends, he often reacted the same way. Like they were an impostor, someone who needed to be kept an eye on. Someone who might turn out to be dangerous. Of course, he had the usual fear that big brothers did: that his sister might get her heart broken. But at the same time, he knew enough from being an FBI agent to know that sometimes, just having a broken heart would be a lucky getaway.

The question was, what kind of suspicion was it that caused Stephen to look at Bradley that way? The normal kind of brotherly suspicion, or something more?

"I've just been to the store for some tea supplies," Bradley said, hefting his bag. He walked in, setting it down on the coffee table, having to step between Laura and Nate as he did so. Then he hesitated, awkwardly, like he didn't know where he was supposed to fit in this tableau of family.

"How did the two of you meet?" Laura asked, which Nate knew was just her way of exploring the situation and starting to get an idea of exactly how Bradley felt about his deceased girlfriend. It wasn't necessarily in the words he said, but in the tone, the body language. Even the look on his face. These things could give away more than a person realized.

"We both work at the hospice," Bradley said. "We're both nurses. Days are long, you end up spending a lot of time in the break room if you can. We've been talking for a long while, but it was only recently that it became anything more than that."

"She used to talk about you all the time," Mrs. Rowse said sadly. "I wasn't at all surprised when it came out you had been out for a drink together. I started to get really excited for her. I thought..." Her voice trailed off, leaving unspoken the story of what might have been. Nate saw how her shoulders seemed to droop, further at that.

"Have you been able to think of anyone that might want to harm Veronica?" Laura asked. "Perhaps there's someone from work, or a friend you had in common? A family member of someone from the hospice?"

"No," Bradley said, shaking his head mournfully. He looked tired and almost deflated, like he'd had all of the life sucked out of him over the past twenty-four hours. "And I don't know if she would have told

45

me, not yet. We were only just getting started, like I said. There are things that you tell your long-term partner you wouldn't tell a friend, or even someone brand new. She didn't seem to be afraid, or to have any worries or fears in the last few weeks. I've been going over it in my head, trying to remember everything she said to me. But there was never anyone like that, not that I can think of."

"That's very helpful," Nate said, nodding. It was always good to encourage people in these situations, rather than just firing questions at them without pause. It made them feel like they were being interrogated, and then sometimes they would clam up. "So, to summarize, none of you can think of anything that might point to the reason why Veronica in particular was singled out?"

"No," Stephen said, and the others shook their heads in agreement, and Nate studied them.

The parents were crushed. Stephen was angry at the world, at the killer, but not anyone in particular. It wasn't the kind of anger that he'd seen in violent criminals. It was a kind of hurt, defensive anger, the anger of a man who had not been able to protect his little sister and knew it. As for Bradley, he just looked like he was in an uncomfortable situation, dealing with something very sad among strangers. That would have been difficult for anyone to deal with, and Nate bought everything he was saying.

He believed them all, in fact. Which meant that they weren't going to get any more leads here.

It was beginning to look more and more like Veronica had been chosen at random. And while it wasn't exactly a surprise for an FBI agent to be brought in on a difficult case, he found himself wishing that, just for one time, they would have had something a bit more straightforward to deal with.

Random victims were always the hardest to trace. There was no way of knowing where the killer would strike next, or why he had chosen the victims he had, until they worked out some kind of psychological profile. That could take a long time. More to the point, it could end up taking another death.

Laura looked over at him, and Nate found that he was strangely comforted to see her giving him that same look she always did when she felt that an interview was over and wanted to check that he felt the same. Over the last three years and more they had slipped into an easy pattern, a working relationship that flowed. The last case, the one where they hadn't been speaking, had been awkward and abrupt and off kilter. Coming back to normal now, it was so much better. Even if he was still worried about how he was going to help her with the delusions she was suffering from, at least they were talking now.

"Thank you very much for your time," Nate said, nodding at all of them in turn. "We'll leave a few of our cards here so that you can give us a direct call if you think of anything relevant. Please, don't hesitate to call if you think of anything. Even if it seems small, even if you're not sure. Any little thing could help. As for us, will be in touch as soon as we have any updates to pass on to you."

"You're going to catch him, right?" Stephen snapped, locking eyes fiercely with Nate. Nate wondered if he could kind of sense the big brother energy that Nate carried, that thing they had in common.

"That's what we're here for," Nate said, stopping shy of making an actual promise.

He and Laura left the room, nodding their goodbyes as they filed through the hallway and then out of the house. It was only when they had reached the car again that Laura sighed, speaking to him quietly before he got into the passenger seat.

"Dead end," she said, a statement of fact rather than a question.

"There's still one more opportunity, though," Nate said. "We've still got to talk to the husband of Stephanie Marchall."

"I hate to say it, but I really hope we're dealing with a homicidal, abusive asshole to make this easy for us," Laura said.

Nate didn't even need to smile to lighten the message as he replied. "You and me both," he said. "I'm still hoping I can get you back to your little girl in time for the weekend." And he was gratified to see the look on her face, the gratitude, the relief.

Sometimes, knowing that someone else had your back could make all the difference. And he hoped against hope that knowing he was there for her would allow Laura to get past the delusions she was suffering from - and that they could use her newfound focus to get this case solved as quickly as possible.

CHAPTER NINE

Laura stood behind Nate as he knocked on the door to the small but neat property, set in a suburban development some way from the city center. It was a quiet street, and she found herself glancing up and down, thinking about the kind of people who lived in a neighborhood like this. Quiet people. The kind who kept themselves to themselves. They couldn't have imagined something like this would come to their doorstep.

The door opened silently, without a word; the man behind it just stared at them for a moment. His eyes were bloodshot and red-rimmed, set into a pale face. For a terrible moment, Laura thought he was just going to shut the door again. He didn't look quite in his right mind.

She couldn't exactly blame him for that.

"Ross Marchall?" Nate asked, his voice soft. There was hardly any need to ask. It was clear that this man was the grieving husband of Stephanie. His demeanor, the sadness and shock that seemed written throughout every line of him. The gold wedding band on his finger that was ringed with red skin, as though he had been twisting it constantly in his distress. "We're from the FBI. We want to talk to you, if we can. Ask a few questions about Stephanie."

"I spoke to…" Ross said, seeming to have some trouble getting through the sentence. He was in his late thirties, perhaps his early forties. A black beard and thick black hair, albeit with a slightly receding hairline, seemed somehow out of place on him just now. Normally taken as a sign of masculinity, strength – the look didn't fit this grieving, broken-looking man. "I spoke to them. You. The police."

"We're not the local police," Laura said, hoping her own gentle voice could lend some calm to the situation. It was cold out, the breeze whipping itself up into a wind, stinging at her exposed cheeks already. "We're following up to see if we can shed any more light on what happened. It's very important for the investigation."

Ross Marchall opened and closed his mouth a couple of times before stepping back, letting them in. As she passed him still holding the door, Laura noticed he was wearing a pair of furry slippers. Pajama bottoms, too, matched with a more formal-looking shirt. He wasn't together at all.

That was one of the hardest parts of dealing with victim families: their emotional state. Not only because it was difficult to witness, but because it made them difficult interview subjects. They could be distracted, angry, too sad or shocked to listen. To remember important details. It was why Laura always left a card, asked them to call later. Sometimes, a little time passing would help them to recall something that was very important indeed.

There was almost a crime scene in the living room. It was neatly decorated, clearly well-kept, but also a scene of some devastation over the past few days. There were a couple of empty casserole dishes still with spoons poking out of them, which she guessed was how Ross had been sustaining himself since his wife died. Tissues, screwed up into used balls, littered the whole of the floor. There were some clothes discarded on the floor, blankets on the sofa all mussed up as though Ross hadn't left there for a while, and several framed photographs lying on the coffee table.

Photographs of Stephanie and Ross, in happy times. Their wedding day. Another formal event that had required them to dress up. On vacation.

Ross had been sitting down here, Laura thought, probably unable to face going back to the marital bed. Looking at photographs of his wife, crying, and doing little else.

"Ross," Laura said, keeping her voice gentle still as he sat down on the sofa, leaving them no room to join him. There wasn't need to stand on ceremony, not in that way, not here. The grief-stricken could shut other people out in so many ways. Most of them were not intentional. They just needed to get on with the interview, even if it meant another stretch of uncomfortable time standing in front of a victim's family. "We need you to tell us as much as you can about Stephanie, and what might have happened to her."

"Her phone," he said, his voice barely above a whisper. He cleared his throat slightly, shaking his head. "That's what I keep thinking about."

"Her cell phone?" Nate prompted. He chose to squat down behind the coffee table, facing Ross. He placed one hand on top of it to steady himself, putting himself under Ross's level. In his line of sight, given that Ross didn't seem willing or able to lift his head.

"Why did he leave it on?" Ross said. "He must know. Everyone knows. You can trace a cell phone."

Nate twisted his head slightly, catching Laura's eye. He had a slight look of alarm. A look of, *is this guy making sense to you?*

"Maybe it didn't occur to him," Laura said. She figured that Ross could only be talking about one thing. About Stephanie. How they'd found her body. "That the police would be able to use it to track her down."

"He must have known," Ross said, squinting his eyes. He looked up at Laura like he was looking into the sun, and it was blinding him. It didn't give her the feeling that she was a bright object. More like he was just too far down in the dark. "Did he want us to find her?"

The words sent something of a chill down Laura's spine. It was fairly common for people to speculate on what had happened to their loved ones. To spend hours, days, weeks, even years trying to put it together in their heads. It was only natural. Wanting to know the answers.

But something about the way he said it… it wasn't only the utter grief that was weighing him down. It was the horror of it. Of a sadistic killer, deliberately setting things up so that someone would find the awful game he had set up. A woman left to hang in an abandoned gas station. A clock around her neck. A timer stopped for midnight.

Twelve.

Like there was some horrible meaning behind it all, some riddle. It was the kind of thing that Hollywood scriptwriters dreamed up, not real people. Not the kind of thing that really happened.

"Did Stephanie talk about anything weird happening in the last week or so?" Nate asked, breaking Laura's thoughts. "Did she seem worried, or tense? Any different than usual?"

"No," Ross said, his voice croaking and cracking. "Everything was fine. She was happy. Nothing ever happened to us. Not like this."

"She didn't have any feuds at work or in the neighborhood?" Nate pressed. "No ex-boyfriends, anything like that?"

"She was friends with her exes," Ross said. A ghost of a smile passed over his face, and only left it cracked wider open in its wake, a raw wound. "It used to drive me mad. And she got on with everyone. She had this hippy-dippy thing. I always thought she let people take advantage of her. Just so she could be nice."

The man was obviously in a great deal of pain, but at least he was talking now. Making sense. Laura moved a step closer to the coffee table, looking at the photographs spread out there, thinking of her next question.

She saw one that made her reach out, almost without thinking. She would never normally pick up something belonging to the victim's family, not without permission, but…

She grabbed it, and was rewarded with a flash of pain through her temple. A headache. She'd been right to go for it. The framed photograph was of three people – Ross and Stephanie Marchall, and another man, a man standing with his back to the camera and pointing over his shoulder at the number on his baseball uniform –

Laura was looking at a clock. It was an old analog clock, the kind that used to hang on kitchen walls. Old-fashioned. Probably didn't work unless you wound it. You'd have to wind it often.

He was winding it now.

He was setting it to twelve noon. Twelve, again. Laura watched those fingers move the clock face. She strained for any detail, any that would help her make sense of it. The clock was slightly different than the one she had seen before. There was a mark, a mark on the clock face itself, like a stain or maybe even a burn mark. As if someone had pressed a cigarette against it.

It was a different clock.

Two clocks, two timers.

Today? Tomorrow?

Both?

He was going to kill again. Laura felt her panic rising, even inside the vision, felt the fear of it. He was going to kill twice more. At least. One of them could be standing on a platform now, struggling to get free. And if they didn't save her, another would be next, would be right on her heels. If they didn't find enough information to stop him…

Laura blinked and she was still holding it, her hand lingering on the glass of the frame. Lingering over the number on the baseball uniform.

The number twelve.

It couldn't be a coincidence. She touched a picture of this man, and there the vision was. And the number. Twelve.

It had to mean it was him.

"Who is this?" she blurted abruptly, too shocked by the discovery to temper her words into something more gentle and respectful.

Ross looked up at her, startled. Something in her own speed and abruptness seemed to flip a switch in him, as though it had woken him up. Or maybe startled him into reacting, before he could think instead. "That's Brad," he said. "Brad Milford."

"He's a friend of yours?" Laura asked, placing the photograph back on the table now she'd had a good look at it. Ross's eyes followed it, like he needed the prompt.

"Kind of," Ross said. He swallowed. "Stephy's friend. He… they dated. He was one of those exes. But they stayed friends."

"He's a baseball player?" Laura asked. It wasn't that obvious of a question. There could be any reason for a man to be dressed like that, and for it to have nothing to do with baseball. It could have been a dress-up party, like Halloween or something. He might have been wearing it for a dare. For a special event. Maybe a one-off game that he never played again.

"Local minor league," Ross said. He frowned up at Laura like he was seeing her for the first time and starting to wonder why she was there. "Why?"

Laura bit her tongue. Now wasn't the time. You didn't go around spouting suspicions to the families of victims. Not if you didn't want them to go off the handle and attempt some sort of vigilante justice before you had the chance to stop them and get the real answers. Nate was giving her an odd, questioning look, but she ignored that, too.

"I'm just curious," she said. "Were they in contact often? Spending a lot of time together?"

"Not a lot," Ross shrugged. "Mostly we'd hang out as part of a larger group. Over the years, I guess we started having less time for that kind of thing."

"Did you ever get the impression there were lingering feelings on Brad's side?"

Ross blinked slowly at her. "I don't know. I don't think so. I don't... why are you asking this?"

Laura took him in, how he was pale and swaying slightly, like it was a struggle just to keep his head up. He wasn't suspicious. He was confused. He was finding all this hard to take, and she couldn't blame him for that. She changed tack, trying to squeeze a little more out of him before he shut down completely. "Let's move on from that. So, there's nothing you can think of that might tell us why Stephanie was targeted in this way?"

Ross closed his eyes, shook his head slowly from side to side. Like it was all too much to bear.

Laura glanced at Nate again, concern starting to override her need for answers. Ross was clearly broken. There should have been a local officer here to support him, but perhaps he'd turned it down. He was a long way down a dark path, and they weren't helping him by asking him these questions. If it had seemed like he wasn't hearing them, or wasn't thinking hard enough, Laura would have wavered. But as it was, it seemed as though he just couldn't think of anything that would make this happen to his wife.

And he looked like he'd spent the past couple of days trying to.

"Thank you, Mr. Marchall," Laura said, as Nate got to his feet again beside her. It was almost unnerving, going from being the tallest person in the room to having him tower over her again. "We'll be in touch if we have any news for you. In the meantime, please call us if anything comes to mind."

Ross nodded numbly, and Laura wondered if her words had made their way inside his head at all, this time.

Laura exchanged a glance with Nate one last time, a hesitant look that showed her they were on the same page. It felt bad, leaving him here alone. But they had to. Their job was to catch the killer, not to look after the families of the victims. As much as he needed someone, it couldn't be them. A call to the precinct could maybe get someone out here, someone who was better placed to help him out.

They left, with a reluctant slowness, just in case he would call them back at the last minute.

Outside, Laura sighed, rolling her shoulders back. The overcast sky seemed to match the mood, as did the cold air. Still, it was bright winter daylight, which seemed not to fit. It should have been the dead of night, judging how it felt inside that house.

"We should call someone to come down here," Nate said, echoing her own thoughts. Trust him to show that he, too, could empathize deeply with these people. Could spot the worrying signs and actually care that they were dealt with.

"Yeah," Laura said, digging out her cell. "You drive. I'll call Blackford from the car."

They sank into their respective seats, though Nate did not start the engine right away. He rested with his hands on the wheel, his back braced, and for a moment Laura thought he was going to say something.

Given their most recent conversation – the one at his home – Laura had a sudden and strong feeling that she didn't want to hear what it was. She dialed the number quickly, pressing the phone to her ear so that Nate couldn't interrupt.

"Yeah?"

That was Blackford, surly and short. At least he'd answered.

"Couple of things," Laura said. "We're going to need someone with trauma training over here at the Marchall house, keep an eye on the husband. Second, I need you to look up a name for me."

"What is it?" Blackford grunted, with a considerable air that suggested she could have asked a more junior member of the team than the Captain.

"Brad Milford," Laura said. "I wondered if you have any information on him in the system."

"Oh, you're looking up the boyfriend?" Blackford said. "We already checked him out."

"Ex-boyfriend," Laura corrected, her heart sinking all the same. That was one viable lead gone.

"Where'd that intel come from?" Blackford asked. "We have him down as current from all the family members. Even him."

Something began to dawn on Laura. Something she maybe should have seen right away but hadn't. "Whose boyfriend?" she said.

"Veronica Rowse."

"Shit." Laura looked at Nate, her eyes wide. The photograph in the house had been a few years old. Bradley Milford had longer hair then, and the angle was bad. She hadn't recognized him.

Even though she'd only see him a short while before.

"What?" Nate asked, catching her look with an alarmed eyebrow raise.

"Back to the Rowse place," she said. "Right now. We have a suspect."

A man who'd dated one of the victims in the past. Was dating one of them now.

And he wore the number twelve on his jersey.

It couldn't be a coincidence.

They had him already – just so long as he was still where they'd left him.

CHAPTER TEN

He settled back in his seat, watching the barn.

He wouldn't stay for long. It wasn't safe to be around here. There were any number of things that could go wrong, and he knew that. It was why he was so careful. But at the same time, he wasn't really worried about getting caught. How could he be?

Everything had gone so very smoothly so far.

He turned slightly, glancing into the backseat. He was thorough, liked to check things over again and again. It was clean, the whole space clear of anything that might make him stand out during a routine stop. He liked to keep it that way.

He liked the riddle of the farmer, the fox, and the hen trying to cross the river. The farmer couldn't put the hen and the fox together on either side of the river, because then they would eat one another. He saw things a bit like that.

If he travelled with a kill kit, the tools required to put together the rigged platform, and the victim all at the same time, it would be pretty obvious that he was the one responsible for all of it.

That's why he liked to do things in stages. First, scout out a nice remote location, like this one. The old barn on a condemned property. A place no one was ever going to go, not until the land was sold and the barn cleared – which could take decades to ever take place.

Then he'd take his tools over there. Set up the platform, get it rigged up nice and secure. If anyone happened by, they might not even know what they were looking at, once it was all set up. And if they did, well, he wouldn't be anywhere nearby. All he had to do was turn around and drive away if he happened to notice other vehicles around the property when he was coming back to it.

As for the victim, well, that was so easy. So easy that it almost seemed like it shouldn't be true. But then again, they deserved to die. Maybe it was the universe intervening, making things right. Paving the way.

Or maybe people as a whole were just that stupid that they made it easy for him.

He sighed lightly, running his mind over the events of the last day. How he'd gone ahead and found the next one, right where they were meant to be. Even keeping track of a few different potentials, it was surprisingly easy to build up an accurate picture of someone's schedule. To stay in the shadows and watch them until you could predict with a high degree of accuracy where they would be on any given day at any given time. People were creatures of habit.

From there, you could easily spot the times they were the most vulnerable. The sweet spot was that combination of routine and vulnerability. Crossing under a dark underpass for the very first time, a person might feel scared, might have their wits about them. Ready to run. But walking to a car in a parking lot that was almost always empty of other people at that time, when it was something that you did every day? Most people didn't even look up from their phones in that kind of situation.

So, it had been easy to get the latest one into the trunk of his car.

After that, it was easy to get them out of the trunk and set up inside. A matter of minutes. In and out so quick, there was little chance he was going to get caught. It was the perfect set-up. Minimum risk, just for a little extra effort.

He got out of the driver's seat, finding that thought about the journey here crossing his mind. It was always worthwhile to check. He opened the trunk, casting an eye over the interior. He used his fingers to sweep across the sides of the area, just in case there was something small that had managed to get caught up in the seams. You never knew. Something tiny like an earring – it could be his undoing if he missed it.

There was nothing. He relaxed, walking back to the front of the car.

He took one last look at the barn, before settling behind the wheel and starting the engine. He didn't need to stay until the end. He knew what the ending was going to be. All he had to do now was get on with the next job. This one was done.

There was another routine to check, another location to set up. He couldn't rest now. There were people out there who deserved this, and he was going to make sure they got what they deserved. Cheaters. The kind of people who needed to die, to set things right.

He drove away from the barn, glancing at it only once in his rearview mirror. He wasn't going to be coming back.

This job was as good as done, and he knew no one was going to make it out of there alive without help. And if help did come, well, he was better not being in the vicinity to get caught. In the meantime, he had those boards to get off the window at the new place he'd seen – the perfect place to set up another of his platforms and make everything right again.

CHAPTER ELEVEN

Laura tried to focus on the road, not on Nate's questions, as they roared through Atlanta towards the house they'd only left a short while before.

"It was some Sherlock Holmes level observation, that's all I'm saying," Nate said. He was looking out of the window, not at her, and his voice had that tone to it like he was trying very hard to keep it casual. "I just glanced over the photographs and didn't notice anything."

Laura shrugged, speeding through an intersection just before the light turned red. "I wasn't enjoying looking at Ross's face," she said. "Studying the photographs was less awkward. That grief – it was so raw. I hate having to talk to people like that."

"Yeah." Nate's voice was sympathetic, heavy. Laura knew he felt it too. "Still, kudos. I didn't catch it. And it was a hell of a coincidence to pick up on, that twelve."

"I guess our minds analyze facts in different ways," Laura said. "I've been playing around with that twelve hours, twelve noon, twelve midnight collection in my head all day. That's why it jumped out at me."

It was all true enough, of course. This time, Laura was glad she could actually tell him why she'd fixated on that detail. The vision had helped to reinforce a sense of timeliness in her, a deadline that was coming up. But noticing the number twelve on the photograph had been all her.

It was nice to remember that she was actually good at her job, sometimes.

"It's a good link," Nate acknowledged.

Laura pulled the car to a screeching halt outside the property, looking up at it. The same cars were still parked on the road as before. It didn't look as though anyone had gone home. "It's tenuous," Laura admitted. "But the fact of being the boyfriend of both of them – that's much stronger than the number connection."

"And he's our first lead," Nate grinned, getting out of the car. Laura followed suit, straightening the front of her jacket in a subconscious effort to prepare herself. She hoped he was going to come in for questioning without a fight. With so many other people there, things could get awkward. People could be hostages. Could get in the way, impede a chase. There were a lot of reasons why she so much preferred when these confrontations went down as the suspect was alone.

"Let's do this," Nate said, nodding sharply at her and turning for the door as soon as she nodded back.

Within seconds he was hammering hard on the front door, making sure that he would get someone's attention. It was the older brother, the one they hadn't spoken to, who opened it. He had a look of surprise on his face, like they were the last people he was expecting to see.

"Bradley?" Nate asked, keeping his voice low. Not loud enough to be heard by the people inside.

"No, I'm John," he said, his expression blank and confused.

"No," Nate hissed, leaning forward to keep his voice low while being understood as clearly as possible. "Bradley. Is he still inside with your parents?"

"Oh." John blinked again, then slowly shook his head. "No, he had a practice session to get to."

Nate looked over his shoulder at Laura, his eyes wide. "When?" he asked, turning back.

"Right after you left."

Laura was running calculations in her head. When they first interviewed everyone, Bradley had only just been returning. He'd been out somewhere – to the store, he'd said. She had no idea how long he'd been gone for prior to that. Long enough to head out before noon, set up his victim, swing by the store on the way back, and then pretend it was all innocent?

And now – why had he left again? Was he really playing ball, or had he gone to check on his latest victim?

"Where?" Nate asked, following up with the obvious. Behind him, Laura was already pulling out her cell phone and dialing Captain Blackford's number. She turned her back on the conversation and moved towards the car, already preparing to get into the passenger seat so that Nate could drive while she talked.

"Captain Blackford," he said, his tone surprisingly pleasant.

"This is Agent Frost," Laura rattled out, opening the door and getting into the car. "I need you to trace a registration plate for me. Then we need to put out an APB. Our suspect is on the move."

"Name?" Blackford barked. It was funny how the man could put so much emotion into one single word. Laura heard how his tone had hardened, realizing who he was talking to. But she also heard a note of grudging respect, no doubt towards the fact that they had already managed to get a suspect on a case that had proven difficult for his men.

"Bradley Milford," Laura replied. "He's a minor league baseball player for a local team, if that helps."

"I know the man you mean. We just spoke about him," Blackford replied, with a light trace of irritation in his voice. There was a kind of rustling noise and then clacking, like he'd moved to a computer and started typing. Somehow, it didn't surprise Laura that he was interested in the local sports scene. Nate got into the car beside her, behind the wheel, and started programming the GPS with whatever location John Rowse had given him.

"We're told he's at practice right now, but if we don't find him there, we'll have high reason to believe he's on his way to set up or check on a new crime scene," Laura said, as Nate started the car and began to drive. "No idea on whether he'll be armed, so best advice your people to approach with caution."

"Got it." Blackford's typing stopped. "I have it here. You got a pen handy to note it down?"

Laura pulled out her notebook to jot down the registration, as well as the make and model of the car – a newer black coupe. "Thanks," she said. "We'll keep you updated."

Blackford ended the call on his end with a grunt, as if that stood in for a sufficient goodbye.

"You got it?" Nate asked, his eyes flicking overhead to take in the lights as they sped across the city once again.

"Yep, and his guys will keep an eye out," Laura said. She was feeling a surge of adrenaline, a kind of excited hope that they might be on the right path already. If this was him, it was going to be thrilling. Done with a troubling case in less than a day. She wouldn't just have the weekend with Lacey, she'd have the whole week before it to catch up on paperwork and get ready, too.

"We aren't far," Nate said, checking his mirrors. "Sounds like Bradley wasn't entirely honest with us. You think he genuinely works at the hospice?"

"Maybe he's part time. Or a volunteer," Laura said. "These minor league guys, they make... what? Peanuts, really, compared to the majors."

Nate nodded. "I don't think it's a high-A team," he said. "But it's still shady that he didn't mention it. You'd think he'd want to bring it up, if he wasn't hiding something."

Something like his number. Laura couldn't help but agree. Nate was already turning through a set of gates that opened up onto a baseball field, the parking lot to the left scattered with just a small number of cars.

Among them, as Nate found a spot, Laura craned her head and found a black newer-model coupe. The registration matched up.

He was here.

"That's the car," she said, nodding towards it as she opened the door and jumped out. Nate had to hold back to switch off the engine and put the car in park, joining her just as she was done looking through the windows to see if there was anything incriminating left out on the seats. She shook her head – the car was clean. Almost too clean. Like he'd made sure of it before coming out. And who exactly went to practice the day after their girlfriend was murdered, as though nothing was happening?

Maybe someone who didn't quite feel the emotional impact they claimed to. Maybe, Laura thought, someone who had done the killing themselves and didn't need to stay at home and deal with the shock.

"Inside, then," Nate said. Laura followed his lead as they marched across the lot and towards the ticket kiosks guarding the entrance to the field, which were currently manned by a bored-looking teenager in a reflective vest.

"We're closed for practice today," he called out as they approached, his voice coming out strangled with that scratchy quality of late adolescence, not yet fully deepened. "No members of the public."

"Then it's a good job we're not members of the public," Nate said, flipping his badge open. The kid's eyes got wide. "We're looking for one of the players. Are they all on the field?"

"Yes, sir," the teenager said, making an awkward movement with his arms. It was like he'd had the urge to salute, realized it wasn't appropriate, and tried to suppress it. "Um. Should I call my supervisor?"

"That won't be necessary, son," Nate said. Despite the gravity of the moment, Laura had to try hard not to smile. Nate was probably less than twenty years older than the kid, but he was obviously leaning into the fearful respect he was being given. "Just close the gates behind us. We don't want anyone leaving without our having spoken to them."

"Um." The kid looked to the left and then to the right, like he was afraid something was about to happen right now. "What about the other entrance?"

"Where is it?"

"Straight shot down that side," the kid said, pointing. "We have one at either end of the lot, so it's not too crowded on game nights."

"Thanks," Nate said, glancing at Laura to make sure she'd heard. "Maybe you ought to radio that supervisor after all, get him to shut up shop over there too. Got it?"

"Yes, sir," the kid said smartly, nodding and yanking a handheld radio from his belt.

Laura and Nate walked past him, hearing him excitedly pass the message onto his supervisor over the radio as they did. Then there was a creak and a clang of the pedestrian gate closing. He was doing what he'd been told.

The field wasn't a big one. It was set up a lot more casually than some of the stadiums Laura had seen: the seating areas for fans were smaller, closer to the ground, not built up in a full circle around the field like they were for the majors. The ground was dry, the grass a little on the brown side, as they walked unimpeded right onto the field itself. A cohort of players in white uniforms were set up in various practice areas, running through the motions of different types of training.

Laura shaded her eyes as Nate did the same, both of them scanning the men as much as possible. Although the field was wide, Laura started to feel an increased prickling of alarm. She didn't think she could see the man they'd met at the house.

"Hey," she said, calling out to a man jogging by. He looked like a junior coach or some kind of assistant, judging by how he was dressed. "Excuse me – can you tell me where Bradley Milford is?"

"Are you scouts, or something?" the guy asked, coming to a stop not far from them. Laura walked a few paces closer anyway, not wanting to shout the information loud enough for it to be overheard by others.

"Something," she said. "We're with the FBI. Just want to talk to Mr. Milford about something we think he may be able to help us with."

"Oh," the coach said, paling. "Yeah. I heard about his girlfriend. It's super sad. I don't think he's having a good time of it, today."

"Is that why he isn't on the field?" Laura asked, nodding towards the other players. They already knew he was here, somewhere. Unless he'd left his car behind as evidence that he'd gone where he was supposed to, then walked away. Would he do that?

"He's in the locker room," the coach said, turning and pointing back in the direction he had come from. "We told him he could go home if he wanted, but he said he just needed a little break and then he'd come back out. I don't blame him. Playing can take the mind off things, but it's hard to let go in the first place, you know?"

Privately, Laura thought: *no. Neither of us probably know. How could we know what goes on in the head of a killer?*

"Thank you," Laura said, nodding at him. "We'll take it from here."

The coach, or whoever he was, seemed hesitant. Like he didn't want them to go back there. But he didn't say anything, letting them pass by.

They were probably lucky. Someone with more authority on the team might have put up an argument. Something about how non-team personnel weren't supposed to go back there, or especially how women weren't supposed to be in the men's locker room. But they had a killer to catch. That went beyond the normal rules of who was and wasn't supposed to be in a particular place.

Passing inside the building, a scent immediately hit Laura: something like old socks and body odor. She wrinkled her nose, glancing at Nate, who only laughed.

"You get used to it," he said. "The gym I go to smells like this, too."

Laura shook her head and rolled her eyes. "I don't think I would like to get used to it. You should come to my gym. They actually clean it."

"They clean mine," Nate protested. "It's just we take working out seriously. The scent builds up again, you know?"

Laura shook her head again, pointing to a sign on the wall that indicated the direction of the locker rooms. They passed along a narrow hall with Lino floors, smooth and polished, and the scent only got stronger. "I think what you're trying to tell me is that boys smell."

"I think you could have worked that out a long time before now," Nate laughed. It was a strange sound to hear just then. Considering how long it had been since they'd been relaxed enough to laugh together, it was odd for it to happen right when they were approaching a suspect. But Laura felt it, too. The adrenaline. Being close to your quarry was a rush. Knowing you might have to be prepared for anything – but in this case, there was less fear, because they had no indication that the killer would be armed at all. It wasn't as though they were investigating gunshot wounds or stabbings. For all they knew, he didn't use any weapons at all in claiming his victims.

Just rope and gravity.

They stepped through an opening that led down a twisting hall and back on itself, a kind of privacy feature that left the locker rooms somewhat open while also preventing anyone from seeing in from the hall. Laura let Nate go first, figuring that if she was about to get an eyeful of something unexpected, at least Nate's frame would block the view until the guy had had a moment to scramble for something to cover himself with.

But as she emerged behind him and took in the scene in front of them, she couldn't see anyone at all.

The room was set out almost exactly as she'd imagined it: rows of lockers all around the outside, then benches in front of and between them so that players could sit down to change, most of them already strewn with discarded bits of clothing. A rack divided the center of the room, hung with all kinds of coats and jackets, no doubt left there by the players who'd come dressed for winter. It concealed the back half of the locker from their view, but as Nate looked around it –

He gave a shout, distracting Laura from her glance around the rest of the room. Before she could even react, he took off running, and Laura had no choice but to follow him. She didn't know what he'd seen, but she knew what she would bet on: Bradley Milford, running for it.

CHAPTER TWELVE

As far as Laura was concerned, the locker room was a series of tripping hazards, one after the other. There was a bench set at an angle, maybe left there messily or maybe nudged deliberately before Milford ran, and Laura caught one of her shins on the very edge of it as she attempted to take the shortest route she could across the back of the room. There was another of those winding corridors on the other side, leading to a shower room – thankfully, with none of them turned on, there was no steam obstructing their vision. Nate ran past but Laura hesitated for a moment, checking the large communal shower space was empty, not knowing if he still had Bradley in his sights or not.

It was only a moment's pause, but when Laura chased after him, Nate was already fully around the next bend. When she'd turned it, he was there in front of her again, his large and tall frame filling up the corridor enough that she couldn't see around him. She cursed herself in her head, wondering why she hadn't stopped to grab something in the locker room. If she'd been able to get a vision of where Bradley was going…

She threw herself down the hall as fast as she could, aware that she was little help right now. Nate was closer, and there was no way past him anyway. But she had to keep up. If the path diverged at all, it would be important for them both to be close. To be able to chase him down, no matter where he went.

Nate shot out of a doorway ahead, and when Laura followed, it again took her a moment to get her bearings in the new setting. There were corridors branching off in all directions, doors everywhere, from a wider hallway that was more decorative: plants at set intervals in pots, a noticeboard with things pinned to it, labels on the doors describing whose office they were… The sound of her own shoes squeaking on the polished floor echoed back to her, obscuring any clue of the footsteps ahead.

Laura raced ahead, putting on a surge of energy to get up to Nate again, then realizing it was only because he had slowed slightly. He was looking around, and Laura knew then that he had no idea where their suspect had gone.

"Left," Laura panted out, darting in that direction down the hall that split off to the side. She didn't wait for his reply, but she heard him running onwards, towards the rest of the halls and wherever they led.

Laura was lost quickly. She had no idea where she was. It felt like they had gone downwards on a slope after leaving the field, and by the turns they had taken since, she guessed they were underneath it now. Or at least, she was. Nate could have been in Kansas by now, given how far and sprawling the corridors seemed.

There was light up ahead. Laura put on another burst of speed, feeling that if she were on the run, she'd want to move towards the outside as soon as possible. Get back to her car. Be gone before anyone could figure out that she was no longer on foot.

Laura stumbled upwards into the daylight again, a strange contrast to the yellow lights of the underground halls that made her head hurt. The players were still on the field, carrying on like normal. But a few of them, those closest, had turned and were looking up. Looking...

Looking at the stands, where Laura could now make out the figure of Bradley Milford running, zigzagging across rows and leaping over chairs to get higher, with Nate running behind him.

They must have emerged from another doorway, somewhere nearer to where she'd left Nate, right into the stands. Laura was below them now, picking up speed again after a momentary pause, tracking them along the flat surface of the field. There were no impediments in her way like they had, nothing stopping her from getting up to full speed. She looked ahead, calculating, trying to strain to make out the unfamiliar layout of the field.

The stands – there were openings at the tops of each side, no doubt leading to staircases. People would file up those stairs with their tickets and their snacks when they were coming in from the outside. That must be where Bradley was heading – to get down the stairs and out to the parking lot through the visitor entrance, hoping to use his knowledge of the stadium and his fitness to outpace them!

Laura dashed headlong towards the spot where she and Nate had entered the field in the first place, putting her all into concentrating now. Above her, she could hear them clattering across the metal stands and didn't need to look up. They were still on course for the far edge of the stands, the opening she had seen. She took one glance as she reached the corner, saw Milford almost reaching it, Nate falling behind. He must have tripped or stumbled getting over some of the seats, letting Milford take more of an advantage.

It had to be on her now.

Darting down the narrow opening between the two stands was the biggest risk of it all. Laura was cut off, unable to see either Milford or Nate now, only hoping that her theory had been correct, and she was about to emerge in the right place. She aimed for the place where the wall of the stands beside her stopped and the path opened up again, towards the entrance, running as fast as she could –

She was knocked to the ground as she went bodily into him, colliding just as Milford came to the bottom of the stairs and leaped outwards. He had been looking behind him, the only piece of information she managed to gather in the flash of seeing him before they hit one another. Laura rolled, saw him sprawled across the ground next to her and threw herself forward again, only for him to recover his senses enough to lunge out of the way at the same time.

Right into Nate, who was barreling down the stairs fast enough to leap for him.

"That's enough!" Nate shouted, pinning him to the ground successfully this time. Laura assessed herself quickly, checking for injuries. She had probably a good enough bruise developing on her right shoulder, but that was all in. She grabbed her handcuffs from her belt and used them to restrain Milford, allowing Nate to get up.

She looked over in time to see the young security guard, the one who had let them in, walking out a few paces from his post and staring at them wide-eyed. He blanched immediately, as if realizing that he had been caught leaving the place they had told him to stand watch and disappeared back towards the gate.

"I swear, it was just for me," Milford said, his words coming out high with panic and strained as he turned his head against the ground. "I wasn't going to give them to anyone else. I'm not distributing, or anything like that. You have to believe me!"

Laura blinked.

"What are you talking about?" she asked.

"The drugs," Milford said, as if it was obvious that was what they were all here to talk about.

CHAPTER THIRTEEN

Laura stepped back to allow Nate to haul Milford to his feet, setting him back down again at the foot of the metal stairs. Propped up like this in a sitting position, with his hands still cuffed behind his back, it was easier at least to talk to him.

"Okay," Nate said. "Start talking. Now."

"W-well," Milford stuttered, looking between the two of them uncertainly. "I, I don't know, what..."

"Cat's got your tongue now, has it?" Nate said, his words sharp and angry. "You've as much as admitted that you have drugs in your possession. I think you'd better start telling us everything."

Milford nodded, his shoulders sagging in recognition of the fact that they had him dead to rights. If he had been smart, he would have kept quiet right from the beginning, instead of trying to clear his name and only incriminating himself even further. "Okay," he said. "They're in my pocket."

Nate stepped forward, quickly patting both sides of Milford's hips until he found a pocket that rattled. He pulled out a small bottle of pills, unmarked except for a mysterious letter printed in large font right on the front.

"What are they?" Laura asked. They would probably have to run a full toxicology report on them at the lab in order to make any kind of arrest stick, but it would be better to hear it from him first. To know exactly what they were dealing with.

"I just..." Milford sighed. "I needed a bit of an edge, you know? Something to make me faster, stronger. I wanted to make it to the majors. One of the boys on the team has this supplier, he told me they can't be traced yet. They won't show up in any tests they make us do."

Nate opened the bottle, shaking it a little and eyeing the pills suspiciously. He tipped one out into his hand, examining the markings on it closely. Then he barked out a laugh. "If this is what I think it is," he said "you've been tricked. They absolutely are testing for these kinds of things now. You'd have been caught within five minutes of stepping anywhere near a major league team."

"What are they?" Laura asked, frowning. "Side effects?"

Nate shook his head. "They're not steroidal. No violence or aggression expected."

She sighed, folding her arms across her chest. It would have been nice if they could chalk all this up to drug induced rage. It would have made a nice neat little court case, the kind of thing that a jury could sign off on pretty quickly. But, no. Apparently, they were going to have to work for it.

"Wait a second," Milford said, looking between them with an owlish expression. "You didn't come here about the drugs?"

"They do, however, come with a nice serving of paranoia," Nate commented dryly.

"No," Laura said. "We didn't come here about the drugs. We came here to talk to you about your girlfriend."

"Oh," Milford said, dropping his head down to the ground again. "Veronica. Damnit. I've been so jumpy ever since all the cops and you guys came to the house, I thought you must have figured it out about the drugs. I thought that's why you came here, instead of finding me at home."

"No," Laura said, finding it difficult not to start yelling at him for his selfishness. His girlfriend was dead, and he was worried about his drug habit? He was looking more and more suspicious in her eyes by the minute. Surely, only a psychopath would care this little about her. "Not Veronica. Stephanie."

There was a pause. Milford looked up at her, frowning and squinting his eyes. Then his expression cleared a little, though he looked no less mystified. "You mean, Stephanie and Ross, kind of Stephanie?"

"Stephanie Marchall," Laura confirmed. "Your ex-girlfriend, isn't that right?"

"Yeah," Milford said, but he shook his head again. "I mean, a long time ago. She's married now. To Ross. They've been together for ages. We ended up staying friends, all three of us. I wouldn't even think about calling her my girlfriend anymore. It was so long ago, it barely even registers."

"It would seem so," Laura said. "You're not even that upset about it, are you?"

Milford frowned again, his brow turning into a jagged line. "Upset about her marrying Ross? No, not really. He's a great guy. From what I heard, they're happy together. I've moved on, anyway."

"Not about her marrying Ross," Laura said. "About her dying."

68

Milford's face dropped, almost comically so. The color drained out of him once again, and he looked over at Nate as if he was trying to figure out if Laura was telling the truth.

"She's dead?" he asked, his voice dropping to barely a hoarse whisper.

Laura felt an impatience growing at the back of her mind, in the pit of her stomach. He would have to be one of the best actors the world had ever seen to be able to pull this off. First there was the whole thing about the drugs, and now this. It was like he really didn't know that Stephanie was dead. She had seen a few local news reports, knew that they were just naming the dead as 'local women' for now. Captain Blackford had given some kind of statement to the press a couple of days ago about not being able to give the full name of the first victim before her whole family had been notified.

The shock on his face, in his voice, it seemed genuine. Which was very bad news for them, because it meant that Bradley Milford was probably innocent.

"Where were you yesterday between the hours of eleven AM and midnight?" Laura asked, deciding to get right to the point.

"I was at my coach's house," Bradley said. "We had a team party."

"Did you stay all day?" Nate asked. "Or did you come and go to the store, like you were doing earlier today?"

"No, I was there all day." Milford shrugged his shoulders. "Coach needed help with this bathroom upgrade he's doing, so we all pitched in and then afterwards we cracked open some beers and had a good time. I was still there late, so I slept in the spare room, then in the early hours I got woken by the phone call about Vee and headed right to her parents' place instead. That's why I had to go to the store to get supplies. I needed to brush my teeth, all of that kind of stuff, before coming out to practice. After your visit earlier, I ended up just coming straight here and using the showers. Luckily, I usually keep a spare uniform and change of clothes in my locker, just in case. But, is it true? Is Stephanie really dead as well?"

"I'm afraid she is," Laura said. It seemed like it was cut and dry now, no way to avoid the truth. He had an alibi. He couldn't possibly have put Veronica in position on that platform if he was working hard on a DIY project all day. And, yes, there were sometimes issues with allowing someone to use their parents as an alibi. There was a certain amount of bias involved. But that stacked up against the way he was acting... it was a convincing show. "And two days before that, what were you doing?" she added, just to be sure.

"I was here," Milford said. "We had practice, and a game in the evening."

That ruled him out for Stephanie Marchall, too. He wouldn't have needed to be there at the end, when he could have snuck away after the game to get to the gas station before midnight. That wasn't the timeframe they were most concerned about. It was earlier in the day, when Stephanie was set up on the platform. That was when it was sure the killer had to be around.

And if he'd been here, there were enough witnesses and doubtless enough security camera footage to back him up.

"I'm going to call Blackford, get someone down here to take him in for the drugs," Nate suggested. From his tone, Laura could hear that he'd come to the same conclusion she had. He wasn't their killer.

She watched Milford in silence while Nate walked away a distance to make the call. Her mind was on the vision she had seen earlier. The clock ticking down. The killer had to have his victim in place already by now. That meant that every false lead, every dead end, was ticking down her life.

If only Laura's vision had given her more information, a wider view. Some clue about the location, even the identity of the victim. Any flash at all of the killer themselves. But she had nothing.

Not for the first time, and almost definitely not for the last, she found herself wishing she knew how to control this. It was getting into the early evening already, the lights over the field starting to tick on in the early darkness of the winter day. It wouldn't be long before real dark set in, even though people were only just starting to leave their workplaces and travel home.

Laura had always thought of darkness as the domain of killers. There was something about it. The way it hid. So many of the cases she worked involved people who were attacked and killed at night. This one was different, and yet the same. The abduction may have been happening during the day, but it was the night that held the death.

Midnight. A firm deadline. One they couldn't ignore.

They were going to have to work fast, now, to get this done.

Nate walked back over to join them, his cell phone still in his hand. "What are you thinking?" he asked Laura, in a low tone. They both glanced at Milford, who showed little sign of listening in, and walked a couple of steps away anyway. Not far enough that he would be able to get any great distance on them if he decided to run again, but far enough for a quiet conversation to remain mostly private.

"I'm thinking that we're running out of time," Laura said bluntly. "We don't know what kind of timeframe he's working on, but this killer has already given us a view of his MO that we can't ignore. If he has his next victim already, we only have about five and a half hours before they're dead."

Nate checked his watch, verifying her count. "In a case like this, I think we assume he has a victim until we have some kind of conclusive proof that he doesn't," he said. "I would normally point to the fact that there was a two-day gap between the first and second victims, but we both know that killers escalate. And if he's smart, he'll know that the chance of getting caught increases as the deaths rack up, and he'll want to get as many done as possible."

Laura couldn't help but shiver. It was chilling, to hear it in those terms. As many as possible. Yes, that was normally what sadistic, brutal killers like this went for. Putting as many people through their tortures as they could. Racking up a body count. Whether it was some kind of conscious decision, some crusade to clean up the world or end personal grudges, or simply an insatiable hunger to keep doing it again, the count was often part of the point.

"And we have no leads," Laura said. She closed her eyes momentarily, rubbing the bridge of her nose. She'd had more challenging cases than this one, but hardly by much. There were so few clues to go on, and she hated the idea that they might need another death in order to start putting the pieces together.

Two was a coincidence. Three was a pattern. Everything they thought they knew… it could still be changed.

"Maybe," Nate said, thoughtfully. "We do know that both women had to have been abducted more than twelve hours before they died. That's a long enough time for someone to get suspicious."

Laura looked at him, starting to understand what he was saying. "Someone doesn't come home from work, or turn up for their shift, or answer calls about how they were supposed to meet a friend for dinner."

"Maybe they didn't even show up to work this morning," Nate pointed out. "We could have a missing person report already."

"So, we start there," Laura nodded. "Prioritize any local women who have been reported missing in the past day. Get Blackford and his team going out to conduct interviews, get as much information as possible. Anyone whose disappearance is out of character, especially."

Nate put his phone to his ear again, nodding. "I'll call again, get this all set up. I just hope there are enough leads to make this work. I don't know how many missing person cases there can be in such a short space of time. And there's always a chance the next one, whoever she is, might fall through the cracks. No one noticing until it's too late."

"Then we use the other piece of information we have," Laura pointed out. "The locations. He always chooses abandoned locations. We should have as many units as are available sent out to any abandoned buildings they know of. Even if he's still in the process of setting up a new platform somewhere, we could find it, set a team to stake it out and wait for him."

"Good idea," Nate said, turning around to make the call.

Laura watched Milford, making sure he wasn't about to make another break for it, without really seeing him.

If they didn't get any immediate leads, this was about to be a long night. She hooked her hands under her arms, crossing them tighter across her chest, thinking about how the temperature was going to drop as night fell. Somewhere out there, in a cold, abandoned building, she couldn't help but picture another woman. Bound and alone. A clock ticking around her neck.

And they only had a handful of hours to check all of the abandoned places in a city as big as Atlanta.

What were the chances, Laura wondered, of them actually getting it right?

CHAPTER FOURTEEN

Lincoln tried and failed to get his breathing under control, attempting to remember some techniques a therapist had told him once, years ago. What was it? Count five things you can see?

Well, that wasn't easy, in itself. The light outside was fading, and though he'd been able to see a little further earlier, now he was barely able to make out anything. The clock on his chest, that was one. It only had a few hours left on it, now. The timer ticking down.

A fresh wave of panic ran through him at the thought of that timer. He'd asked. He'd been conscious enough when the stranger was setting him up on the platform that he'd been able to ask, even if he wasn't able to struggle away.

No, don't think of that now, Lincoln told himself. He needed to calm down first. Calm down, work out a way out of this, and then consider everything that had happened later.

What else could he see?

The ropes around his body. That was another thing. They tied his hands together and his ankles, and wound across and over his chest as well, pinning his arms to one side. He felt like a pinata, about ready to drop. He couldn't see the one around his neck, could only feel it.

The third thing he could see was the window opposite him. It was so filthy that it barely let in any light and seeing anything through it was mostly out of the question. At least he'd had a little muted daylight, earlier. Now that was gone, too.

The fourth thing was the platform he was standing on, which he could make out if he tilted his head. It was some kind of rough wood, not polished or painted, and clearly only a temporary construction. The fifth thing he could see was the floor, not so far down he couldn't make it out but definitely far enough to be out of reach.

Okay, good. He was doing it. Now, what was next? Oh, yeah – four things he could feel. The ropes, that was easy, because it felt like they were cutting into his skin. The fabric of his jacket, right under his fingers if he tried to stretch them out. What else? He felt... cold. It was cold in here. And he could feel the bounce of the platform under his feet, how unstable it was if he tried to move. The wood was kind of springy. Maybe because it wasn't attached to anything at the other end, like a diving board. He'd been afraid, at first, that it wasn't going to hold his weight.

Next was three things he could smell. Huh. It was musty up here; he could smell that. Like the place hadn't been disturbed in a long while. And a faint smell of something that he thought was probably the rotting hay he'd seen in the corner when the sun was still out. He hadn't ever smelled it before, but he had a feeling it had to be that. And the gag that had been pushed into his mouth, wrapped around his head so it wouldn't come out, that had a kind of oily smell to it. At least, he thought so.

Two things he could hear. He listened, hard, for a moment. The ticking of the clock. And out there… nothing.

No, not nothing. Some kind of bird call. He didn't know anything about birds, didn't know if it was an owl or a sparrow or something he'd never heard of before. But Lincoln could identify it as a bird. Which in itself worried him, because he wanted to hear traffic and people's voices and things that might save him.

The last thing was something he could taste. He could taste his own blood. He'd bitten his tongue trying to get the gag out of his mouth.

Lincoln breathed deeply, trying to surround himself with the immediacy of it. That was what his therapist had said to do. Be in the moment.

Okay, well, in this moment, he was trying not to die on a goddamn platform in the middle of an abandoned building with a timer telling him exactly how long he had to live.

As it turned out, meditation techniques weren't much use in this kind of situation.

Lincoln thought back, trying to retrace the conversation he'd had with the man who left him here. The stranger. He'd been so calm. That was he weirdest part of it. And firm, too. Like Lincoln was a little kid acting up and the stranger had a job to do, and he wasn't going to take any sass from him.

Lincoln wasn't sure if he'd been supposed to come around when he did. He'd looked up, found himself lying on the old wooden floorboards, and made some kind of noise. A gasp, or something. If he'd been more awake, he would have kept himself quiet, but then it was too late before he had a chance to realize. The guy had been working on something up there, on a ladder, and he'd come down to check that Lincoln was still securely tied up.

He'd tried to struggle, of course. But the ropes were holding him so tightly. He couldn't even crawl effectively. And when the stranger

74

pulled him over towards the ladder and then hauled him up by the ropes, Lincoln hadn't been able to do anything at all. Once they got up high, he'd stopped struggling out of fear that he would fall to the ground and break both his legs, or his spine, or his face. Without his arms free, there was nothing he could do.

"Why are you doing this?" he'd asked, before he even really understood what 'this' was.

And the stranger had stopped and looked at him with that odd kind of strict calm. He'd said, "Because you cheated."

And Lincoln had no idea what he was going on about.

There had been some kind of desperate rush in his head to try and understand. To connect it to anything he could. To his fourth-grade math test, when, yes, he'd looked at his friend Bobby's answers because he'd forgotten to study the night before and couldn't remember how to do a certain sum. And that was the only thing he could think of, and it was totally stupid, but he'd blurted it out anyway. "At school?"

And he could have sworn the guy looked at him like he was an alien. This guy, who had hauled him up a ladder to a section of half-rotted floorboards up on a second level of the building, and then onto a short, homemade platform. The thing he'd been setting up when Lincoln woke.

"No," he'd said. "You cheated death."

And Lincoln had realized exactly what he meant, and at that moment something inside of him went very cold. Because he'd known. He'd known that much was true.

"What are you talking about?" he'd asked, anyway, because why not? He had to try and get out of here. Keeping the stranger talking meant at least they were having a conversation, and nothing worse than that was happening to Lincoln. At that moment, he'd still had no idea of the full extent of what was coming.

"You cheated death and got a second chance at life," the stranger had said, with that weird patience, working on something just outside of Lincoln's field of view. "That's not fair. That's not how it's supposed to work."

"It wasn't really my fault," Lincoln had said, starting to feel more than a little panicked. "I didn't ask to get saved, or anything. I mean, I'm grateful I was. But it's not really cheating. Not if you don't do it on purpose."

"Even so," the stranger said. And then he reached over and hauled Lincoln to his feet, and that was when he put the rope around his neck for the first time.

And by the time Lincoln had thought to try and get away, somehow, anyhow, the noose had hit the back of his neck and the front of it at the same time, and he realized there was no way to get out of it.

Not without his hands.

"You're gonna hang me?" he'd asked, his voice coming out high and strained and weird to his own ears.

"Yes and no," the stranger had said. "You're going to hang. I won't be here. I suppose you could say that time is going to hang you."

"What the hell does that mean?" Lincoln had asked, struggling to try and get his arms free. Fruitlessly, of course.

"Well, if you look down, you'll see a timer," the stranger had said, with that same eerie calm. Lincoln looked at the clock on his chest. It was set for 0:00. Then the stranger reached out and started to push buttons, changing it. Above the timer was a clock face, and Lincoln realized it was almost exactly twelve noon. "Now, when this timer goes off, this platform that we're standing on is going to drop. You see that hinge over there?"

Lincoln looked, taking it in. "What?" he'd said, which was about all his terrified mind could manage.

"That's going to swing downwards, pretty quickly," the stranger said. "I've been making some tweaks, trying to make sure it will drop fast enough. It ought to break your neck. It's going to be quite quick, don't worry about that. The point is: your time is almost up."

"Why give me the time?" Lincoln asked desperately. Not because he wanted to push the guy into hanging him right now. Because he wanted to stop him. To make him think. To maybe, against all odds, make him see that he was doing something crazy.

The stranger didn't answer. He pushed a final button on the timer, setting it going, and stepped back with a look of satisfaction. "I'm going to have to leave now, Lincoln," he'd said. Like a teacher telling a child fairly and calmly what was going to happen to them as punishment. There was no anger in it. Just like it was a thing he *had* to do. Not his own choice, but not something he disagreed with either. "I would recommend that you use this time wisely. I've not been through it myself, but I imagine it will give you a chance for some introspection." And he'd tied the gag around Lincoln's mouth.

And then he'd gone.

And that had been more than six hours ago.

Lincoln let out a desperate whine behind the gag, wishing at least this bit of cloth was out of the way so that he could breathe properly, so he could call out. That was the point, obviously.

He turned in a small circle, the most amount of shuffling his legs could manage. He'd already tried to walk towards the hinge. The rope wasn't long enough. He pushed against it again now, feeling it scrape against the skin of his chin and neck. Maybe if he forced it...

Lincoln pushed forward until he was forced to give up, stepping back with a cry that was felt more than heard in his throat. It was too tight. Step that way, and he'd pass out before he got anywhere.

He turned in a small circle again, looking for something that might help him, tears spilling over his cheeks as he saw the same nothing again and again with each rotation.

He only had a handful of hours left before it was all going to be over.

CHAPTER FIFTEEN

"Nothing yet?" Laura asked, searching Nate's face for signs of an answer.

He shook his head grimly, making her shoulders sag.

It had been hours of searching, and they were still no closer to finding the location of the killer's next victim. "How many spots do we still have left to search?"

Nate took the map from her, spreading it out across the dashboard of their parked car. It was already littered with rings and marks and lines, the first of them drawn on hastily during the briefing Captain Blackford had put together and the rest updated throughout the night. Whole areas of the outskirts of Atlanta, plus some central spots, were shaded out. Marked as checked.

And nothing had been found.

"We're here," Nate said, finding the old church they were standing in front of and marking it off with a wide-tipped blue pen. It was burnt out, almost completely. There was nowhere for a platform to even attach, and even if there had been, it wouldn't have been easy for the killer to hide what he was doing. "The latest updates have crossed off everything marked in the east. Those teams are going to move up, split up through the city and cover any properties that we aren't yet aware of, doing a grid pattern search through the city blocks."

Laura looked over the map again, feeling the frustration mounting. All she wanted to do was slam her hand down on the dashboard and swear loudly, but she didn't. Both because it wouldn't help, and because she didn't want to inadvertently set off any airbags. Or stress Nate out any further, which he didn't need either.

"Where are we going next?" she asked.

Nate pointed to a larger circle on the map. "Here," he said. "I think it's probably time we split up. It's already past ten, and we only have a couple of hours left. We need to cover more ground."

"We only have one car," Laura pointed out.

"I know that," Nate said, giving her a look in the harsh yellow glow of the car's overhead light. "This here is a whole industrial complex that fell out of use. According to the map, it's a factory and a bunch of warehouses. Probably some smaller outbuildings as well. I'm thinking you drop me off there and head on to the next site. It'll take me long enough to get through them all. If I need to, I can call you to swing back and pick me up, or I can get a cab or something. Anything to speed this up."

"What if the killer's there?" Laura asked, a fear seizing her. She hadn't touched Nate in a long time, deliberately so. She knew that if she did, even for a brief moment, that shadow of death would be waiting for her. Waiting for him. Waiting to claim him.

What if this was the moment? He went off alone, and the killer found him and attacked him before he could raise the alarm?

"I'll be careful," Nate promised. "I've got my cell phone, and I've got your number on speed dial alongside Captain Blackford's. I've got my radio. I'll stay quiet and cautious. What else am I supposed to do?"

"You're supposed to stick with your partner so you're at less of a risk," Laura argued.

"If he can ambush me and take me down, then he can ambush both of us pretty easily anyway," Nate said. It sounded like he was trying to be reasonable, but he was actually only making Laura more nervous for his safety. "And what else are we going to do? Let him get away with it? Let someone else die? We only have two hours left, and even with all the other teams searching right now, Atlanta is a big city."

Laura took a breath. He was right, of course. If it was the other way around, she wouldn't hesitate to put her own life at risk in order to save the life of a potential murder victim.

That was part of the job.

She sighed out that breath heavily, starting the engine of the car. "Fine," she said. Not because she was definitely agreeing, but because she figured the drive would give her more time to think of objections. And because Nate's point still stood. The night wasn't getting any younger.

Laura watched Atlanta flash by outside the window. Not a great neighborhood. There was more graffiti and broken glass than there were open businesses, by what she could see. Leaving him alone here was even more of a concern, not that he would listen. She just had to think of something. But then they were pulling up outside a security fence bolted with a heavy chain, and Laura still hadn't thought of anything.

"There's a number on the sign," Nate said, nodding ahead. "I'll see if I can get hold of the guy with the keys. If I can't, I'll just hop the fence. I'm sure the security service will either see me doing it and come to try and arrest me, or they won't see me at all. Either way, I'll get in.

You're heading out to this one next, right? The closed-up grocery store."

"Right," Laura said. She was still hesitant. She felt like she was about to lose him, and she was letting the opportunity to stop that from happening slip through her fingers.

Her fingers...

And she did it, without letting herself think. She reached out and put her hand on Nate's wrist, felt the bare skin under hers. He was surprisingly warm, given the cold of the night.

But Laura barely even registered that, because swirling all around her was that death. That blackness. So hard to quantify, but there, hovering around her like sickness, making her want to throw up. To get away.

The feeling that he was going to die.

She fought for breath, for the nausea to go away. At least it hadn't changed. She would have expected it to be darker, deeper, more choking if he was about to die right now. She would have hoped for a vision.

But then again, she didn't really understand how it worked anyway. The only other time she'd really, fully experienced it had been with her father, and one shadow of death didn't necessarily have to act like all the others.

But, still.

"Nate," she said, choking the words out and trying to sound normal while she did it. "Be careful."

He gave her an odd look, something almost sentimental, and nodded. "I will," he said, opening his door and getting out of the car, pulling away from her hand.

Laura sat back in the driver's seat as he slammed the door shut and walked towards the gates in the glow of the headlights.

She'd had no vision, she told herself again. If death was waiting for Nate inside that complex, there was nothing she could do about it. That was cold comfort, but it was something. He wanted this. It was his choice.

She still felt sick and afraid as she drove away.

"Okay," she said out loud, as she looked down at the reprogrammed GPS and tried to focus on going in the right direction at a good speed. More to hear the sound of her own voice than anything else. To try and reassure herself.

It didn't really work.

It was only as she pulled up outside the grocery store that Laura remembered she had her own safety to think about, too. Going in distracted would be a much bigger risk than going in alone. She had to focus, think. Get her head back into the right place.

She just wished a vision would come. Something about Nate. Something about the case. Anything. Right now, she felt like she was fumbling in the dark. And even though this must have been how most people felt all the time, without the promise of a vision ever to enlighten them, she hated it.

The property was all boarded up, heavy padlocks on the front door and wooden coverings over all of the windows. Still, it hadn't stopped someone from getting in. There was graffiti all over the exterior and scattered broken bottles and empty cans lying in the short section of what would have once been landscaped grass before the street. Either teenagers, or homeless people, Laura had to bet.

She moved around the property once, first in a circle, checking out all possible entrances and exits, her mind on high alert. She couldn't risk being ambushed, alone out here. In the front of the store, there was enough light coming from nearby streetlights to still give her enough to see by. Round back, though, the shadows were long. She had no choice but to switch on her flashlight and point it around, lining it up with the barrel of her gun just for safety's sake. If someone sprang out of those shadows at her while she was looking, she wasn't going to get caught unaware.

The radio she'd been given to keep track of the investigation crackled at her belt, and Laura jumped, swearing. She retreated back to the street before turning it up to listen in, taking it off her belt and holding it to her ear.

" – New report," someone was saying, a male voice she didn't recognize. "We've just had confirmation the woman has returned home. She wasn't missing, just told us some story about losing her cell phone and getting stuck out of town. False alarm."

"Thank you." That was Captain Blackford, his tone sharp and businesslike. "HQ, report. That's how many missing women left unresolved?"

"That was the last one, Captain," someone fired back, a woman this time. "All new missing women cases from the past twenty-four hours are marked as resolved."

"Alright." A pause. "Let's go back further. Past forty-eight. Keep searching."

Laura turned the volume down again, partly relieved and partly dismayed. The local police were doing their jobs, despite how unwilling Captain Blackford might have seemed. They were marking off every task that Laura and Nate had asked of them. The missing women – whoever this new victim was, it was looking like she hadn't even been reported as gone yet. As the night wore on, that might change. But for now, it was only the locations that could give them anything.

Laura turned her radio down to the minimum volume and approached the closed-down store again, this time looking for the entrance point.

She'd seen it, round the back. A boarded-up window where the nails had been wrenched out on one side. The boards were still hanging in place, but it didn't take an expert to see how easily they could be moved aside to let someone in.

Laura approached cautiously, listening hard, first pointing her flashlight at the window itself and the surrounding area. It had rained within the last few days, and there were no footprints on the ground beside it. That would have been a dead giveaway if someone was inside now. But then again, the soil looked solid now, like it might not take prints too easily. Maybe it was possible someone had gone in within the past day.

Laura crouched by the window, looking down. On the ground, her flashlight had picked out a glint of something. A nail. It must have been one of the ones torn out of the boards. The head was rusty from where it had been sitting in the elements since the place was boarded up. The rest of it, though…

Laura reached out and touched it, seeing how the part of the nail that had been inside the wood was still clean and rust-free. A headache sparked in her temple as she realized what it meant: that it must have been pulled out recently, because otherwise it would also have rusted by now, or at least picked up more dirt than this. It might even have been moved away by the elements or by foraging city animals –

Laura saw it like a flash. A glimpse of something within the darkness, like a lightning flash illuminating a scene. A white barn. Falling apart. The paint peeling back away from the dark wood underneath. A high window so obscured with grime it was impossible to make it out.

An old tree beside the barn. Twisted up towards the sky, bare branches reaching for something. An old scar down the trunk, something like an old lightning hit or the blow of an ax that had never returned to finish the job. Dead leaves on the ground around it.

From one strong and thick branch, almost improbably, a rope swing holding a tire. Something that had once come off a tractor or some other piece of farm equipment. Big and bulky. The rubber cracked and worn in places now and dropping away, the rope dark with age, like it might snap at any moment.

Laura blinked, clearing her head. She dropped the nail and wiped her hand on her pants leg, thinking. What had she seen?

And why?

She concentrated, putting it together piece by piece in her mind. Her visions showed her the future, but not always the future she was interested in. Not always murder or terrible things. But there was always some kind of connection, some trigger.

The nail had set off the vision. So, what was she seeing? The place where the nail would end up? That seemed unlikely. The head was rusted already, and it had been dropped on the ground. How likely was it, really, that someone was going to gather it up and go use it to board up another place?

Then it had to be something to do with the person who had pried the nail off the board. And if that person was the killer...

Laura stood up, filled with new resolve. The entire time she'd been here, she hadn't heard any movement from inside. Nor had she seen anyone skulking around the place, watching her or it. It seemed as abandoned as it was supposed to be.

She was going to have to take the risk that her assumption was correct.

Laura reached out and grabbed the edge of the lowest board, finding it loose enough to swing out past the edge of the window frame and down. She lowered it until it hit the ground, watching the other boards follow suit without it propping them up. The window was wide enough and high enough up that the boards left an opening behind – an opening big enough for someone to climb through.

There was no glass behind it. The window itself was long since gone, not even a single shard of glass intact.

Laura leaned forward, shining her flashlight into the hole. She swept the narrow beam of light across shelving units, caked with dust and cobwebs, some of them still containing the odd abandoned can of something. A few of them had been tipped over, maybe moved back purposefully.

She swung the beam of light up from that spot –

And then she saw it.

A platform, set up high above the cashiers' lines, rigged in position. There was a rope hanging from the beams of the roof, dangling ominously with nothing inside it. There was no one here.

But she was on his track.

And she knew where he must be now.

CHAPTER SIXTEEN

Laura sat back inside the warmth and comfort of the car, away from the potential exposure of the store. She pulled the radio off her belt and spoke into it urgently.

"Unit required to the abandoned property marked with key A152 on the map," she said. "We have a hit on a future location setup."

There was a flurry of crackling over the radio in response, as though several people had all pushed their buttons at once in knee-jerk surprise.

"Unit seventeen, please respond," the operator at HQ came back.

"Unit seventeen, en route."

"Agent Frost?" that was Blackford.

"Go ahead," Laura told him.

"You have a platform setup?"

"Affirmative," Laura replied. "No sign of suspect or victim. The property is at this moment empty."

"Unit seventeen, stay alert," Captain Blackford said. "You too, Agent Frost. No telling when this guy will show up."

"Agreed." Laura paused, wondering if she should say it, and then gave into her instincts. They needed to track this new place down, the one she had seen, in case it was where he was now. Yes, she was probably going to sound crazy if anyone asked her how she knew what she was looking for. Yes, if Nate heard, he was going to think she was hallucinating or something. But there was a life on the line, and none of that mattered if she could save it. "Can I get local assistance identifying a locale? I'm looking for a white-painted barn. Abandoned."

There was a short pause. Then, "Ma'am, there are a lot of abandoned barns around the outskirts of the city. Might need to have more data on that one."

Laura thought for a moment. "There's a big tree outside, looks like it got struck by lightning or something. Huge tire on a rope swing, like a tractor tire."

There was another pause, longer this time. Silence. Laura was about to repeat her request, wondering whether no one knew what she was describing or whether the message simply hadn't been clear enough, when the radio crackled to life once again.

"I can't be absolutely sure, but that sounds like the old Thousand Oak property." It was a new voice, one she hadn't heard before. "It's not within the scope of our search right now, given the location and the type of property not matching up with what we've been seeing so far."

"Thousand Oak?" Laura repeated, already using one hand to type it into her phone's map search. "Is that the name of the farm?"

"Yes, ma'am. It's out by Interstate 285, down off the way a bit."

Laura found it on her search, quickly inputting the information into her GPS. "Thank you. Unit seventeen, what's your ETA at marker A152?"

"ETA two minutes," came the voice which had first confirmed they were on the way.

Laura started the engine, waiting impatiently for them to show. As soon as they were here and able to surveil the place, she could go.

She dialed Nate's number, knowing she was going to need back-up – but he was going to have to find his own way there. She couldn't spare the time to go back in his direction.

Because she knew where the current victim was hanging – and they had another hour to get there. But that didn't mean she wanted to waste a single minute. Not if that person was hanging there even now, trying to tear the skin off their own hands to get out of their ropes.

***

Laura wrestled the car into submission along the old dirt track, cursing every time she hit a rock or tree root in the path and jolted herself up and down. She'd switched the headlights down to the lowest possible setting, needing to see but also dreading the idea of being seen.

If the killer was still around here, there was every chance that he would try to stop her from interfering. That he would be watching and waiting to make sure his victim died as intended. And she was alone.

If he took her out, then Nate might arrive too late.

"Come on," Laura muttered to herself, leaning low over the steering wheel as she strained to see. Up ahead, it loomed like a ghost out of the darkness: the white-painted barn, glowing in the lights from the car.

Laura killed the engine immediately, taking only a moment for her eyes to adjust to the new darkness. Even though the city wasn't far away – just a couple of minutes back through twisting back roads to get within sight of the interstate – it was private and dark here. The trees formed a natural shelter, and the overgrown fields close around the farm were another barrier to the rest of civilization, so near and yet seemingly so far away.

The farmhouse itself was in bad repair, a very visible hole in the roof even from here. There were no cars parked outside, no sign of anyone else around. Laura waited only the shortest time she possibly could to be somewhat confident there was no one hiding in the shadows before grabbing her flashlight and cell phone from the seat beside her, slipping the phone into her pocket and holding her gun instead. She left the radio on her belt but turned it to silent. If someone was here, the last thing she wanted was for them to hear her coming.

Laura didn't hesitate as she got out of the car, closing the door as quietly as she could and advancing the rest of the way on foot. The farmhouse was directly ahead of her, but the barn was off to one side, a short walk further on. The tree stood outside just as she had seen it, hanging silently, the tire waiting like it was a trap.

There was barely a sound outside, other than a few bird calls that seemed to retreat further away. No doubt fleeing the presence of a human in the area. She hoped their killer was not an ornithologist, someone who could read distress calls and know that the birds were issuing a warning. But it was all down to chance, now. If he was here; if he wasn't. If he attacked her; if he didn't.

All she could do was proceed with caution, and hope.

She couldn't wait any longer – not when someone's life was in danger.

A cloud lifted from over the moon, and in the stronger light the barn seemed to glow a ghostly white. Laura looked at her wrist and was able to make out the time: it was just before eleven. She still had time. There was still an hour before the platform would drop.

If her visions had been accurate, she still had an hour to save a life.

She might have paused then, approached things more carefully, but the image of Veronica Rowse's destroyed hand was there behind her eyelids when she blinked her eyes. There was no getting rid of it. She needed to get in there, and now. No waiting for Nate. No putting him into the line of fire again, either. He would be much safer if he simply joined them when it was all over.

Laura half-ran up the slight incline towards the barn, as fast as she dared while still being able to keep her gun steady in front of her. Her eyes darted from side to side all the time, looking for some hint of movement. Something that would tell her it wasn't safe.

Her shoes crunched on dead leaves as she passed by the tree, a slow breeze stirring them around her but not strong enough to lift them into the air. They only rustled, so many sepulchral fingers at her feet. She felt a familiar tension running up her neck, adrenaline flaring through all of her nerves as she darted towards the front of the barn.

The huge doors that blocked the entrance were closed, but there was no padlock or chain on them. Laura didn't need to look for another way in, but this one was dangerous. She gulped in breath of freezing cold air. There was no time. She had to do this now. She had to get in there, before it was too late.

She touched the door handle, grabbed it hard, and yanked it back, completing the motion by pulling her hand back to the gun as quickly as she could.

She stood there for a long moment, unable to make out anything in the gloom of the inside of the barn. The moonlight didn't penetrate this far, and she stood with her legs planted apart and her gun up, ready to fire. Ready to fire at anything that tried to walk out of there, or move in the corners of her vision, or lift a glinting weapon of its own…

There was nothing. No movement on the floor. She lifted her eyes. Was there movement up there? She couldn't make out enough to see. The cloud had drifted over the moon again, leaving her almost blind. There was no sound, nothing that told her of anyone moving towards her…

And then she heard it. A creaking noise. A dry, rhythmic creaking coming from somewhere up towards the top of the barn, where the hayloft ought to be.

With shaking hands, Laura reached down and grabbed the flashlight she had stashed in her pocket. She lifted it again to place it along the barrel of the gun, to hold them both steady together in case she still needed to fire.

She turned on the flashlight.

And the beam of light hit the man swinging from the rafters of the barn, tied completely with ropes around the whole of his torso, a clock timer on his chest showing a countdown to zero.

No.

Laura froze, staring up at the body in dismay. She was supposed to have another hour. There was supposed to be more time.

How could she be late, when it wasn't midnight yet?

Laura jumped, turning around with her gun outstretched at the sound of a noise behind her. When she realized it was a car, she immediately ducked inside the barn, hiding to one side of the doors. Using them as cover. If she needed to, she could fire from here. Maybe get a good shot off before he even saw her…

She aimed her gun at the silhouette emerging from the car, ready to pull the trigger.

**

Nate got out of the car and began to move towards the barn, keeping the headlights on to illuminate the interior of the building. There was no one framed in the doorway, but...

Then someone stepped out, and Nate's hand went to his gun immediately.

"It's me," Laura said, heavily, sounding like she was relieved – but also dismayed at the same time.

"Laura?" Nate called out, his voice louder than hers, breaking what felt like a sacred silence around the farm. "You alright?"

"Yes," she said, but her shoulders slumped as she said it. "The victim is inside. We're too late."

Nate turned to the cops who had given him a ride, the two of them only just now filing out of the car behind him. "Get around the perimeter and look for the suspect," he said. "He might still be out here. Keep your wits about you."

They both nodded, setting off at a rapid pace. Nate walked forward instead, towards his partner. She had turned away from him, looking back and up at something on the inside of the barn. As Nate stepped closer, he saw what it was.

The man hanging from the ceiling, still swaying slightly from side to side like a macabre pendulum.

"A man," he said, out loud, because the surprise was almost too much.

"Yeah." Laura's voice was low, down. Dejected.

"He's changed his MO," Nate said, rubbing the back of his head with one hand. This was shaping up to be a real headache of a case. "Targeting a man and changing the timings. That's... is it a change, or an escalation?"

"I don't know," Laura sighed.

"But killers don't just change their MO," Nate said, as if saying it out loud would make the universe go back on what it had done and make things simpler again. He was almost pleading. "We already have a victim profile."

"Looks like we were wrong," Laura said. She glanced at him with a humorless smile. "Third victim proves the rules. And we don't know most of them, it turns out."

Nate hesitated, looking at her. For as hard as he was taking this, she seemed to be doing worse.

She'd sounded so sure that this was the place where the killer would be, on the phone. On the radio, too, she had described it exactly. Nate glanced around from his position in the doorway, taking it in. The white-painted barn. The tree with the large tractor tire hanging on a rope swing. It was like she had described. She got it spot on. But how had she known?

When she called him, she had sounded so urgent and frantic that he hadn't taken the time to ask. He just trusted her, like he always did. It always seemed to be that way, with the two of them. Laura telling him things she had discovered, but never how. He'd thought that they were finally getting to the bottom of things, given that she'd said she was seeing to righting things and he had been able to offer her support. But now it was occurring to him, more strongly than ever, that she still knew things. Things he couldn't explain.

And if the visions weren't real, then he was still missing the true answer.

"How did you know to come here?" he asked, keeping his voice pitched low. The two cops weren't back yet, still completing their circuit around the large barn. Still, he didn't want them to overhear this. "Was there a picture, or something?"

Laura shot him an odd look. "What? No. What do you mean?"

"I heard you on the radio," Nate said. "You described this place exactly. How did you know to come here?"

Laura looked away from him, as if she did not want to see the expression on his face. As if she couldn't meet his eyes. "I just... you know I have my ways."

"We're back to that again, are we?" Nate asked, only just holding back from making the words come out as a growl. "Hiding things from me?"

"I'm not hiding things from you, Nate," she said. "I just know that you're not going to like the answer."

He could have pressed it, right there. He should have. If it was anyone else, any other topic, then the good cop inside of him would have asked. Got to the bottom of things.

But something about her tone, the way she said it and the way she wouldn't look at him, made him stay quiet. He mulled over her words in his head. He *wouldn't like the answer*, whatever that meant.

He hoped it didn't mean what he thought it meant. But he couldn't see how it could mean anything else.

90

It meant that she had already told him how she knew, and he hadn't believed her.

But it was ridiculous, wasn't it? To believe something like that? Psychic visions - they didn't exist in real life. This wasn't a TV show. They weren't caught in some high-budget Hollywood movie. This was real life.

It wasn't possible. What she was telling him could not be real.

And yet, how could she possibly have known to come here if she didn't find any physical evidence pointing her in the right direction?

He knew Laura. He knew that there was no way she would hide evidence if she'd found it. Not even to make herself look better. If there was a photograph, then it would be solid evidence for an upcoming trial. If she had any inkling of who the killer was, she would be telling him, trying to track the guy down.

So if she didn't have any evidence, and she didn't know who it was and wasn't trying to track them down, then...

It only seemed to leave one possibility.

A possibility that Nate just could not accept.

CHAPTER SEVENTEEN

He was parked further down the street, like he always tried to be. The further away you were from the location you were actually going to, the less likely it was that someone would connect you with it. His favorite thing was to park outside of a residential property, making it look as though he was simply visiting the people who lived there. Or perhaps that he was the homeowner himself.

It was a simple trick, and yet it was effective. People didn't usually ask what you were up to. Except for the homeowners themselves, and then it was simple to say that you were visiting a neighbor. Not that anyone had ever actually asked. He just held the excuse ready, in case it ever came up.

But it was the fact that he was parked down the road that had saved him in this case. When he had his tools with him, he would park a little closer, because he didn't want anyone to see him carrying the duffel bag. When he had the wood for the platform, or the bound victim, he would park as close as possible and then immediately move the car right afterwards to make sure that he was as far away as he could be. There were degrees of risk involved in each position, of course.

On this occasion, he had neither tools nor victim to carry, so he'd parked a good distance down the street. He just wanted to check on things, make sure that everything was working. He liked to carry out a test run of the platforms before actually bringing someone in, making sure that they were set up correctly. This was all very DIY, and even though he had managed to master most of the techniques involved, it wasn't like he had any real training in this area.

So, he had parked down the street and walked with his hands in his pockets, strolling like he was just enjoying a walk in the neighborhood. That's how he was able to stop some distance away, taking in what was happening while remaining in the shadows himself. That's how he was able to get away without being seen.

He had not expected anyone to find this place. It had been boarded up for long enough, and no one in the local neighborhood even seemed to look at it anymore. It was just one more eyesore, one more failed business that had gone the way of history. People didn't notice it anymore.

But someone had found it. He wasn't sure how. There were any number of ways it could have happened, he supposed. Perhaps it was just a case of a group of teenagers trying to break into a place in order to find somewhere to drink, and then discovering the platform. By now, there were a few details of the deaths that were just starting to leak out to the press. He had read a few of the articles himself. This thing about the platforms, it had been mentioned. They didn't have pictures yet, but they could write about their construction in a little detail.

So, anyone who went into the abandoned grocery store and looked around and saw the platform might think to call the police. That could have been it.

But it was only one possibility.

The other possibility, the one that he didn't really want to think about as he watched the police milling around the front of the store, was that they were somehow on to him. That they had worked out what he was doing, where he was going.

Maybe it was pure luck. If he was a cop, and he'd found two people hanging by the necks in abandoned locations, he supposed that he would start searching in abandoned locations as well. He'd known full well that as soon as he started doing this, the pressure would ramp up very quickly. They would be hunting for him. That was why he had spent so much time beforehand preparing everything.

He had already picked out the victim for this place. He knew who should have been hanging from the ceiling in that grocery store tomorrow night. He was going to have to change his plans, go for one of his backup locations. After putting in some of the preparation already it was a real shame - but what could he do, except accept it? This place was burned. The police knew about it, they were here. They weren't going to let him back in. Even if he tried it, he would inevitably be caught. They were bound to keep this place under surveillance even if it looked like they had moved on.

He turned, his hands still in his pockets, and continued that casual stroll back towards his car. He could be just another local in the neighborhood, someone out to clear his mind at night. On the way somewhere, perhaps. And once he was in the car, he was just one more traveler on the road, one more person driving past the grocery store without so much as glancing at it. He didn't need to look again. He had seen enough. The presence of the marked police car around the front had told him everything he needed to know.

He went over what he had left inside in his head, thinking about it carefully. The wood, which he had constructed into the platform. The mechanism. He didn't think he had left any tools, and when he got home, he would check very carefully to be sure that he hadn't. If it was only the platform itself, he didn't think they would be able to trace it back to him. Oh, and the rope, of course. But he handled everything with gloves even when he was putting it together, for safety's sake. He should still be able to continue going on a little longer.

Now though, he was going to have to get a bit more creative. Worse than that, he was going to have to do it fast. He needed to find somewhere that they weren't going to look, where they wouldn't think to track him down. And he would have to take his time about it, even though he was in a rush. Maybe he should set something up, then circle back and check on it right afterwards, see if the police were looking into it. That might be the best way to do things. Surveillance might have to be a full-time job for him, too, until he was confident that he could set the next person up without risking getting caught.

If he got caught, he would have to stop. He had already prepared so much in advance; it would be such a shame to stop now. He already had the schedule of his next target down, etched into his mind with laser precision. He knew where she was going to be, where he would grab her. But now he needed to know where he was going to take her.

He drove on into the dark streets of Atlanta, his mind working fast. The night was still young, at least for someone like him who was used to roaming the city in the dark. He would find somewhere else. This didn't have to be the end.

He wasn't going to let them stop him - not until he had completed his mission.

CHAPTER EIGHTEEN

"I don't need to get any sleep," Laura said stubbornly, even though she knew deep inside it wasn't true.

Nate just looked at her for a moment. "We're going to check into the motel," he said firmly, taking no arguments. "Maybe you don't think you need the rest, but I definitely do."

He put the key in the ignition and switched on the car's engine, starting it up and rolling out. Laura sighed, looking out of the window. She had given up control of the vehicle to him given that she had been driving for most of the evening, but now she saw that that was a bad decision. It meant he had the power to drive her wherever he wanted to, and she couldn't just take herself back to the precinct. At least, not until after they had gone to the motel.

Truth be told, she was tired. It had been a long day. The flight had not been very forgiving, and she still had all of those worries in the back of her mind about Amy and her new guardian. Not to mention the nerves she was already feeling about having Lacey over on the weekend. Getting back in time to be there was her primary concern but, behind that, she could still feel all of the other little worries building up. Things like whether she would be able to entertain Lacey for a full weekend, what kind of foods Lacey liked to eat, how she had changed since Laura had last been able to have her at home overnight. It was a lot to think about.

All of that, with a case on top of it? A case in which the bodies seemed to already be racking up? It was no wonder she was tired.

But still, solving this case was her responsibility.

Right then, she wished it wasn't. She didn't want to have to have been the one who found this body. The one who failed to save a life. Yet again. It felt like all she ever did was arrive at crime scenes too late.

Somewhere deep in her head, she knew it wasn't true. She knew she saved lives, too, and that she and Nate caught and put killers away all the time. It was what they did.

But the ones who didn't survive, even after they'd managed to get to the scene and take over from the local cops – those were the ones that always haunted her the most.

"We're going to figure this out," Nate said. "It seems kind of impossible right now, but with some good rest and a new perspective in the morning, will be able to do more. Besides, we need to wait for forensics to do their reports and run their tests. We're not going to have anything back from the coroner until the morning at the very earliest. If we go back to the precinct now and continue trying to investigate, we're not going to get anywhere; and by the time we do end up having to go and get some rest, we won't be able to."

"I know," Laura said, sighing again. "You *are* right. I just hate feeling like I'm taking a break when people are dying."

"Yeah," Nate said, in a tone of dark sympathy, an indication that he understood and felt it too. But that was all.

Laura glanced at him out of the corner of her eye, trying not to make it too obvious. Since she'd said what she had said outside the barn, he hadn't spoken much to her. Not in the way that really mattered. He had discussed the case, talked about next steps, and now here he was convincing her to get some sleep for procedural reasons. But he hadn't addressed what she had said. He'd clammed up tightly, going quiet as soon as her words hit home, and he hadn't brought it up again.

Did it mean that he believed her and didn't want to address the fact that what she had said could be real? Or was he secretly plotting ways to get her into therapy, or maybe even have her committed, when they got back?

They pulled up outside a cheap motel not far from the precinct, set up in that old familiar way that motels always seemed to be. The parking lot, the rows of individual apartment rooms with their numbered doors visible from balconies. Sometimes Laura thought that she could walk into any motel anywhere in the entire country and reliably be able to find any given amenity. If they even had any amenities. It seemed like they were always the same, as if the universe was playing a cosmic joke on them and it was only the furniture and the wallpaper that changed, not the actual location.

And if the universe was playing a trick on her, it wasn't the only one. It felt like the killer was messing with her deliberately, moving the goal posts. Laura understood the rules. Twelve hours, from twelve noon to twelve midnight. Why change them, why change them exactly at the moment that she was getting closer?

Did he somehow know?

No, that was only paranoia speaking. In all of her years of searching, Laura had never managed to find another psychic like herself, so it was hideously unlikely that the killer was one. Still, it didn't seem fair. The job was like this: you figured out what was happening, you learned the rules that applied to each killer, and you used those rules to either catch him or track him down via one of his victims. The rules didn't change. That wasn't how the game was supposed to be played.

"Alright," Laura said, unbuckling her seatbelt as Nate parked. "Let's get checked in and get to sleep. I want to be up early and on it right away."

"Agreed," Nate said. "I'll get the bags from the trunk; you go speak to the guy. I'll meet you out here with the keys."

She got out of the car to do what he'd asked, feeling like every step was far too heavy. She had the weight of another dead man on her shoulders.

And if tomorrow didn't go well, she might soon be adding another – something that she could hardly bear to think about.

CHAPTER NINETEEN

Laura shrugged on her jacket, pausing for a moment by the cracked mirror in the bathroom to look at herself. There were dark circles under her eyes, a consequence of another night of barely any sleep.

She'd tossed and turned constantly, swinging from bad dream to half-awake anxiety, until finally the cell phone resting on the bedside table had told her it was an acceptable time to wake up. She'd showered and dressed quickly, thinking of nothing else but getting back to the case and getting it solved.

She let something slip, yesterday. She hadn't been quick enough. She hadn't managed to prevent the killer from taking another life. But she was going to be damned if that was going to happen today.

Laura walked out into the cold morning, expecting to have to knock on Nate's door and get him out of bed. But instead, he was waiting for her, just locking up the door to his own room. They had taken rooms next door to one another, and he must have heard her emerging herself.

"Ready to get to the precinct?" he asked.

"Ready to catch this creep and get out of here," Laura replied firmly, earning a weak flash of a tired smile from Nate.

They got into the car and drove, Nate taking the wheel again while Laura slumped into the passenger seat and wished for the sake of her aching bones that she'd had a few more hours of rest. "We need to figure out where to look next", she said. "I don't have much confidence that we're going to have any fingerprint evidence or otherwise from forensics, given how careful he was at the previous two scenes."

"I would have to agree there," Nate said. "And from what I saw of the guy hanging up there last night, I'm sure the coroner is only going to be able to tell us more of the same. But we do have some very important new pieces of evidence. Two changes in the MO. That means whatever is left has to be considered even more strongly."

"You're right," Laura said. Trust Nate to spend the night coming up with a more positive spin on things. "So, what do we have? A victim set up on the platform, bound with ropes and gagged, and then hung by the neck until dead once the timer goes off."

"It makes the clock look even more important," Nate said. "The change of the time - there could be any number of reasons behind that.

Maybe he thinks that men deserve less time to try and get away, or maybe he has this kind of sick system calibrated to just exactly the amount of time he thinks would give the victim hope but not allow them to actually escape."

"This guy was bound even more tightly," Laura said. "Did you see? His arms were bound around his torso as well as just his wrists. There was no way he was going to get out of that."

Nate made a grunt of agreement. "So it's not about escape. I don't think any of them are meant to, even though they get all this time to stand up there on the platform. Which means that the time is really important to the killer, symbolic of something."

Laura sighed. Her first sigh of the morning, but she thought grimly that it probably was going to be far from the last. "I just wish we knew what it meant."

"You and me both," Nate said. "Look, he's not giving us much in the way of evidence to go on. So that means we just need to look closer at what we do have. I'm thinking we might be able to get something out of these clocks."

"It's the same type in all three, I think," Laura said. "Some kind of custom build, from what I could see. I was thinking that those kinds of clocks are usually used as old kitchen appliances, you know? Where you can use the timer to tell you how long is left on your dish? But the digital timer itself must be a newer edition. The one I remember from my Granny's house; it just had a dial you could turn all the way up to an hour. No longer than that."

"That's exactly what I was thinking," Nate said. "I think our grannies might have had the same one. So, that's our first thing as we get in. We need to look at these clocks. Find out who makes them, where you can buy them. That kind of thing."

He swung the car into the parking lot at the precinct, and Laura was grateful that the drive had not taken very long. Choosing a motel for its proximity to your local investigation headquarters, rather than the quality of the beds available, made for a poor night's sleep but a quicker start to the day's work.

"They'll be in the evidence locker," Laura said, unbuckling her seatbelt. "We should be able to get a closer look at them. Come on."

They walked into the precinct, finding it already buzzing with activity despite the early hour. Most of the faces in the bullpen were unfamiliar, given that they hadn't even had time to make it here yesterday. There were more than a few questioning looks sent their way, though Laura had the feeling that most of them would take one look at their suits and know right away that they were FBI agents.

It wasn't every day that the FBI came down to work a murder case in your precinct. They would have to be very aware that Laura and Nate were coming.

Captain Blackford was, luckily, just heading into the precinct, seemingly only a handful of seconds ahead of them. He was carrying a takeout cup of coffee, which perhaps explained why they hadn't run into him in the parking lot. He was just opening his office door and going inside, a smaller structure set at the back of the bullpen where he could keep an eye on all of his officers.

Laura and Nate followed him, catching up just as he was setting the cup down on his desk and starting to sit down. He looked up at them with barely concealed annoyance, a frown cutting across his forehead. Laura could quite easily see where, in probably less than a year, he was going to have some very deep wrinkles across that part of his head. For all the youth he brought to the job, unusual at this level of the police system, he was going to end up aging very quickly.

"So, you didn't catch him last night," was the first thing he said. So much for people from the South being more friendly.

"We didn't," Nate replied, his tone even. At times like these, Laura was happier than ever to have him as a partner. She wasn't so convinced she would have been able to keep her tone level. "But we have some ideas on how we can stop him from striking again. We need to get a look at the clocks, the ones from all three crime scenes. Are they here at the precinct?"

Blackford nodded, getting up from his desk. There was a weary resignation around the action, like he was already accepting the fact that he wasn't going to get a lot of time to sit down today. He moved past them, leading them out across the bullpen again with a beckon of his hand. Another rudeness, not even bothering to explain where he was taking them. Laura gritted her teeth, telling herself it was far too early to get into an argument at this time of morning, and followed.

Again, crossing the bullpen seemed to draw the eyes of every officer in the place, all of them watching Laura and Nate like they were unusual specimens of some rare animal. Laura was used to that, given that they were always in new places and always ranking higher than those around them. Still, it could be unsettling, especially when you had spent the night watching a man slowly swing backwards and forwards from a noose and then dreamed it over and over again when you were trying to sleep.

At the end of the bullpen, two sets of stairs leading directly out to the street flanked an elevator. Blackford led them here, pressing a button on the inside of the elevator as they joined him to travel downwards.

"Do you have any kind of techs here?" Nate asked. "Someone who knows what they're looking at, when it comes to engineering? Any clock experts, by some happy coincidence?"

Blackford shrugged, shaking his head. "I don't know that we have any experts on that kind of thing," he said. "But I can bring in a local source, if you need one."

"We'll see how we go," Laura said, as the elevator came to a stop one floor down. "It might be that we can figure things out ourselves."

Blackford led them down a short corridor to a room which was guarded by an overweight cop behind a Perspex screen. He looked up at them as they approached, searching their faces and quickly settling back on Blackford's.

"What can I do you for, chief?" He asked, his voice cheerfully pleasant enough despite the early hour.

"Need to take a look at some evidence," Blackford said. "All from the clock killer case. Mind if we just head straight back?" Clock killer. Laura noted that. Apparently, he was already getting a bit of a moniker among the locals.

The cop nodded, pulling out a clipboard with a pen attached by a string. "Sure thing, chief. Just need you to log anything you take."

Blackford nodded, swiping the clipboard off the counter and leading Laura and Nate around to a door set into the wall beside the guard's Perspex screen. There was an internal buzzing noise, then the locking mechanism disengaging, and he pushed the door open to lead them through.

The evidence locker walls, predictably, looked much like Laura had seen in a hundred other precincts. Cages and shelves everywhere, most of them containing brown or white cardboard boxes. Each of these was labeled with a case number, and some of them with names. Some even had letters, indicating that the case required more than one box to store all of the evidence that had been collected. There were also locked cabinets for the kind of evidence that needed to be kept safe, such as firearms or illegal drugs that had been seized.

Blackford led them unhesitatingly through what seemed like a maze of shelving to a specific spot, where he tapped the boxes. "We've stashed them in here, for now," he said. "There's a table at the end of the room. We can examine them here, put them back in the boxes afterwards. No need to remove any evidence if we don't have to."

Laura nodded, biting her tongue on the fact that he didn't need to tell them how to do their jobs. Inside the box, a number of different evidence bags held different items. Long coils of rope that had been cut from around the victim's bodies. Personal effects, found in their pockets. Clothing, most of it also cut in places. The platforms themselves, Laura guessed, were big enough to be held in another part of the locker. But the clocks were here, and Blackford reached in to pull out the evidence bags that contained them before carrying them over to a table set under a high, grated window. The light fell just on it, allowing them to see what they needed to.

Laura and Nate both pulled on evidence gloves, swiped from a dispenser that Blackford held out to them without saying a word. Only the surly expression on his face indicated that they were to put them on, or else. Again, Laura couldn't help but feel patronized. She knew how to handle evidence. She wasn't about to just start touching things and putting her fingerprints all over them. Did he think she'd only just completed basic training?

"Do you have a screwdriver, or some kind of tool set?" Nate asked. He was turning one of the evidence bags over in his hand, looking at the clock through the plastic rather than removing it just yet. "Looks like we might need to do a bit of work on the case to get these open."

"Why do you need to open them?" Blackboard asked. He was almost protective of the evidence, like he didn't want anyone touching it that wasn't from his own team. He was going to have to get over that.

"To see who made them," Nate said. "Or any kind of other hints as to how they were created. You see, this is a custom-built timer. We need to figure out where the killer is getting either the clocks themselves or the pieces to make them, if he's doing it DIY."

Blackford scowled, an expression on his face as if to say that he wasn't stupid and could have worked this out himself. Laura was doing a very good job of biting her tongue, and she didn't want to stop now. However, she allowed herself a moment of crowing in her own head. If he was so smart, he would have never needed to ask the question.

This line of thinking was, of course, pretty juvenile, but that didn't stop her from getting a tiny little kick out of it.

Once the toolkit was produced from the booth where the cop on duty sat, Nate was the one to pull one of the clocks out of the bag and examine it carefully. He turned it over in his hands, and Laura pointed silently to a couple of places where there appeared to be markings on

102

the plastic case of the clock itself. Places where someone might have opened it with some kind of prying lever, for example, to take out one element and put another in.

"Alright," Nate said, taking a deep breath. "Let's get this baby open and see how it ticks."

Laura nodded, unable to resist reacting to his terrible joke even in spite of the gravity of the situation. Blackford, she noticed, did not. His face remained as stony as ever as he watched them with folded arms over his chest.

Laura watched as Nate carefully lifted the unscrewed back off the clock, turning it over. He handed it to Laura as he looked closely at the inner mechanism of the clock and the timer, now even more clearly inserted into the place where a different kind of timer had once sat. It looked a lot more technical than the mechanics of the clock face, with a chip and soldered wires rather than simply cogs and wheels.

"Here," Laura said, showing him the inside of the clock's back. In small letters, engraved just at the same height of the new timer, was a name. *JT Time*.

"I know them," Blackford said, with some surprise. "They've been here in the city for decades."

"Then you'd better take us right there," Laura said grimly.

They were on the right track at last – and though she couldn't resist subtly resting the bare skin of her wrist, above the glove, on the clock casing just before they placed it away, no vision came. They were going to have to rely on old-fashioned police work this time.

And at last, they had a very good place to start.

CHAPTER TWENTY

Laura looked up suspiciously as Captain Blackford slowed to a stop right in front of them, his patrol car parking outside a storefront that did not look very auspicious.

"This is it?" she said, craning her head. She made out, in faded lettering above the store, the words 'JT Time.' She guessed it had to be the right place. At first glance, though, the store didn't even look as though it was open. The windows were dirty, the paint on the sign above cracked and even peeling off, and there were certainly no customers inside that she could see.

She and Nate got out of the car and rejoined Blackford as they headed inside. A bell above the door tinkled to announce their arrival, apparently prompting a flurry of activity from somewhere behind a beaded screen door, set into the back of the shop behind a counter.

The person that was back there took long enough to come out to them that Laura had time to glance around. And time, indeed, was what she saw. There were clocks of all kinds all around the store, upon shelves, hanging on the walls, and even laid out under glass within the counter. They ranged across the board of all the old-fashioned clocks she could think of. Cuckoo clocks, some of them seemingly carved with minute precision in what Laura thought might be a Swiss style. Grandfather clocks, tall and loud, their pendulums ticking above the rest of the incessant noise. It was almost eerie how the entire clock collection seemed to tick on the exact same beat, ongoing so that it started to make Laura feel as though she could only move or speak in time to the same rhythm. There were watches, both small gold pocket watches and the kind to be worn on wrists with leather straps, none of them looking modern at all.

The man who emerged from behind the beaded curtain with a clatter was elderly, to say the least. He was gray-haired, his shoulders and back slumped and slouched forward, a sign of years spent hunched over his work. His fingers and hands, too, were gnarled, another sign that he had spent a long time working with those same hands on small, detailed work. He wore a thick pair of glasses perched in front of watery blue eyes, and his face was thoroughly lined. Laura couldn't exactly say that he looked threatening at all. In fact, he looked rather timid, as if he was unsure of how to deal with these people in his store.

"Hello," he said, the sound a timorous and questioning one.

"JT," Blackford said, greeting him with a grunt.

"Captain," the man - who must have been the owner, presumably this JT- replied. "Has something happened, something I can help you with?"

"Could be," Blackford said. "These are FBI agents. I'll let them fill you in."

Laura turned from giving Blackford a wide-eyed look, trying to smooth her expression as much as she could, as JT looked around at her and Nate expectantly. She knew that Blackford was not exactly going out of his way to help them, but sometimes it felt as if he was actually doing the opposite. Putting them on the spot, not hiding his rudeness. The locals had to pick up on it, and they were sure to trust the local Captain, especially if they knew him, more than a couple of random agents.

Laura cleared her throat and then smiled, figuring it was the best approach with an elderly man who looked as nervous as this one did. "We are trying to trace down a few clocks that we think you may have made," she said. She kept her words calm and light. "We found your name carved into the back of the inside case."

She took a picture they had prepared out of her pocket, placing it down on the counter in front of JT. There was a full color print of one of the clocks, taken not from the crime scene itself but from the moment that the items were logged in as evidence. There was nothing about the picture to suggest it had been involved in any kind of crime, much less clear as to which one. That, she thought, was going to be helpful. It was always good to get an unbiased reaction first, and then be able to assess whether the person they were talking to was genuinely surprised when they announced what the item had been used for.

"That looks like one of mine," JT said, nodding in agreement. "One of the newer lines that we've been working on. It's a shame. I wouldn't make them if I didn't have to, but here we are."

"What do you mean by that?" Nate asked.

JT looked up at him, almost jumping at Nate's deep voice. He looked even more scared of Nate than he was of the other two. "W-well," JT said, stammering a little. "I've always worked with my hands. It's a craft, you know? A trade. I learned it from my father. He learned it from his grandfather. Three generations of us, working on clock mechanisms in the traditional way. Now here we are, and people don't seem to want mechanical clocks as much as they used to. They want these new, modern things. Horrible, really. I've been trying to save the store, and my daughter suggested we try these new techniques. It makes me sick, honestly it does, but I was able to compromise by at least reusing one of the old, more traditional settings for a modern replacement. It's called... what did she call it? Upcycling, I think. Apparently, it's all the rage these days."

"Where do you sell these?" Laura asked. "Just here in the shop?"

"No, well," JT said, scratching the back of his head. His skin made a kind of papery sound underneath his fingernails. "They do this online thing now. I don't really understand it myself, of course. But my daughter, she was helpful in setting it up. So, I suppose, we sell them... On the web, is it? You have to excuse me, I'm not really up to date with all the right terminology."

"Online," Laura muttered under her breath. That wasn't helpful at all. It was looking more and more like this was going to be difficult, more difficult than anticipated. "I don't suppose you remember selling at least three of these, or more, to the same customer?"

"The same customer?" JT blinked, looking surprised. "Why would someone want three of the same clock? They're not selling them at a higher markup, are they?"

"No, JT," Blackford said, his voice a more reassuring one for the old man. "No one's ripping you off, don't worry. We happened to find these clocks at a few crime scenes."

"Crime scenes?" the old man frowned, then his expression cleared. Along with it, his skin paled even more than Laura had thought possible. "I read about some young ladies who were hung after a timer went off. It's not...?"

"'Fraid so, JT," Blackford said. He was leaning against one of the counters, his elbow down on it to support his weight, his legs crossed at the ankles in a casual pose. "It's a real bad business."

"Oh, goodness," JT said. He blinked a few times, looking down at the counter in front of him – though Laura didn't expect he was actually seeing it. "My clocks were there?"

"Not just there," Laura said, feeling the need to speak up and drive home the point. It was all well and good Blackford giving JT some comfort, but there was still a chance that he knew somehow what was going on. She very much doubted that a man as old and feeble looking as he could do any of the work that was required to set up the platforms and take the victims to them, but that didn't mean he wasn't involved. He might have been protecting the person that he had sold the clocks to, or otherwise had some inkling that a son or a grandson or a nephew had taken a little too unhealthy of an interest in the clocks.

She remembered what she and Nate had discussed earlier. Time. This whole case was about time. And here they were, in a place owned by a man who called himself JT, and his shop JT Time. That was a big coincidence. Well, perhaps not exactly a coincidence, since a clock had to come from somewhere. But still, it was something, and she wasn't going to go easy on him just because he was elderly. At least, not easy enough to potentially miss a lead.

"The clocks were instrumental in the crime," Laura continued. "The timer was used to tell the victims how long they had left of their lives."

"Gracious Jesus," JT whispered, his hands clutching onto the side of the counter for support.

Simple shock from a man who had never heard of something so terrible involving his own handicraft in his life? Or a realization that someone close to him could be involved?

"Do you have anyone working with you here?" Laura asked. "Someone who helps out, perhaps?"

"Just my daughter," JT said. He swallowed hard, his Adam's apple bobbing up and down in his leathery throat. "All she does is help with the online sales. I don't know any of that stuff, so she packs everything up and takes care of it. I just make the clocks. Truth is, I wouldn't have enough money to hire anyone else even if I wanted to."

"What about in the past?" Laura asked. "Did you ever take on an apprentice? Maybe try to teach the craft to one of your children, or another relative?"

JT shook his head. "I only have my daughter," he said. "And she's got her boys, but they're too young for this kind of thing."

"We might need to speak to her," Laura said directing this comment at Blackford. He nodded swiftly.

"We can arrange that, can't we, JT?" he said. "When is she next in to do a stock take?"

"I'm not sure," JT said. "I can call you the second she arrives."

"That would be most appreciated," Blackford said, his voice still a lot more gentle than Laura would have liked. She had been thinking it was a man who committed these crimes, due to the strength involved, not to mention the whole DIY aspect. But the truth of the matter was, that was only an assumption. There was no reason a woman couldn't be strong enough, couldn't be handy enough with a hammer. Assumptions, she had to remember, could break cases. Could let people go uncaught for decades and more. Assumptions were like poison to a murder investigation.

"I think it might be better if we get a chance to speak with her as soon as possible," Laura said. "We need to see a list of those online sales urgently. I'm guessing she's the only person who can provide us with that."

JT nodded, starting to shuffle over to a landline phone hung on the wall of the store right next to that beaded curtain. "I'll call Susanna now," he said, and Laura leaned back against one of the counters to settle in and wait.

***

The moment that Susanna walked into the store, Laura's heart sank. The woman was petite, probably only around five foot tall, and carrying a lot of extra weight. When they shook hands to greet one another, Laura found her grip soft and her arm strength weak. There was little chance that Susanna could have been responsible for putting anyone on a platform, let alone carrying the lumber to set up the platforms in the first place. Unless she had an accomplice, Susanna was a dead end. Just like the store was seeming to shape up to be.

But there was still hope.

"We need to see as many of the online orders as you have records for," Laura said, once the initial introductions were over. "Specifically for this type of clock here."

Susanna looked at the picture with a kind of businesslike nod, taking it in. "That's one of our more popular models", she said. "Really does well with the aging demographic. They like to have those modern luxuries, but they also appreciate something familiar."

Laura bit back the response that she wanted to give, which was that she didn't care at all about the ins and outs of the business. She just wanted to know who had bought them, and that was all. While she was busy trying to retract her words from her head and turn them into something more polite before they ended up on her tongue, Nate interrupted.

"Do you have full data on customers from the retailers you stock with, or do you ship them out wholesale?"

"A bit of both," Susanna said tilting her head. "We sell on a few online marketplaces directly, and the rest go out to big warehouses where they can handle larger orders. I can get you the customer data for anything we've sold directly, but the rest might take a while."

Laura was already sighing to herself in her head. This was turning out to be far more complicated than it needed to be. All they needed to get was this information about who had bought at least three of the same clock, and they could go arrest the guy. It didn't have to be this hard. They were so close, and yet here were all these roadblocks coming up to delay them and make things take much longer. It was frustrating, to say the least.

Her phone rang in her pocket and Laura pulled it out to take a look at the screen. She frowned, seeing a name she hadn't expected.

Christopher Fallow.

"You take that," Nate said, no doubt seeing the consternation on her face. "I'll go through the sales records with Susanna."

Laura nodded gratefully, stepping outside of the store. Nate had no need to let her take the call, given that he didn't even know who it was. But it was a one-man job, so she wasn't going to turn him down. Not out of a sense of duty, anyway. And if this was something about Amy, she needed to know.

"Hello," she said, stepping back out into the cold air and wrapping her jacket around herself a little tighter.

"Hi!" Chris said, his voice sounding relieved. "Hi, Laura? It's Chris Fallow."

"I know," Laura said. "Is something wrong with Amy?"

The pause that Chris allowed left her heart missing a beat in her chest.

CHAPTER TWENTY ONE

Laura was about to repeat herself, in case there was any slim chance he hadn't actually heard her, when she heard a deep sigh down the line.

"I don't know," Chris said. "I just... I needed your advice. I know you said I could call anytime, but if it's a bad time for you right now..."

Laura glanced back inside the store. She could see Blackford, still leaning on the counter, talking lazily with JT. Nate and Susanna had disappeared into the back of the store, no doubt to find where the records were kept. "No," she said. "Go ahead. I have a short while. What's going on?"

"It's..." Chris sighed. "Man, this is awkward. Well, it's about the nights. Amy's been wetting the bed, and everything I read online told me she would settle down after the first few nights in an unfamiliar place. But... she still hasn't stopped."

"Have you talked with her about it?" Laura asked.

"With her?" Chris sounded puzzled. "No, well, she's just a child. I figure she probably doesn't even understand why it's happening."

Laura sighed, pressing the heel of her hand against her head. She had a headache, and for once it wasn't even from a vision. She didn't need the added stress of dealing with this, but that didn't matter. It was important. Amy was important. She wasn't going to allow her to slip through the cracks, not in any way, shape, or form.

And it was good that Chris had reached out to her. A good sign. A sign that maybe he was taking this new guardian thing just as seriously as she expected him to.

"Maybe she doesn't, on every level," Laura said. "But you still have to talk to her. If you just ignore the problem, it won't go away on its own. Or, maybe it will, but a long time from now. If you talk with her about how she's feeling, what she's been going through, she might open up and start to realize that she's safe now."

"That's what it is?" Chris asked. "She doesn't feel safe?" He sounded sad, almost sulky. Like a child himself, being told that his favorite toy wasn't working anymore because he hadn't looked after it properly.

"She won't, at first," Laura said. "Think of what she's been through. Kids are resilient, and yes, they do bounce back. But they're not rubber bands. It takes a while."

"How am I supposed to talk about that with her?" Chris asked. Laura had a mental image of the handsome doctor running his hands through his thick, brown hair and pulling it out. It didn't exactly gel with what she'd seen of him, but it was what he sounded like right now. "Isn't it... too much? To talk through the gory details?"

"You don't have to go into the gory details," Laura said. "And, Chris? Remember something. If you think it's too much of a topic for a child to talk about, think about the fact that she actually experienced it. She was there, in that house, while it was happening to her and around her. No matter how heavy you think it might be, it's already in her head. And she needs to know a lot of things."

"Like what?" Chris asked.

Laura took a breath. She was thinking about the survivors of abuse she'd seen in the past. Some who were just starting to cope with it after being saved, usually when she saw them again at the trial. Some who didn't cope with it at all and went on to become abusers or even killers themselves. "That she's safe," she said, starting with the most important thing. "That it wasn't her fault. That you're going to look after her and make sure that it never happens again."

Chris sighed. "I just... I'm..."

"What?" Laura asked, immediately on edge.

"I'm scared," Chris admitted. "Scared that I'm not going to be enough for her. That what's happened to her was too awful, and she's not going to get better."

"Well, not with that attitude," Laura said. Only half of it was meant flippantly. "She'll pick up on that, you know. It's your job now to believe in her. To show her that there is a way forward."

"Alright." Chris said. His voice sounded steadier, more determined. Like he had taken her words on board and decided to follow them. "Thank you, Laura. Can you... I mean, would you mind meeting us again, sometime soon? I know it's really comforting for her to see you. She thinks you're her guardian angel, you know."

Laura chuckled lightly, the sadness and direness of the situation offset by the knowledge that she had at least made some small difference. "I know. And yes, I can. But not right away. I'm on a case right now, and I have custody of my daughter this weekend."

"Right," Chris said hastily. "Right, of course. At your own pace, obviously. We can fit to your schedule. I took some time away from the hospital to make sure she settles in fine, so I'm pretty open."

"Alright," Laura said, glancing up to see Nate emerging from the store. "Well, I'd better go. But... you can call me again, if you need any more help."

"I will. Thanks again," Chris said. "Uh, good luck with your case."

"Thanks," Laura said, before hanging up.

"Anything?" she asked Nate, even though she didn't need to. His face was like thunder.

"Nothing in the records," he said. "I've left Blackford in there, still talking to them. He's going to get one of his guys to call through all the online suppliers we don't have records for, one by one. But it's pointless. There's no bulk orders from anyone, literally ever, in the system. People buy one clock at a time, and that's it."

"He has three of them, though," Laura pointed out. "So, someone out there bought three of them at some point. He must be somewhere in the data."

Nate sighed, rubbing the bridge of his nose and then flexing his shoulders back like his back was aching and he needed relief. "I'm sure he is. It's just a question of whether we find him or not. He must have spread the purchases out over time, and that means there could have been months between them. If he used fake identities every time as well or got someone else to place the orders for him, then we've got no hope of tracking him down."

Laura chewed her lip. "He's been very cautious," she said. "Every step of the way, we can see that. Buying the clocks separately in advance, setting up his kill sites ahead of time, wearing gloves, leaving no forensic evidence. He doesn't even hang around to make sure the death happens. He just gets out of there."

"It's going to make it very hard for us to get any kind of resolution here," Nate said. "How are we going to track him down if he's this careful at every turn?"

Laura felt a momentary despair, but behind it was a determination rising fiercely. The same kind of determination she'd just heard Chris bounce back with.

She couldn't get this case wrong. She just couldn't. Every wrong step they took, every dead end, was a waste of time. And every day they wasted brought them one step closer to her own personal deadline: Lacey's visit.

Laura couldn't let this case drag on. If it did, she would have to stay here, continue working it. She would have to get the job done. That was what was expected of her. And if she did that, she'd end up having to postpone Lacey's visit. Not only would it break her own daughter's heart, but it would give Marcus plenty of ammunition against her.

Her ex-husband could go to the courts. Tell them that Laura had missed her very first mandated weekend with Lacey. Forfeited it. And then where would she stand?

No, it wasn't going to happen. It couldn't. It just wouldn't be acceptable.

Not to mention that she couldn't let any more people die.

"He's going to mess up sooner or later," Laura said, meeting Nate's eyes. "Maybe he already has. And we're going to be there. We're going to see it. And we'll take him down."

Nate nodded after a moment, seemingly awed by her fierce response. He reached out, holding something towards her. "Here's the photo of the clock, by the way," he said. "You left it inside. Figured we might end up needing it again."

"Thanks," Laura said, taking it from his outstretched hand – and feeling a headache hit her square in the temples.

She pulled the photograph back towards herself, trying not to let anything show on her face –

Laura was looking down at her from close above, at her face. She was lying there, still as stone, the life draining from her. Veronica. Veronica Rowse.

Where?

The mortuary?

The funeral home?

Laura could make out nothing past the edges of the vision, past the edges of Veronica's face. There was only her skin, pale white, and her closed eyes. Her lips with that faint tinge of blue.

Laura hovered there, staring. Something was happening. Something to the body. She couldn't see, but it was moving slightly in her vision, the face pulled in subtle directions in reaction to whatever it was. Was she being dressed for her funeral? Prepared by the mortician? What was happening?

Was the killer going to come back and find the body and do something to it?

Why was she seeing this?

It happened so fast; Laura wasn't even sure what she was looking at for a second.

Veronica Rowse with her cold, dead face – Veronica who was in the mortuary already, cut up and sewn back together again – Veronica who was dead, dead, dead...

Her eyes flew open, and she took a breath, and Laura saw that she was alive.

Not just animated – alive.

And it was impossible, totally impossible, because she was dead, and –

Laura blinked, moving to put the photograph back in her pocket. Nate walked past her to go to the car, leaving Laura a moment alone. She caught her own reflection in the window of the store, how wide her own eyes were, and fought to get herself under control.

"Who's driving?" Nate called over, from beside the car already.

"You can," Laura said, without turning. Then she did turn, made herself do it, made herself go and get into the passenger seat like everything was fine.

Once she was buckled in, she could stop focusing on moving herself forward. She looked out of the window so that Nate couldn't see her face as he started the engine and began the drive back. She pretended she was watching people walking around on the morning streets.

But she didn't see a single thing at all.

Inside, her head was in turmoil. She didn't understand. What she had seen, it didn't make any sense. It didn't add up. It had to be some kind of... mistake?

What could it mean?

She saw visions of the future. That much was the one thing she was sure of. And though they were only visions of a possible future, still subject to change, the rule she had relied on for her whole life was that the vision was still possible *at the time she saw it*. When she changed things in real time, the visions adapted, kept up. Showed her how things would be now that the change had come.

They didn't show her things that couldn't happen.

And yet, what she had seen was impossible. She knew it was. She'd seen Veronica Rowse's body in person. She had no doubt it was the same woman. But you didn't just wake up from the dead when you'd been gone for a couple of days. Much less so when the coroner had cut you open to check for any other signs of injury or distress.

Laura brought her hand to her forehead, rubbing it hard. Something was happening here. Something she didn't understand. She couldn't interpret what the vision meant.

114

How was she going to figure out what it meant?

"Captain Blackford, would you mind staying back here to get those records?" she said, as she called his number, even though it wasn't really a request. It was a decision. "Nate and I need to head back to the precinct. Having all three of us working the same angle is a waste of time. We need to keep moving – right now."

CHAPTER TWENTY TWO

Laura trailed behind Nate as they walked into the precinct, back on Captain Blackford's turf but without him. Which meant that the cat was away – and the mice had the place to themselves. The question was, were the mice going to respect the orders of the dogs in his stead?

Or, whatever other kind of complicated metaphor Laura could dream up.

She felt like her head was still spinning as she walked up to an unoccupied desk, glancing around. There was another cop, a detective, sitting at the desk next to it. "Who uses this computer?" she asked, making him look up in surprise.

"Uh, that's Bobby," he said. "He's not in today. Got annual leave."

"You have some kind of tech department here, who can get us set up on the computer so we can use the databases?"

He nodded, but then jumped out of his chair as he realized why she was still looking at him expectantly. "Right. I'll go get someone."

"Thanks," Laura said, turning around.

Nate had stopped to talk to another detective, an officious-looking older man with a gray streak in his hair and a clipboard in his hands. He was showing Nate something inside a file, which Nate nodded at thoughtfully.

"What do you have?" Laura asked, joining them as she waited for her tech man to get back.

"Identity of our third victim has been confirmed," Nate said, handing her the piece of paper. "We've got a male aged twenty-eight. Lincoln Ware. A local resident, just like the others."

"Has he lived here long?" Laura asked.

Nate frowned down the length of the report. "No. See, here – about two years ago, his last address was reported as being in Montgomery, Alabama."

"Two years," Laura said thoughtfully. "You think it means anything?"

"Not that I'm aware of," Nate said. "Not yet, anyway. It could all mean something, I guess."

"Yeah." Laura stood with her hands on her hips, staring into the middle distance as she thought. He was right. Every little thing could be relevant. They didn't know enough yet to rule any of it out.

Which was why she needed to get her hands on that database, sooner rather than later. She needed to go back over Veronica Rowse's file, see as much as she could that might give her some clue about what she had seen.

The last case they had worked, the one out in Milwaukee, was still fresh in her mind. The killer had been targeting twins. That was one thought. Had the vision she'd seen not been of Veronica after all, but her identical twin?

It would be weird if the family hadn't mentioned a sister, but then again, people did weird things.

"What are you thinking?" Nate asked, snapping her attention back to him.

"I'm thinking that we know hardly anything right now," Laura said. "Has his family been tracked down and notified?"

Nate glanced at the detective who had brought him the file in the first place for confirmation.

"No, not yet," he said, making a disappointed face. "They're back in Montgomery, from what we understand. We're liaising with the local department there, trying to get them informed. When we do, I'll be able to let you know."

"Thanks," Nate said, clapping the man on the shoulder. "We'll have to talk with the detectives on the ground there, get them some immediate questions to ask. I'm guessing the family will want to come and see the body anyway, but we need information faster than they can get here."

The detective nodded smartly, moving away just as Laura's contact returned with an overweight and bespectacled woman hustling across the bullpen behind him. Pushing her glasses up her nose, the newcomer looked at Laura and Nate owlishly before returning her glance to the computer behind him.

"You're the ones need access?" she asked.

"That's us," Laura said. She flipped out her badge for the tech's benefit. "We need access to all local and national databases."

"You don't need access to Bobby's files?" the woman asked. When Laura shook her head, she nodded in reply and sat down in the vacant chair. "Shouldn't take me too long to whip up a new user profile. I'll get you all the access you need."

"Thanks," Laura said. She turned to Nate, figuring this was a good time to fill him in on what she'd been thinking during the drive over – if not revealing the cause of those thoughts. "I'm going to dive deeper on our victims. Starting with Veronica Rowse, see if there's anything in her history I can dig up. There must be something here that we can work with, even if it's just some kind of popular hangout they've all been to."

Nate nodded. "I'll work with you on that," he said. "I can do the non-database route. Look at their social media pages, start looking for locations or people in common, that kind of thing."

Laura knew that Blackford would have had his guys looking into those sorts of connections already, but it didn't hurt to look again. A fresh pair of eyes from out of town could sometimes reveal hidden layers of information. Maybe there was a bar that absolutely everyone in Atlanta knew and went to every now and then, and it was discarded by the initial search team as being only a coincidence. A non-local, though, would flag it up.

"All set," the tech woman said, getting up out of Laura's way. Laura thanked her gratefully and sat down in the chair herself, immediately logging in to the local database and starting to look up Veronica Rowse.

There were lots of records she could check, and Laura decided to go for all of them. Birth records was obvious, but searching by Rowse didn't get her anything other than the family members that they already knew about. No record of a twin, or even another sister.

Didn't mean one hadn't been born in shameful circumstances and swept away, maybe given up for adoption or abandoned, with no name filled in for 'mother' on the birth certificate. Medical records could tell her a little more about that.

Laura searched Veronica's mother's information, trying to see anything that would give her a clue about an extended hospital stay or even just a one-night check-in. But there was nothing. Veronica, though, had a fairly serious stay on her records: a car accident, just over a year ago. By the list of procedures that she'd been through, it looked as though it had been pretty bad.

She'd survived it. Only to come out the other end and get herself killed by some kind of monster. What a waste. Of course, it was extra time with her loved ones, time to do the things she loved and maybe make an impact on others. She'd worked in the hospice, maybe made someone's life better. Maybe lots of people. But, still, it seemed like a damned shame to go through all of that and then just die not long afterwards anyway.

Laura checked everything else she could think of, storing each piece of information in her mind. The non-existent criminal record, which told her nothing. Any mention of Veronica she could find in the local paper – which, as it turned out, was only one, a report on the car accident. The details of her family that came up in searches. Everything. Laura had no way right now of knowing which bit of information was important, so she kept it all in her head.

Beside her, Nate was slumped in a spare chair he'd wheeled over, hunched over his cell phone. He was making rapid notes on a page of his notepad, then pausing to scroll up his screen. They would both be here for a while, especially if they found nothing. Laura squared her shoulders and turned back to her keyboard, flexing her fingers above it as she thought.

There was no other way she could think of to search for information. There was only so much data that could quantify someone's life. The real essence of them, that was what you got from interviews with the family.

She put her fingers to the keys and typed in Stephanie Marchall instead.

What she saw made her lean forward and frown, focusing more closely on the screen. The medical records were... interesting. Stephanie had only been in her mid-thirties, but according to the report, she'd been brought in after suffering from a heart attack some two years before. All manner of scans and tests were listed on her record, until she had been diagnosed with a congenital heart problem that had never previously been noticed. She had a prescription for heart medication. She must have been taking it on the day she was abducted, or the stress of the event would probably have been enough to trigger another cardiac event. Since the coroner hadn't mentioned it, Laura guessed it hadn't come into play during her twelve hours on that platform.

There was more data to go through, more information to find. But Laura had a hunch that something was up, here. Something that she couldn't quite put her finger on yet.

Instead of looking through all the other checks for Stephanie Marchall, she focused on the medical records, this time looking up Lincoln Ware.

He, too, had a whole batch of tests on his record, and within the last six months. They all occurred on the same day. Tests for arterial blood gasses, a CT scan, blood and urine tests, a chest x-ray, an EEG. Something must have happened to him. The record didn't show what, and the tests had apparently all come back clear.

Whatever it was, it was clear he'd had some kind of medical experience. Something dangerous, judging by the seriousness of the tests he underwent. The same as the other two.

An accident within the past couple of years. That was what connected all of them.

Was that what her vision had been trying to tell her?

But, then, why had it come through like that?

"Nate?" Laura said, getting his attention with an uncertain note in her voice. "I think I have something here."

"What is it?" Nate asked, dropping his pen. "I haven't come up with anything at all, yet."

"Look," Laura said, showing him the three records that she'd kept open on her screen. "All three of the victims we have so far were involved in some kind of accident or injury over the past two years. Serious ones, too. I would even guess they were all life-risking scenarios."

Nate frowned. "Could that be enough?"

Laura shrugged. "I don't know. But it's all we have right now."

Nate stood up, snapping his notebook shut. "Well, then we better chase it down. Where first?"

"The Rowse family," Laura said. She gave him a faint smile. "If we get lucky and Bradley Milford has already been released and gone back to them, we might be able to hit two birds with one stone."

***

The Rowse house was darker and emptier than it had been the last time they visited. There were only two cars parked outside now, which quickly dampened Laura's hope of being able to speak to Bradley Milford. A call back to the precinct verified that he'd been transferred for processing before his court appearance, after a much larger stash of pills were found at his home. At least they knew where he was if they needed him again.

Laura knocked on the door, feeling Nate's presence behind her as a reassuringly solid shadow falling over her own. She wasn't quite sure anymore just how stable the ground was beneath her. This whole thing with the vision of the dead woman coming to life, with the killer tricking them about the times – it was all throwing her off. And her visions hadn't been coming often enough, or giving enough detail, through the whole case. It was like she was reaching out for things she'd relied on for years, only to find them no longer where she'd left them. And she needed them to be where she'd left them.

The door opened to reveal the brother who had been helpful before – Stephen, Laura remembered. He took one look at them, sighed, and then stepped back to allow them inside.

"Good morning," Laura said, because she felt like someone should say something. She walked in, her feet taking her by instinct back to that same living room they'd met in before. There was no one else in the room this time, the sofa empty, the whole space seeming smaller and sadder now that it wasn't full to the brim with people.

"My parents are resting upstairs," Stephen said, his voice low. "Let's try not to disturb them. Unless you're here to tell us that you've caught the guy?"

"Unfortunately, no," Nate said, his tone one of regret. "We actually have a few follow-up questions. We're getting closer to catching him all the time, and the information you can give us might help us get there."

Stephen sighed again and sat down, gesturing for them to do the same. "What do you need to know?"

Laura sat beside him on the sofa, finding the seat cushions uncomfortably flat and sunken, while Nate took an armchair to the side. "I believe Veronica was in a car accident not too long ago?" she said, posing the words as a question.

Stephen looked at her with a frown. "Yes. What's that got to do with anything?"

"Let us be the judge of that," Laura said, gently but firmly. She found that relatives often had the tendency to become armchair detectives, especially if you didn't get the case solved quickly enough for their liking. They had to be reminded from time to time that actual detectives couldn't just share all the information on the case with everyone they spoke to – that most of it had to stay classified so that the killer wouldn't escape. "Can you tell us about what happened?"

Stephen glanced away, towards the wall, his eyes clearly looking inward to his memory instead of outward. "It was a pretty bad smash. Totaled the car. It wasn't her fault at all – some loser was drunk behind the wheel, and she happened to be driving home after staying late at work. T-boned her car at an intersection."

"What about her injuries?" Laura asked. "Her medical records suggest it was pretty serious."

Stephen snorted. "Serious?" he said, shaking his head. "It was a miracle she survived. She almost didn't."

"What do you mean?" Laura asked. She could hear a rush of blood in her ears. A thing she didn't want to acknowledge was coming rapidly towards her, like the very vehicle that had hit Veronica's car.

"Her heart stopped before they even managed to get her out of the car. The EMTs had to resuscitate her at the scene," Stephen said. "She had months of problems. Broke her leg in two places. She had to practically relearn how to walk on it by the time the cast came off. Broke her collarbone too, and she had some pretty nasty cuts on her side from the broken glass."

Laura had a flash of herself, standing in the morgue, looking down at the body. From the other side. She hadn't gone around to examine Veronica from all angles, had never noticed the scars. The coroner hadn't mentioned them, but why would he? They weren't relevant to the cause of death.

"She died, and came back to life," Laura said, saying the words almost to herself. She felt like she was floating for an odd moment. Like she was looking down at herself having this realization.

That was what she had seen. Veronica Rowse coming back to life. And now that she thought harder about the vision she'd had, the images that were burned into her memory, she could see details. Like the glint of broken glass in Veronica's hair, just at the edge of the vision. Like the fact that Veronica was only just dead, or she would have looked completely different, as she had in the morgue. This was something that happened not long after her heart stopped. She was resuscitated. The movements Laura had seen – they must have been caused by the EMTs pumping her chest.

Laura felt her own heart pounding and constricting oddly, her head swimming. The sound of her heartbeat echoed in her ears. She hadn't seen the future.

She'd seen the past.

CHAPTER TWENTY THREE

Laura was still reeling as Nate made their goodbyes. She hadn't even heard whether he'd asked any more questions, or what Stephen might have said in response to them. She was too shaken. Still trying to understand what all of this meant.

She'd never seen the past before. It had always been the future. This was a complete change, a one-eighty, something so far out of left field she had never expected it. And she had no idea what it meant. Why it was happening.

If the foundations had felt shaky before, now they were entirely gone. Laura was falling through quicksand, and she had nothing to hold onto. She followed Nate out of the house numbly, slumping into the passenger seat, able to do nothing but simply stare ahead blankly.

"Laura?" he said. His tone was urgent but soft, like he didn't want to startle her. "Laura, are you alright?"

She turned her head to look at him, feeling how slow the motion was. She couldn't seem to speed up. Couldn't snap back to normal. It was like she was inside a dream; and in the dream, she was swimming in treacle, and nothing was working properly.

Nate swore quietly under his breath.

"Laura, what's going on?" he asked, reaching out to touch her arm. "Talk to me."

The second he touched her, bare fingers on bare wrist, there it was again. The shadow of death. It was dark and roiling and visceral, and Laura felt it hit her stomach before she had a chance to even react. She recoiled with horror, brushing his arm away with a half-whimper, half-shout, unable to bear it. For a moment she thought she was actually going to throw up, right there in the car.

Nate looked at her even more intensely, his eyes wide with what Laura realized was fear. He was afraid for her.

Or of her?

"Just take a deep breath with me," Nate said, his voice going lower and rhythmic. "In, okay? And out. You're doing great. In… and out."

Laura followed his instructions mechanically, recognizing their value. They'd had the same training, after all. She breathed with him until her mind started to clear, the fog dissipating slowly like mist coming off a river when hit by the sun.

"Are you back with me?" Nate asked, when she was able to meet his eyes without feeling her own glazed over.

"Yes," Laura said, finding her mouth dry. She swallowed hard.

"What was that?" he asked, the inevitable follow-up. The one she didn't want to answer.

Laura paused, thinking about how she was supposed to answer him. What she was supposed to say. How could she explain something that she didn't even understand herself?

"I saw something," she said, at length, then looked back at him to see his reaction. Better to start small, with something like this. Something non-specific.

"What?" Nate asked. He looked back at the house. "Something in the living room?"

"No, Nate," Laura said, holding up a hand to bring his attention back to her. "I mean, I *saw* something. Like we talked about."

Nate paused, looking at her. She didn't look up to meet his eyes again. Suddenly, she was feeling incredibly tired. So tired she wasn't even sure how much of this she could manage.

"Laura…" he said, trailing off like he was struggling to think of how to put his words together. Then: "How did you know where to go last night? The barn?"

Laura nodded slowly, meeting his eyes again. "You already know. I've told you."

"No," Nate said, shaking his head. "I mean it, Laura. How did you know which barn you had to go to? Did you see a photograph or something? Did someone give you a description?"

"I was alone," Laura said. "You know I wouldn't hold back evidence if I'd seen a photograph or some kind of physical proof. I saw it in a vision. I was at the site the killer had set up for the future, in that grocery store, and I touched something he had touched, and I had a vision of the barn."

Nate's eyes flicked down to her wrist, the spot where he had just touched her. He must have been thinking about how she'd reacted. Like she'd been burned.

"But, you didn't really, did you?" Nate said. His tone was becoming uncertain, almost pleading. "That's not what really happened. You just don't want to tell me the truth. Maybe you don't want to admit the truth. I thought I knew you, but… maybe you would

124

do this. Maybe you would hide evidence and claim you had a vision just to get… What? Attention?"

"I've been hiding this from you for three years," Laura said, her jaw tightening. "Do you really think I'm telling you this for attention?"

"But you do get attention," Nate said. He was talking faster, like he was figuring something out. Like he was having a revelation. "Back at HQ, they talk about you having this intuition. Like you've got some kind of sixth sense. People say that about you all the time. They call you a natural detective. You must love that. And I can see how you'd want to keep that going, even if it meant hiding things now and then."

"No, Nate," Laura said, feeling a painful squeeze in her chest. "I hate it when they say that. I've told you that before. It just makes me self-conscious. I'm only trying to do my job. I wouldn't cheat like that, not when anything we find could make the difference in court."

Nate was looking at her strangely, slowly shaking his head backwards and forwards. "It's like you're a stranger to me," he said. "And just now, this whole panic attack thing. It's an act, isn't it? Now that you've got me on the hook, you're just trying to string me along and get my attention."

"No," Laura said again, but Nate was shaking his head more rapidly now, holding up his hands.

"I don't want to talk about this anymore," he said. "I'm not going to keep encouraging you by giving you this attention. You know what? I'm going to call the precinct, get them to send out someone in a car for me. I'm going back to the clock store, going through the records they've been downloading. At least there we might find a concrete lead. You… you do whatever you have to do."

Laura's mouth was drier than she could ever remember it being as he got out of the car, leaving the door open and striding away a few paces down the street. She watched him get his cell phone out of his pocket, heard him speaking quietly into it as he'd promised.

Laura got out of the car, but she didn't go and get in the driver's seat immediately. She walked over to him instead.

And he saw her coming and turned and walked further away.

"Nate," Laura said, desperately now. She ran a few paces to catch up, then reached out to catch at his arm. Even though she knew it was stupid. Even though…

The shadow of death was on him, on her, so strong she could barely breathe. So dark and deep and intense, so much more than it had been a moment ago.

125

"Don't," Nate said, shaking her off. "I need some time. Let's just get this case solved before someone else dies."

Before someone else dies. His words were almost prophetic. Laura shivered, but he was turning away from her again, deliberately, shoving his hands into his pockets and squaring his shoulders. He wasn't going to listen.

She turned and went back to the car, getting behind the wheel because she didn't know what else to do. He was determined, apparently, and his pickup was already on the way. She started the engine and set off in the direction of the precinct, but she didn't go far. As soon as she was out of sight of Nate, she turned down a side street and parked a little way down it, resting her head in her hands.

She needed to process this. The shadow of death that she had seen hanging over him all of this time had fluctuated during the months that she had been seeing it. There were times when it had seemed stronger than ever. There were even times when it had seemed to go away completely. Looking back over all of those times, Laura couldn't help but notice a distinct pattern emerging.

Whenever she thought about telling him that she was psychic in the past, the intensity of the shadow had either diminished or gone away completely. But whenever she decided not to tell him, and now when he declared he didn't believe her, the shadow had become stronger. So dark it was almost overpowering.

The parallel was impossible to ignore. She had seen the shadow of death hanging over her father for a long time before she actually learned that he was going to die of cancer. And that, in itself, was a long time before he had actually succumbed to the disease. But it wasn't like her visions. She had no way of measuring how long it would take for the shadow to progress to a real threat on Nate's life. Even if she had a preconceived notion of it, now, with things as they were, she wasn't sure that any of the rules were the same anymore.

But what she saw now was very clear. If Nate went on thinking that she did not have psychic powers, that it was all a made-up lie, he was going to die. Sooner rather than later. Certainly not at the age of one hundred with all of his grandchildren around the bed. But if she told him, and made him believe, and made him see that it was real, then he wasn't going to die at all. At least, not for a while.

She had a duty to make him see. She had a duty to save his life.

Not just because she cared about him, which she did. But because this was her job. Her whole reason for being. Laura was an FBI agent because she wanted to stop people from being murdered. She wanted to save their lives. If she couldn't even save the life of her partner, when all it required was for her to be honest with him, then what good was she?

She was going to have to find a way to convince him, to make him see.

But right now... he was clearly having a hard time taking it in. What he'd said had been hurtful – accusing her of making it all up for attention like that. He knew, deep down, that Laura hated the kind of attention she got for solving cases. That was the only reason she was able to keep it together herself and forgive him for that kind of accusation, something that went so hard against everything he knew about her. He was struggling with the concept of her being psychic in itself, and while there would be opportunities to show him proof, they wouldn't just pop up randomly if Laura trailed around behind Nate like a lost puppy dog. She still needed to do her job.

Just as much as she needed to save Nate's life, she also needed to stop the killer from taking another. He'd had his next kill site set up already at the grocery store, which meant it was highly likely he was already stalking his victim. She couldn't just drop everything to try and change Nate's mind, not right now. There would be time for that in due course.

Right now, she needed to work the case. And working the case meant she needed to find the next lead. Looking at medical records and speaking to family members was only going to get her so far.

Laura turned the key in the ignition, starting the engine again with a new determination.

If she wanted answers, she was going to have to go right to the source. The hospital.

She zoomed out on her GPS and found it, the one place where all of the medical records so far had come from. The same hospital. How she hadn't seen that connection and jumped on it before, she had no idea. She'd been distracted, too much in her own head. But she saw it now, and she was going to get to the bottom of this before the day was done. Whatever it took.

***

"So, this is for the clock killer case?" the administrator asked, looking at Laura with an intensely measured look over her shoulder. Laura didn't flinch.

"That's right," she said, following the tall, sharply dressed woman down the hall towards the records office. "We're chasing down a lead that might be crucial in solving it."

The administrator nodded, her heels clicking on the linoleum floors at a rapid pace. Even in her sensible flats, Laura found herself hurrying to keep up. "I wouldn't normally do this," she said. "But I understand that time is of the essence here, and I want it to be on the record that we're doing everything we can to help you stop this public menace."

Public menace. It was a funny way of describing a rampant murderer. "Of course," Laura said, instead of responding to that. "Your help is much appreciated."

They'd reached a door marked with a plaque reading RECORDS in old-fashioned font, and the administrator pushed her way in before holding it open for Laura. She followed into a small room which was mostly occupied by a desk and a single computer. Behind it, a partition hid a number of shelves stacked with cardboard archive boxes. Laura couldn't see how far back they stretched. She didn't think she wanted to. The computer was much more promising.

"I'll have to access the system for you, of course," the administrator said primly, sitting herself down and smoothing out her pencil skirt. "But you can tell me what you want me to look up, and I'll get it for you."

"Alright," Laura said, because she was in too much of a rush to argue – and definitely in too much of a rush to have to go out and get a warrant signed by a judge if this woman decided not to help after all. "I need to see the details of three patients who've had procedures done here. The first is Veronica Rowse."

"And what are we looking for?" the administrator asked, her hands already moving over the keyboard.

Damned if I know, Laura thought. She was hoping this would be one of those things that she would know when she saw it. "She was involved in a car accident about a year ago. I need everything related to that event."

"Everything?" the administrator said, raising an eyebrow. She turned back to her screen, then glanced at Laura. "I've got a lot here. EMT reports, scans and tests, results, signed orders for medication…"

"All of it," Laura confirmed. "If you can run me off a copy of everything in that file pertaining to the time of the accident, I'll start looking through it while you find the data on the other two."

"Alright," the administrator said, with a heavy tone in her voice that implied Laura was pushing her luck. But Laura didn't care. This was all she needed, and it had to show her something.

It had to.

She scanned page after page of the documents, trying to record as much of the information in her head as she could. Doctor names. The date and time of Veronica's admission. The medication she had been administered. All of the tests, and the results they showed. The amount of coverage she'd had with her insurance, and who her provider was. The amount she'd owed. The name of the physiotherapist who helped her to walk again and the number of weeks she'd spent in physical therapy, and the name of the center where she did it. All of it could be relevant.

When Laura finally moved on to look at Stephanie Marchall's file, the administrator was watching her with clear impatience, looking at her watch repeatedly.

"You can go if you're busy," Laura said, not looking up. She could see enough in her peripheral vision, and the files needed her attention more. "This could take a while."

"I'd better not leave you alone with the files," the administrator said in a supercilious tone, and Laura was glad she hadn't been making eye contact at the time. The woman might have seen something ugly cross Laura's face in response.

She was an FBI agent. If the administrator wasn't going to trust her, then who was she ever going to trust?

It didn't matter. Laura refocused, reading through the files again. This time with an even finer-toothed comb, given that she didn't know all of the details already. The heart attack had happened when Stephanie was at work, according to the EMT report. It looked as though they were called out to the scene, where…

Where her heart had stopped, and she had to be resuscitated.

Laura sat up a little straighter in her chair. Of course. A heart attack, and a near-fatal car accident. Both women had to be revived. That was a link. The first one she'd really seen so far, other than the hospital. Without a vision to help her out, the hospital was too vague of a connection to build on. But this seemed like it would take her one level deeper. This…

Laura reached for the first few pages that had been printed from Lincoln Ware's file. She had no idea what kind of accident he'd suffered, only the tests that he'd had done for it. She flipped to the EMT report and started to read…

He'd been swimming, at a friend's house in their own pool. He'd been drinking, too. They all had. Things had gotten out of control, apparently, and the ambulance had been called after he'd slipped under the water and not come back up.

When the EMTs arrived, they'd found him unresponsive, his lips blue. They'd had to resuscitate him. He'd been clinically dead for at least a minute or so.

His heart had needed to be restarted.

Laura felt her own pound in her chest again, as if in response to the idea of a heart failing. All three of the victims had already died once before, and not too long ago. All over the span of the past two years, all in Atlanta, and all were brought here afterwards to recover.

Their lives had been saved. They'd been given extra time. Time, which seemed to be so important to the killer.

Was this it?

Laura studied the text of all three reports again, trying to get something else to jump out at her. She scanned the lines all the way to the bottom, where they were signed off by the responding EMT. The first one was a guy named Paul Payne. He'd been the one to resuscitate Veronica. And the one who responded to Stephanie Marchall was...

Was Paul Payne.

Laura heard herself gasp out loud, a sharp intake of breath as she saw the link. She hurriedly grabbed Lincoln Ware's report and read through it, but – the name at the bottom was different. A Holly Randall had been the one to respond on that occasion.

But this was something very important. Laura could feel it. The same man had been present at two out of three of these near-death experiences.

"The EMT who signs off on these reports," Laura said. "They don't work alone, do they?"

"No, ma'am," the administrator said, in a kind of stern tone. "They work in pairs, always, if not in groups when responding to larger accidents. Why do you ask?"

"The names on these reports," Laura said. "There's only one."

"That would be the person who had seniority at the time and therefore had the responsibility to write the report," the administrator said.

Laura saw what this meant. There was someone else at the scene when Lincoln Ware nearly drowned. That someone else could have been Paul Payne.

She didn't have evidence yet, but surely it would be easy to find.

"I want to speak to one of these EMTs," Laura said, looking up at the administrator decisively. "Where can I find him?"

CHAPTER TWENTY FOUR

Laura studied him from a distance for a moment before moving closer. Paul Payne was dressed in the standard gray shirt of his profession, a radio hooked up on his shoulder, ready and waiting to call him in for any new emergency. He was talking casually with a colleague, a young woman sitting in the back of the ambulance beside him.

It was lucky that he happened to be on shift, right here at the hospital, exactly when Laura needed to speak with him.

He was young enough himself, no more than forty years old. No, Laura would have guessed even younger, actually. Maybe around the same age as the women who had died, or around her own age. No younger than thirty, given the fine lines he wore around his eyes and across his forehead. He was handsome enough, too, with straight, dark hair worn swept to one side and cut slightly longer across his temple and pale blue eyes. Laura remembered reading somewhere that having dark hair and blue eyes was actually extremely rare in genuine genetics, and that was why such a large percentage of actors and actresses seemed to have them. It was viewed as rare and exotic.

A kind of natural advantage, giving someone a charm that could override a nasty reputation. Laura took that into account as she approached him. In her experience, the handsome ones were the ones you had to watch out for. They got away with so much just by being admired.

"Excuse me," she said, as she reached the back of the ambulance where the two EMTs were sitting. "You're Paul Payne, is that correct?"

"Yeah," he said, sitting up a bit straighter. His expression smoothed out, like he was putting on his customer service voice. "How can we help? Do you need some assistance?"

"You could say that." Laura dug her badge out and showed it to them both, glancing at the young woman who was sitting beside Paul. She didn't need an audience. "I wonder if we could chat for a moment?"

She felt tension thrumming high in her veins. If he was the killer and she was about to get herself left alone with him, she could be in danger. But what was she supposed to do? Nate wasn't in the right frame of mind to do this with her, not right now. She couldn't let him just carry on roaming the streets. She had her gun. And at least here, on the hospital grounds, there was a good chance of there being a witness at all times. That might make him think twice, if he really was the killer.

"Sure," Paul said. He followed her glance at his coworker, and evidently recognized her hint towards privacy. "Uh, I was actually due a break anyway. I'll head inside with you – there's a little room we use near the canteen. Sandy, can you take us off call for fifteen?"

"Sure," the other woman nodded brightly, though her eyes kept flicking over Laura uncertainly.

Laura was sure it wasn't completely unusual, an EMT having to talk to the police. There were cases they would have been involved in, treating victims and so on. Sandy didn't argue, only watched curiously as Paul got down from the back of the ambulance and walked Laura inside.

"What's this about?" he asked, when they were inside the doors, walking down the hushed halls. Even though it was still daytime, there was a kind of quiet to a hospital. The people sitting in the main waiting area were subdued, many of them looking blank as though they'd been there for a long time, even the ones clutching bloodied towels against hands or foreheads. A baby was crying, but even that was shushed as they walked by.

"It's regarding an ongoing case," Laura said. "I'd feel better discussing it when we're in your break room."

"Of course," Paul nodded. They were surrounded by people, so it was hardly an unexpected request, Laura thought. He led her to a small room, as promised, which was occupied by only one other person. A slightly overweight man with headphones jammed in his ears, a paperback and a bowl of kale and chicken salad in front of him, and the same uniform as Paul. He nodded a greeting when they entered, but that was all.

Laura instantly felt better. A witness, but also one who wasn't going to be listening in to their conversation. The best she could have hoped for.

The room held three tables surrounded by chairs, as well as a wall of lockers and a fridge, sink, and cupboards for plates and mugs. Paul led her to one of the tables, then hesitated as she sat down. He turned to get a smoothie out of the fridge, marked with a piece of tape that had his name written on it in black pen. Then, at last, he sat down to face her.

133

"So, what is it?" he asked. "Is it about that stabbing last week?"

"No, this is about some older cases," Laura said. "Well, older for you. There are three that took place over the last few years. I'd like to get your perspective on them, if I can."

"Oh, sure," Paul said, flipping up the top of his smoothie shaker and taking a draught. "Anything you need."

"Alright," Laura said, reaching into the inside of her jacket. She'd stashed a file there containing the things she wanted to show him: the three EMT reports for Veronica, Stephanie, and Lincoln. "I have your name on a couple of these reports, so I want you to take a look at them and see what you remember."

Paul took the first one, his forehead furrowing as he looked it over. Something he saw made his eyebrows lift and eyes widen, his face going pale. "Oh, God. Wait. Is this about the clock killer?"

"What makes you ask that?" Laura replied, instantly on guard.

"The name," he said. "Veronica Rowse. I saw it on the news earlier today. That's one of the victims, isn't it?"

Laura silently cursed in her head. Captain Blackford hadn't been able to hold off the media forever. There went the element of surprise. Still, it wasn't like it was unusual to deal with members of the public who already knew some details of the case. She needed to watch him carefully, figure out if he knew more than he should. One slip, and she would have him. "Yes, I'm afraid it's about that case," she said. "This is one of the victims."

"And the other two?" he asked.

Reluctantly, Laura nodded.

Paul sighed heavily, passing a hand over his mouth and shaking his head. "Damn. That's... wow. I resuscitated her. And now she's dead anyway." He flipped through the other two pages, stopping at Stephanie Marchall's. "This one, too?"

"You see why I wanted to talk to you in particular," Laura said, glad he'd picked up on the connection. "It seems like you would be best placed to tell me anything that stands out about these two cases."

Paul's eyes roved over the reports again and he shook his head slowly. "I don't remember anything in particular that isn't already written down here," he said. "They were... well, pretty much like any other callout. We did good. Saved their lives. I just... I can't believe they're gone now."

"What about the third one?" Laura asked. "Do you know anything about that? Did you happen to be there as well?"

Paul glanced over the third sheet. "Lincoln Ware – it doesn't ring a bell. No... No, I definitely wasn't on shift that night."

"How can you be so sure?" Laura asked, watching him closely. She couldn't get a read on whether he was genuine or not. Had he reacted properly to the name, like he really hadn't heard it before? She couldn't tell. "This happened six months ago. You remember what you were doing on that night?"

Paul gave her a brief smile. "I'm sure," he said. "That's my birthday. I was out with family."

Laura leaned back in her chair, sighing internally. He had an alibi for that night. He still would have had access to the records, of course, but it became less of a connection if he wasn't personally there at all three of the near-death calls.

"Who were you working with on the other two nights?" she asked. "Do you stick with the same crew, usually?"

"Sometimes," Paul shrugged. He looked between the sheets of paper which held information about Marchall and Rowse, as if he was looking into his memory at the same time. "I don't think... no, these two nights were different crews. Holly was there for both Lincoln and Stephanie, I think, but she wasn't there when we responded to the car crash for Veronica. It all depends on who's on shift, you know?"

Laura nodded. She made a note of it, anyway, in case it turned out to be relevant. She could always track this Holly down and interview her next, if she got desperate. It looked like a dead end, but you never really knew.

She was about to ask another question when the door opened, letting in a couple of EMTs who were loudly laughing and talking among themselves. They stopped when they noticed Laura, their expressions dropping from the over-exuberant to simply cheerful.

"Oh, sorry," one of them said. "Didn't realize you had a guest in today, Paul!"

"Oh, I don't," Paul said, though he was smiling back at them. "This is Agent – Frost, wasn't it? She's with the FBI."

"Hope you're not looking into Paul," one of the newcomers, an older guy who was rail-thin and had tightly muscled arms under his shirt, joked. "He's one of our best. We need him on the team!"

Paul laughed and shook his head. "Don't listen to him," he said. "He's just trying to get me to cover his weekend shift."

"You know it," the older EMT laughed. "No, I'm not kidding. He's got a better record than most of us out here."

"Is that so?" Laura asked, looking back at Paul.

He had a faint blush on his cheeks, which was kind of funny to see on a man who was so handsome, self-possessed, and obviously confident in his work. "I don't really pay attention to the records," he said modestly.

"Well, those of us that do know he's got a hell of a lot of saved lives ahead of most of us," the older man said. "What are you chatting about, anyway?"

"It's a case," Paul said, sliding the pieces of paper back across the table to Laura. "I... guess I'm not supposed to talk about it?"

"If you could keep it to yourself for now," Laura replied, tucking the sheets back away into the folder. "Thanks for your time, anyway. I think that about covers it. But if you do think of anything relevant..."

Paul took the card she was offering him with a nod and a smile, immediately slipping it into his breast pocket. "I'll call you right away," he said.

"Thanks again," Laura told him, getting up. "Enjoy the rest of your break."

"Thank you," Paul said. "And, good luck. I hope you catch whoever did this. It's... well, it's a tragedy."

Laura nodded, skirting the three other EMTs who now made the small break room feel crowded on her way to the door. She found her own way out of the hospital, back the way she'd come in, until she was standing outside in the cold air of the morning again. It was still early. Early enough that, if the killer was planning on starting a timer today, it wouldn't have been set up yet.

But not early enough that she had any confidence she was going to get this done.

It was almost starting to seem impossible. Paul Payne had been her best lead yet, and she had even started to feel excited that she might be getting somewhere in this case. But now that she had met him in person, she had no qualms about ruling him out of the investigation. Not only was he charming and obviously cared a lot about his patients, but he had no connection to the third victim. Lincoln Ware had been revived when Paul wasn't even on duty, and his coworkers seem to think highly of him as well. From what Lauren knew of the Angel of Mercy-type killers, usually there was a lot of suspicion among their colleagues. People noticed when deaths happened around a certain person. It was just that the system often allowed them to get away with it for longer than they should.

Which left her back exactly where she had been yesterday, and the day before that, and even really where she'd been before she'd even heard of the case. Yes, she knew now that it must have something to do with the fact that all three victims had once been clinically dead, only to survive. But where did that get her? She had no way to link it to any particular person, and there must be so many hundreds or even thousands of people living in Atlanta who had once almost died.

Nate wasn't talking to her again; or if he was, it made no difference because she had no idea where he was now. Lacey's visit was still coming up, and Laura felt another day slipping out of her grasp slowly as they failed to get anywhere with the case. Another day closer to having to forfeit her first weekend with her daughter, and maybe something even more serious than that if she couldn't get back in time. And there was Amy, who needed support and help. If Laura had been back home, she would have gone round there, to help Chris out as quickly as she was able to. But she couldn't. Everything had to be on pause until this case was done.

Add on top of that the fact that her visions were playing up, and she had no idea why, and Laura was starting to feel like the weight of the world was on her shoulders with this case. She had no idea how to push through it. Or what she was going to do now.

All she knew was she couldn't give up.

Laura walked back to the rental car in the parking lot, shut herself inside, and leaned over the steering wheel, trying hard to think. There must be something she could do to either trigger a vision that actually told her something or move this case forward.

She just had to think.

CHAPTER TWENTY FIVE

Jenny sighed, looking out of her window at the car. She wished she didn't have to go, but she was going to have to.

This was how it had been, lately. Staring out at that car, trying to work up the courage to go and get into it. Knowing she had to.

Jenny pushed her hair back from her face, the scars on her right arm catching her eye as she did so. She felt like she couldn't go anywhere without seeing a reminder of what had happened only a few months ago, even if only on her own body. The bandages had been off for a while now, and the cuts had healed to red lines, but that didn't mean she didn't remember what it felt like when they were fresh.

When the glass from the car window had sliced her open.

She shuddered, shaking her head.

No, she wasn't going to do this. She wasn't going to allow her fears to get in the way yet again. Every week, she had the same fears, the same anxieties. She'd been working with the therapist on getting over it, and she remembered now what she'd been told. Think about the likelihood. Think about the severity. How many times had she driven a car in the past without anything bad happening at all? Hundreds of times, surely. Being in one car accident one time, well, that left a several hundred to one chance of anything like that ever happening again.

Of course, her traitor brain reminded her, the likelihood was even lower if she didn't get back in the car at all.

But she had to. She had to get back to normal life. She pulled her head away from the memory of the sound of twisting metal and breaking glass, and moved towards the doorway, her motion a little off-balance.

The physiotherapy was going well, at least.

Jenny took her car keys from the peg by the door and stepped outside, moving towards the vehicle. She kept it parked under a little overhang beside the house, not really a full garage but still something that provided shelter. That was one more consolation: the fact that her neighbors couldn't see her having this same freak-out every single time she tried to get in the car to go to her appointment. At least none of them knew how fragile she was, how weak she could be sometimes. It was pathetic, she told herself.

And then she heard the voice of her therapist in her head reminding her that she was doing great and taking things one step at a time, and not to let negative self-thoughts get in the way of things. And she sighed again.

It was always like this. The constant battle between her head and the things that she knew she was supposed to think.

Jenny paused, patting her pockets. She'd forgotten her purse and everything in it. She moved back inside the house, grabbing it, and then finally made her way back to the car again. She had to walk all the way around it from this part of the house, slipping around the front of the car in order to get to the drivers' side door. She was looking into her purse, rummaging around inside it to see if she'd remembered to pick up any breath mints, when it happened.

Something hit her in the back of the head.

Her first thought was that she was having a stroke or something. That the injury she sustained in the crash was finally catching up with her. She had done a lot of reading about head injuries ever since it happened, working herself up into a frenzy of terror. She knew that sometimes there could be no symptoms at all, and everything could seem as though it was fine, and then one day you would just drop dead from a blood clot or something like that. Her first thought was that it was finally happening.

But she staggered forward, catching herself on the car, and when she was able to focus on her own reflection in the window glass, she could see that there was someone behind her.

She turned, managing to get the strength to push herself against the car, using it as leverage so that she could stay standing up.

"Sorry," the man said, his tone actually apologetic. "I'm usually a lot more precise. I meant to hit your neck, knock you out cold."

"What?" Jenny said, not quite comprehending what he was saying. Her head was muddy, confused. Something was ringing a distant alarm bell. She frowned. "Do I know you?"

He didn't answer, but she was sure of it. She knew him. Where did she know him from?

He moved closer to her, and Jenny shrank back, but she was unable to go anywhere. The car was the only thing supporting her weight, her legs seemingly turned to jelly. The right leg, the one that had been injured in the accident, was threatening to give way at any moment.

She wasn't far enough along in her physiotherapy for it to handle this kind of stress.

"It's okay," he said, his voice calm and gentle. She remembered it, remembered him speaking to her before. "Don't worry. I'm not going to hit you again. I just need to make sure that you stay asleep for a little bit longer."

And when his hand flashed out, holding a needle, she remembered where she knew him from. She was still reeling from the realization when he plunged it into her neck, holding her steady with the other hand. It was like there was nothing she could do to resist him, so dizzy and groggy and out of control of her body. Her eyes fluttered closed, as whatever it was that he injected into her neck slowly began to filter its way into her system, and all she could think of was how beautiful it would be to sleep now instead of having to worry about any of this anymore.

CHAPTER TWENTY SIX

Laura rested her head on the leather of the car's steering wheel, as if it could bolster her brain and give her the strength that she needed to get through this thought process. She hardly had anything to work on, but that didn't mean she couldn't do it. She'd solved cases before with less, she knew. Sometimes, all it required was a bit of faith in your own abilities and a reminder that this was your job. The thing you'd been training for your whole adult life to do.

She reviewed everything in her head as much as possible, trying to put herself inside the shoes of the killer. The first thing was that they knew he was obsessed with time. That had to be a huge part of it, just like Nate had pointed out. The clocks, the timers, they had to mean something. It had to be something to do with the way he chose his victims, too.

The victims had died and then been resuscitated. Now he was killing them. It was like he was enacting some kind of cosmic justice, like he thought that no one should be given a second chance.

Was that it? Was it linked, somehow, to how long the victims had been given in the world after almost losing their lives?

No, that didn't quite make sense. Stephanie Marchall's accident had happened a couple of years ago, while Veronica Rowse had been in the car crash one year ago. They had both been suspended on the platform for the same length of time, twelve hours. While Lincoln Ware, who had had an extra six months of life, had been standing up there for only ten hours. The difference didn't make sense. There had to be some kind of math that explained all of this.

Laura opened the file again, going through the EMT reports with a closer look, trying to spot anything that related to time. There was one thing: in each of the reports, the EMT specifically noted how long the person had been clinically dead for.

And that was very interesting indeed.

According to what Paul Payne had written, Veronica and Stephanie were each dead for an approximated full minute, or sixty seconds. Both of them had been in serious conditions when he arrived, but he had been able to note the moment that their hearts stopped beating due to the quick actions of others in calling for help. Stephanie Marchall's

141

heart attack had only really gotten into full swing after the ambulance had arrived, with a concerned coworker recognizing the signs that it was about to happen from having witnessed the same thing in her father.

As for Veronica, the injuries she had sustained in the car accident had been bad, and when Paul Payne arrived with the ambulance, the firefighters were just cutting her out of the vehicle. It was during this transition that her own heart had stopped, before she could be laid down on the ground beside the car for Paul and his colleague to bring her back to life.

One minute each. The time matched.

Lincoln Ware was the final data point, the point they needed to match in order for her theory to be proven correct. Laura scanned through the document again, noticing even as she did that the style of the report was noticeably different. It was easy to see that it had been written by a different EMT. Here, though, Holly had written that Lincoln was thought to have been unconscious for only fifty seconds.

It worked.

Laura grabbed her notebook out of her pocket and started scribbling down the numbers, checking her math. If she worked it out as one hour of time on the platform for every five seconds the victim had been dead before revival, then it worked. A full minute for Veronica and Stephanie gave them twelve hours on the clock. Fifty seconds for Lincoln equated to ten hours on his timer. It worked.

Laura stared at the numbers again, running them through in her head a third time just to be sure. It was hard to be completely confident. As always when looking at any kind of data, more points would allow you greater certainty about a theorem or formula. In this case, they only had three. And Laura wasn't complaining about that. She didn't want him to add any more for them.

It was as close to being sure that she could be. The numbers worked. She understood now. She could see the way the killer saw the situation. These people had died. They should have remained dead, according to him. They had been out for a short period of time, and now he was re-creating that time in 1:5 scale for them to consider the end of their lives before it happened.

It was the kind of twisted thought process that someone might have if they actually thought they were being compassionate. Doing the victims a favor by giving them that last bit of time. Giving them one more chance to cheat death again. If they escaped, maybe he would be satisfied to let them live. If they didn't escape, they died.

But just like the old, arcane methods that would have been used for testing a witch, there really was no way out. They weren't being given a completely fair chance. They were tied up in ropes so tight they had little chance of ever escaping – certainly not without great cost, like Veronica had paid. And she hadn't even made it out in the end, either.

Laura sat up straight behind the wheel, taking a deep breath. It made sense now. And what could she do with the information?

She had to use it to track the killer down. He had to have known about the reports, somehow, or he couldn't have known exactly how long to leave each person up there on the platform. Paul Payne had confirmed for her that no one, not even him, was on all three teams of first responders. That meant it had to be someone who wasn't at the scene but would have been able to read the reports.

She got out of the car, having not even moved it during the whole time she was sitting inside, and marched back towards the administrator's office.

***

The administrator seemed much less pleased to see Laura than she had the last time. "I don't know what more I can tell you," she said, gesturing frustratedly from her position seated in front of the archival desk. "I printed off every bit of information that was in those files."

"I know, and I'm very grateful for that," Laura said. She was having to concentrate hard not to snap, not to fire her words out at a mile a minute. She was almost there. She almost had him. She checked her watch; it was coming up to twelve noon. She was on a deadline here, quite literally. If she didn't get to him soon… "I actually did make some great progress with what you gave me, so I'm thankful for that. Now, I need to know who would have access to this information in any way."

"Access to it?" the administrator asked, blinking quickly. She uncrossed her legs and crossed them again in the other direction, like she was nervous. "Well, there's me…"

Laura glanced over her, quickly. Then she dismissed the idea entirely. The administrator might have been tall, but she certainly didn't look strong. Her manner was wrong, too, and more to the point, she had finely manicured fingernails that ended in precise points and were decorated with little flowers. There was no way that kind of manicure could last on someone who had spent the last few days

143

dragging unconscious victims onto platforms and building DIY dropping mechanisms.

"Who else?" Laura asked, impatiently. "Anyone who could see the files themselves or was involved in an administrative way in getting the reports together."

"The supervisors would have seen the reports from the EMTs, the doctors, and the technicians separately," the administrator said, her eyes going up to the ceiling as she pulled the information out of her own mind. "Then the doctors would have seen most of the reports over time, in order to follow up and make sure that they had provided the best possible care. Plus, they would receive verbal reports from the EMTs when the patients were brought in."

Laura shook her head thoughtfully. She'd already seen the names of the doctors involved in treating each patient, the techs who ran the processes, and the supervisors who signed off on each report. They were different in each case. Depending on who was on shift, as well as the specific treatment that the patients needed – they'd mostly been in different departments, except for a small few areas of overlap that Laura already knew gave them nothing.

"Someone else," she said. "Who would have the information in the EMT reports, specifically? Forget about the others for now."

The administrator tapped one of those decorative nails against her lower lip thoughtfully. "Hmm... I suppose, the dispatcher? They would be able to review the first responder reports after calling in help. They add their own reports, if needed. Usually it isn't, because we have the recording of the call in the first place."

"Recording?" Laura asked, her ears pricking up somewhat. "So, you have access to those on the computer?"

"Not here," the administrator said, shaking her head regretfully. "You'd have to go direct to the dispatchers' office for that."

Laura nodded, trying not to feel too disheartened. In the past, being able to hear the voice of the killer, or even the sound of his breathing, had helped her to trigger visions. She'd been able to solve cases based on that, figuring out where he would be next. But this time, it wasn't going to be that easy. Of course, it wasn't.

"Do you have a record of the dispatchers that dealt with each call?" Laura tried, thinking that might be more fruitful.

"Actually, I can find that out," the administrator said, reaching out her hands for the files that Laura already had in her possession. "We use a certain code, which we use to identify staff members. I can tell you what it means."

Laura handed her the files, watching her flip open the page to the EMT reports sitting right on top. "Here, see? At the top of the page." She tapped on a five-digit code at the top of the page, next to the letters 'DIS' and above the space for the details of the time and date the ambulance was sent out.

Laura had seen that code before. She'd assumed it was some kind of regional code, a code to show that they'd all come from the same hospital.

She'd assumed that because all three codes were the same.

"Who does that correspond to?" she asked, with her heart in her mouth.

The administrator tapped around on her computer screen. With the angle she had it turned at, Laura could just make out her opening a spreadsheet and scrolling through it. "Let's see... Here we are. That staff code belongs to a dispatcher called Earl Regis."

"And where can I find Earl?" Laura asked, already getting up from her chair.

CHAPTER TWENTY SEVEN

The dispatch headquarters was easy to find. Laura strode inside on a mission, well aware that time was ticking down. She hadn't heard from Nate all morning since they'd split; she had no idea whether that meant he'd found nothing and was still looking or had found something and was looking into it. Either way, she needed to keep going. She fired him a quick text explaining what she'd found and where she was as she waited at the reception desk for someone to take her inside. Let him do with the information what he would.

"Hi." An older woman with dreadlocks tied back behind her head emerged from the doorway into the main center of the dispatch unit, letting out a stream of conversations before the door closed behind her again. "I'm told you're looking for Earl?"

Laura nodded, lifting her badge to show it. "That's right. I need to speak with him regarding an open investigation."

"I'm afraid he's not working today," the woman said. She had a badge pinned to the front of her shirt that marked her out as a supervisor. "Can I help you in any way?"

Laura hesitated. She wanted to get moving on as quickly as possible, go and find Earl and drag him into the precinct. But if he wasn't home, she would be right back to square one, trying to find him somewhere across the whole city. And given that it was past noon now, she had a feeling there was a good chance he wouldn't be home.

"Yes," she said, decisively. "Is there somewhere we can talk privately?"

The supervisor nodded, leading Laura through another doorway into a quiet and cozy room set up with a soft armchair and a small coffee table. There wasn't much room for anything else, but as soon as the door closed, Laura felt like they might have been out on the moon for how isolated it was. There was no sound from outside at all, and with the door closed and a small window only showing the briefest glimpse of the leaves of a tree outside, there was no way you would imagine you were inside a dispatch center.

"We use this as a little booth for when things get too overwhelming," the supervisor explained. "Somewhere for the staff to retreat to and process things. No one will disturb us while we're in here."

Laura nodded gratefully. "How long have you worked with Earl?" she asked, getting right to the point.

"Oh," the supervisor said, her eyes going to the ceiling. "Wow, let me think. Probably... six or seven years, I'd guess. I don't know exactly when he joined, but it was before my promotion."

"So, would you say that you know him quite well?"

The supervisor shifted, moving her arms and then settling again like she wished she had a cup of coffee she could pick up. "I think so. Why?"

"What's he like?" Laura asked, avoiding the question. "His character, personality? What can you tell me about him?"

"Um, he's a good guy," the supervisor said. "Very detail-driven."

"How so?"

"He gets things worked out very precisely," the supervisor replied, making a loose shrugging gesture. "I don't know how to explain it. Well, for example, he can tell you exactly how long the average response time would be from any given hospital or precinct to any given location in the city. He's really good with data and working things out like that."

The word *time* seemed to chime in Laura's head. A red flag going up, an alarm bell sounding. "He's interested in time?"

"Oh, yeah, definitely," the supervisor nodded. "He likes to review each of the calls after the fact to make sure that things are as efficient as they can be. He's even called up the hospital before and suggested new routes for the ambulances to help them get there quicker. I'd be lying if I said they appreciated it, but he's got a good heart. He's just trying to help."

Laura thought for a second. "Does he keep his own records of this kind of thing? It sounds like it requires a lot of working out."

"Yeah, he keeps a journal on his desk where he records everything," the supervisor said. "I think he does it all in his head, and on the paper. You know? No calculators. He's super smart."

"Can I see that journal?"

The supervisor hesitated, obviously reluctant to break the trust of a coworker by showing someone else his private notes.

"It's extremely important," Laura said. "Like I said, this case is currently ongoing."

The supervisor bit her lip. "It's not..." She glanced down at her hands before continuing, like she was unsure she wanted to finish. "It's not the clock killer case, is it?"

"What makes you assume that?" Laura asked.

"You got really interested when I said he was interested in time," the supervisor pointed out, almost shyly. Gingerly. "But... I don't think he's got anything to do with that. Earl's a lovely guy, really. He took this job instead of retiring. He just wants to help people."

The mention of his age wasn't necessarily promising, but then again, it wasn't the end of the lead either. If they stayed in shape, Laura knew there were sixty- and even seventy-year-olds out there who were stronger than she was. "At any rate, I'd really like to talk to him and see that journal, just to rule him out of our investigation," Laura said. She kept her tone soothing, as though she believed what the supervisor was saying completely. It was the best way to ensure compliance. "If he's as good a guy as you say he is, then I'm sure it's nothing to worry about. And I'd love his help in shedding some further light on the case, given that he was the dispatcher on duty at a number of important moments that could really give us some good clues."

"Okay," the supervisor said, wringing her hands for a moment. Then she got up, hesitantly, but at least she was doing it. "I'll go and fetch it for you now."

Laura checked her cell phone while the woman was out of the room, seeing if she had any messages. She didn't. She sighed to herself, wondering if Nate was sulking. Maybe he'd gone to call Chief Rondelle and get her yanked off the case or something. If so, it was more important than ever that she work fast on this.

Laura got up and left the quiet room, stepping back out into the reception area. The supervisor appeared from the dispatch room almost immediately afterwards, holding a journal and a scrap of paper.

"I wrote down his address for you," she said, still holding both items firmly in her own hands, close to her chest. "I think he should be at home today. He didn't say anything about having plans."

"Thank you," Laura said, then held out her hand pointedly when the supervisor still didn't make a move.

At last, she handed over both the journal and the address, biting her lip as she did so.

Laura turned to leave the moment she had both of them in her grasp. "I'll let you know if we need anything further," she said over her shoulder, walking right out to the parking lot. It felt like time was of the essence. There was every chance that nervous supervisor would call

Earl and warn him that the FBI were coming. There was no telling what he would be able to hide or prepare if he was given enough of a chance.

But even so, as Laura stepped out into the parking lot, she stopped dead.

Nate was there, standing by the car.

She cleared her throat, trying to pretend that she hadn't really come to a complete halt in surprise as she walked over to him. His hands were in his pockets, but he took them out and straightened as he saw her.

"I got your message," he said, his voice kind of strangely shy, like he wasn't sure how she would react to him being there.

"I've got a new lead," Laura told him. "Address of a potential suspect. A dispatcher who is obsessed with time, and just happened to be the one dealing with all of the calls when each of our victims was reported as being in distress the first time."

"Sounds good," Nate said. He hesitated. "Laura, I'm not... I'm not saying I accept what you've been telling me. About your... about you. What I said earlier, I didn't mean it. I don't think you're hiding things for attention. I know that's not you."

"Apology accepted," Laura replied, though she couldn't keep a little testiness from creeping into her voice. So, he knew he was wrong – but still wouldn't admit she was right? Where did that even leave them?

"I don't know about all the rest," Nate continued, his voice back to the reasonable, logical, soothing Nate that she knew. He always had the right thing to say, even if they'd been fighting. He knew how to settle things down. "But you're right about one thing. We need to solve this case."

"Then let's go arrest our suspect," Laura suggested, extending an olive branch of her own, and she was relieved and gratified beyond measure when Nate turned around and got into the car to go with her.

CHAPTER TWENTY EIGHT

The second the door opened, Laura was moving forward, holding out her badge and making sure to get her foot inside the doorframe. She wasn't going to allow him the chance to slam it in their faces or try to run, especially not if he'd been forewarned.

"Earl Regis?" Laura said, waiting a bare second for his stunned nod before continuing. "You're under arrest on suspicion of murder. You have the right to remain silent. Anything you say can and will be used against you in a court of law. You have a right to an attorney. If you cannot afford an attorney, one will be appointed for you."

"Wh-what?" Earl said, his eyes as round as saucers behind round-rimmed glasses.

There was no treading lightly here. He was the absolute best match they had, and they wanted him off the streets. "We're going to need you to come to the precinct with us," Laura said, holding out a pair of handcuffs. "Please hold out your hands in front of you, wrists together."

Whether he was too shocked to argue or just naturally meek, Earl complied immediately. Laura snapped the cuffs on his hands and then stepped aside to steer him down the short path back to the sidewalk and the car, where Nate was already waiting. He'd allowed Laura to take the lead on this one, but he was still in a ready stance, able to take off running after their suspect if he should decide to try and escape.

Laura assessed the man she was leading, his strength, his ability. He was old, yes. But he was still physically capable. She could feel it in him. He didn't stumble on the walk. He didn't shuffle like a more infirm man would. He had a good stride, an upright posture. Age, apparently, hadn't slowed him down enough to make him an unviable suspect.

Nate made sure he didn't hit his head as he helped Earl into the car, and then got into the driver's seat with a glance at Laura. She nodded, walked around the car, and got inside – sitting next to Earl in the back.

As Nate started the engine, Laura brought out the journal and put it on her lap, placing it so that Earl couldn't help but notice she had it. There wasn't any time to lose, given that it was mid-afternoon already. If Earl had already taken a victim to another platform, like they suspected, then they needed to crack him sooner rather than later. They needed to get to that person before their timer stopped, and there was no telling when that might happen.

"Earl, I'd like you to talk to me about this," Laura said, tapping the cover of the journal to show him what she meant. "We'll have an attorney for you at the precinct, if you want." This mention was intended to remind him of his rights – making sure she'd ticked off that box. If he didn't ask for one now but continued to answer her questions, he was as good as ceding his right to any legal representation for the duration of the conversation. Or until he did ask for one, at least.

"M-my journal?" Earl said, looking at it with a look of complete confusion. "Why do you have my journal? Oh, my... my door, we didn't lock..."

"Don't worry about that," Laura said. "We've got local detectives who'll be along just in a minute to keep an eye on the place for you. I need you to focus on this right now. We've had a good look through this journal of yours, Earl, and it's very interesting reading."

"Do you think so?" he asked, frowning slightly. "I mean... why?"

"You don't agree that it's interesting?" Laura asked. This was a cat and mouse game, and she was more than willing to play. She could bet any amount of money that she'd come across tougher customers than this sixty-something-year-old man. Either he was weak-willed and nervous, or he was trying to play that part to avoid suspicion. Whichever was the truth, it wouldn't be anything Laura hadn't dealt with before. "You're the one who wrote it all down."

"I do, but... no one else ever does," Earl said. His eyes only ever left the notebook to wander around the car as if in search of something, before returning straight back.

"What do you find so interesting about all these numbers?" Laura asked. She flipped to a page – seemingly at random, though in truth she had prepreared it. "Like these, for example – you have the dispatch call time, the minutes and seconds it took the ambulance to respond, how long the patient was dead for before revival..."

Earl swallowed visibly. "I like to make sure we're being as efficient as possible," he said. "Brain death can occur from as little as three minutes after the heart stops. A delay of even a second can make a difference in those critical cases."

Laura nodded thoughtfully as though she was taking this in. "And it's your job to make sure that they get there as fast as possible, is it?"

"Well… no," Earl admitted. "I just decide what services are needed and send them out and give the caller advice over the phone to help them have the best chance of survival until our guys arrive."

"So, then," Laura said, looking right into his eyes. His nervous, flitting eyes, which quickly returned to the journal again. "Why do you take it upon yourself to record this information?"

"Because it's important," he said, his voice almost pleading. "Someone has to do something about it. If there are failures in the system, then…"

"How does it make you feel, when there are failures in the system?" Laura asked. She glanced up, just a momentary glance while she was sure Earl was staring at the journal, towards the central console. There was a red light showing on the device she'd set up there, confirming it was working. A voice recorder. She wasn't going to have anyone say that the evidence they heard on this car ride didn't count. She'd read him his rights, done everything by the book.

"I don't like to think about people dying," he said. His voice was almost a pleading whine. "Not when we could have got there and saved them."

"You don't?" Laura said. She kept her voice deliberately curious, so that the impact of her next words would be all the stronger. "So, then, why are you killing off the ones that did make it?"

Earl opened his mouth to reply, but then paled, his eyes going to hers. "E-excuse me?" he asked.

"Our theory so far has been that you don't think they deserved the extra time," Laura said. "That's what it's all about, isn't it, Earl? Time?"

"N-no," he stammered, staring at the book again. "Well, yes, but – I didn't…"

"You tell us, then, if we've got it wrong," Laura said, leaning back casually in her seat. "If it's not about deserving more time, then what is it? Are you trying to raise awareness, trying to show people how important time can be? Are you trying to improve the system?"

"Yes!" Earl said, but then his brow lowered again in confusion. "I mean, that's why I keep the journal, not… not why I… I mean, I don't kill anyone. I haven't killed anyone!"

"Are you sure about that?" Laura asked, conversationally. "I have to tell you; judges are usually inclined to be rather more lenient with those who confess readily. And I myself have spoken to a number of people in the past who say that it's like a weight off their shoulders to have it all out in the open. Don't you think it's better to just get it over with and admit everything now?"

"No!" Earl said, bringing his hands up to his face only to remember that they were cuffed together. "I... I mean... I..."

"Alright, Earl," Laura said. They were only a block away from the precinct now, but the mid-afternoon traffic was heavy enough in this area to slow them down. "Let's try something easier. Where were you, yesterday?"

"W-when?" he asked.

"All day, if you can."

Earl's mouth moved soundlessly, before the information he held readily inside his head seemed to take over for him. "I was alone in the morning," he said. "My wife passed a few years ago, so it's only me, but I like to rise early and get things done around the house. Then I had lunch, and I got ready for the late shift at work."

"And what time did that start?" Laura asked.

"Four o'clock, sharp," he said.

Laura didn't need to run the numbers to know that he would have had plenty of time to set up Lincoln Ware on the platform in that abandoned barn and then return home, clean up, probably eat something, and get ready before heading out to work. He had no witness to say that he wasn't doing that, no alibi. He was starting to look better and better.

"Aren't you leaving something out of your day, Earl?" Laura asked. "You did something else, didn't you?"

Earl looked at her with a kind of puzzled fear. "N-no," he said. "That was all."

"No, you saw somebody else, didn't you?" Laura said. Nate was pulling into the precinct parking lot, close to the entrance where newly arrested suspects could be led in and processed. "You saw someone who can't tell us what you were up to, because he's dead now. Hung."

"Oh, God," Earl groaned. "No, no, I didn't, I swear to you!"

"Well, let's take a break now," Laura said, very aware that Nate was turning off the engine. "We'll talk a bit more inside, when you've been processed. But think about what I said, Earl. The judge is going to like you a lot more if you confess everything without too much work. There's still time."

Nate came around to Earl's door to get him out of the car, and Laura switched from interview mode to thinking about everything they needed to do to process him. This part could take a while. He hadn't given her anything in the car, which was a real shame. They could be hours now, waiting for him to get an attorney he approved of, to get set up in the interview room. He might delay further by claiming he needed medical assistance, given his age.

Laura followed behind as Nate led him inside, handing him over to the duty staff for processing and booking. Taking his fingerprints and getting him entered into the system could take a while in itself, and they allowed the local team to handle it while they stepped off to one side.

"We should go and organize our materials," Laura said quietly, so that only Nate could hear her. "Get ready to hit him hard. We need to do this fast, just in case someone is already out there waiting to be saved."

"Alright," Nate said. He cast a glance over at Earl, as though he was worried that the locals weren't going to be able to look after him properly. "You go grab everything. I'll watch him and get him to an interview room so we can move as fast as possible."

Laura nodded, quickly departing and heading through the bullpen to the desk they had commandeered. They had left only a few small things there, but it was enough: files, records, and photographs, mostly. The kind of things they would need to have on hand in order to make their points in the room.

Laura opened the top file to start checking through it, ignoring the buzz of the bullpen around her, single-minded in her focus on finding the right materials. There were the coroner's reports, the crime scene photographs... she remembered she still had the photograph of the clock in her pocket and pulled it out, almost recoiling as a stab of pain went through her forehead when she touched it.

She continued to draw it out of her pocket, ready to put it in the file —

She was focused on Veronica Rowse's face, appearing in close-up. Her eyes were closed, her lips faintly tinged blue. She had a pale sheen to her skin. Almost bloodless. Like she'd been bleeding for a while, all of it drained from her face and gone somewhere else.

Her whole body was shaking, though Laura could only make out her head. And then, at some unheard or unseen command, her lips moved to take in a breath, her eyes opened...

Laura put the photograph back into the file, confused beyond measure. It was the same thing she had seen before. Why? It didn't make any sense. She had already seen that, and she'd gone and made the arrest off the back of it. Why was she seeing it again? With nothing changed?

Unless…
Unless she hadn't made the right arrest at all.

CHAPTER TWENTY NINE

Laura sank into the chair at the desk, her mind reeling. She had been so sure. All the signs added up. Earl Regis had access, knowledge, even a twisted kind of motive. He definitely had opportunity, and it wasn't a hard stretch to think that a man of his age might know how to do a few DIY things. He fit.

But now, Laura saw, he didn't fit at all.

She couldn't be a hundred percent sure, even still. All she'd seen was a vision of the past. She didn't even know why it was the past and not the future, like normal. For all she knew, they did have the right guy and her visions were just... broken.

But even as she thought it, she knew it wasn't true. Earl Regis did fit, in all the ways except the ones where he didn't. He was old. He was timid and nervous. He had a thing for numbers because he wanted to save lives. Turning around and ending them instead didn't make sense.

It only looked like he was the right person. And it looked so convincingly like he was that Laura was going to have a hard time telling anyone at all, much less Nate, that he wasn't their man.

Or, again, maybe he was, and she was just losing her grip on her visions and her sense of reality to the point that she couldn't even tell what was going on anymore.

Laura stood a little unsteadily, gathering the files she'd come for even though she didn't really believe that she needed them anymore. She walked back to the elevators and took them to the next floor up, where she knew Nate would be waiting outside the interview rooms.

She found him pacing the corridor, his arms folded across his chest, his black suit almost looking like it was going to split across the shoulders.

"Hi," she said. "I have the files."

"Great," Nate said, but he tossed his head with an expression of disgust towards the closed door of the interview room he was pacing outside. "He's invoked his right to an attorney. Got someone from across town he wants to come. We could be here for a while."

"That's alright," Laura said. "I..."

She hesitated. He was looking at her with this kind of annoyance on his face already. Like a caged animal who wanted nothing more to spring out and get back to the hunt. This was going to make him mad; she couldn't help but think.

But she had to say it anyway.

"I've been thinking," she said, giving herself the soft introduction that she needed for the topic.

Nate groaned immediately.

"No, Laura," he said. "I don't like it when you think. Not about things like this. What's going on now?"

"I don't think it's him," Laura admitted, letting it pour out of her in a rush. "I think we have the wrong guy. Which means someone is still out there, and while we can't question him anyway, I think we ought to be looking for them."

Nate stared at her, shaking his head minutely from side to side, his wide eyes seemingly fixed in place. "I don't believe this," he said. "You're the one who was so sure he was the right guy in the first place!"

"I know, I know," Laura said, putting a hand to her head. "I get why you might think I'm messing around, or just following a whim. But I was working on the evidence I had when I went after him. On paper, he looks great."

"Right," Nate said. "He does. So, what evidence do you have now that contradicts that? All you did was go pick up the files!"

"It's…" Laura hesitated. She could barely meet Nate's eyes, but she had to. What good was getting it all out in the open between them if she still couldn't use her ability to tell him what she knew? "It's not evidence, exactly."

Nate's head rolled to the side, looking at her from a tilted angle, his stare going harder. "You're not going to tell me this right now," he said, warningly.

"No, I am," Laura replied. She took a breath. "I have to. Look, Nate, I saw something. Okay? And I don't exactly know what it means or anything specific. It's just… I don't tend to see the same thing twice if we've made a difference. I shouldn't be seeing it again, do you understand? It means we're on the wrong track."

"And what did you see?" Nate asked. If he didn't already have his arms crossed tightly over his chest, Laura had the feeling he would do it now.

She swallowed. "Veronica Rowse," she said. "Coming back to life."

Nate narrowed his eyes. "I thought you said you saw the future," he pointed out. "That's not accurate, is it? She's dead. Very dead. We both saw that."

"I know, and it's confusing the hell out of me too," Laura said. She wished she had a better explanation for him. Maybe it was too much, throwing this information out there as well as everything else. Maybe she should have fudged the truth, just told him enough to make him see that it wasn't normal. When the rules were changing and she didn't even understand it herself, how was she supposed to convince him that they existed in the first place?

"Laura, I can't..." Nate paused, sighing and shaking his head before continuing in a softer tone. "We've been here before. And I can't keep doing this. Putting up with this... this investigational whiplash. First, you're absolutely sure one thing is right, and then you're absolutely sure the same thing is wrong. It's not normal, the way you make these leaps and jumps. There's no logic behind it."

"There is," Laura said, her voice quiet. "It's just that you can't see it. If you had the visions, you'd understand how it can be. How one thing leads you in a certain direction, and then you see something else, and you figure out another clue."

"But I don't have visions, Laura," Nate said, in a tone which very much suggested that maybe she didn't either. "And I can't do this. I have to follow the evidence that we actually have. And that evidence shows us that Earl Regis is our most likely suspect. What do you expect me to do? Just drop everything and let him go because you've got a hunch? What if your hunch changes with your next 'vision' and you realize it *was* him after all?"

Laura nodded, keeping her head down. "Okay," she said. She was blinking, trying to keep the emotion out of her voice and the water out of her eyes. "Okay. You're right. I'm sorry."

Nate relaxed very slightly. "So, you're going to come in with me and do this interview when the lawyer gets here?"

"No," Laura said, wishing she could give him an answer that he would like more. It didn't matter. She knew what she had to do. Her duty was first and foremost to the victims – the ones that had already been, and the ones that were yet to come if they didn't solve this. "No, I... I'm going to have to follow this lead. I know you can handle the interview on your own. Maybe with Captain Blackford, if you feel you need backup. But I just... I don't feel like I can let this go."

Nate stared at her evenly for a long moment before passing a hand over his eyes. "Fine," he said, at last. "Fine. So long as it doesn't get in the way of the investigation, I don't see why you can't keep going. I guess it's a good idea not to be too married to one suspect anyway, just in case. Good investigatory practice."

"You're not mad?" Laura asked.

Nate sighed, looking away from her. "At this point, I don't know what I am any longer," he said. "Mad, worried, afraid, frustrated. Nonplussed. All I can tell you is that I want to solve this case. Like I said, if it doesn't get in the way and it might help, then… you do what you think you have to do."

"Thank you," Laura said, even though she didn't quite think he was doing it for her. More like he was trying to preserve his own sanity. But so long as it worked, it worked.

Laura stepped away, backwards, leaving the file in Nate's outstretched hand as she went. He took it without looking at her and started flipping through the pages. He didn't look up when she called the elevator, or when she stepped into it, or when the doors closed in front of her and cut them off from one another.

Laura had about a thirty-second chance to compose herself in the elevator before it reached the bullpen, and then she had to be right back to it.

She had no time to feel sorry for herself, not right now. There was a killer on the loose, and she needed to go back to the records to try and find him.

**

Laura sat at the desk, staring at the records on the screen in front of her.

The hospital administrator had given up. For all her talk of the sanctity of the records, she was clearly beyond frustrated by having to look up something new for Laura every hour of the day. She'd left her sitting at the desk and walked away, muttering something about a meeting, and Laura was on her own with the digitized files.

The system was easy enough to learn. Once she'd got the hang of it, she could filter by certain factors – one of which being actions taken by medical staff. Searching for people who were resuscitated brought up a huge list, even when she narrowed it down to the last two years. It made sense. A hospital was for people who weren't exactly in good health, after all.

But how was she going to narrow this list down from hundreds – thousands – to enough people that she could actually use the data?

She sighed, rubbing her forehead. Maybe another look at the victims they already knew about would help. She refined the search by Lincoln Ware's name, and then moved to click on the record for his near-drowning incident.

And froze.

There was a second record under his name, also marked with resuscitation. The administrator hadn't said anything about that before.

But then, Laura had asked her about the first incident they'd learned about. She hadn't thought to ask if there were more, and without being able to look at the screen herself, she hadn't known there were more.

She'd relied on a woman who clearly resented having to do the work for her, instead of getting a warrant and going through everything herself.

She'd made a big mistake.

Laura clicked the link and read the report hurriedly, her eyes skimming down the whole page. Lincoln had been readmitted to the ER just a couple of weeks after his first visit. She saw a diagnosis of untreated pneumonia on the first page – apparently, the tests they'd done in the first place hadn't picked it up. He'd gone home with the infection, assumed he'd just caught a cold from the water of the pool or that his breathing was affected by the trauma and treatment he'd gone through.

But it had been pneumonia.

Even in a young man, untreated pneumonia could be serious. Laura clicked open the EMT report and read it with bated breath – and there, right there in black and white on the screen: he'd called himself, reporting respiratory distress and pains, and the ambulance had responded. They'd started checking him over, but things had worsened rapidly, and he'd ended up having a minor heart attack right there in front of them. Even though they were right there on the scene, the complications of the illness meant it took them approximately fifty seconds to revive him again.

Fifty.

Laura knew it before she even looked. She read it in the tone of the report. She let her eyes drift to the bottom of the page, where it was signed off by the EMT who wrote the whole thing.

Paul Payne.

It had been him all along.

He'd been right in front of her, and she'd let him slip away. She'd been fooled by his lies, his innocent act.

Laura grabbed her jacket and ran towards the doors for the parking lot, knowing she had no time at all to lose.

CHAPTER THIRTY

Paul sat on the steps down into the basement, watching. With the lights off, he was shrouded in shadows. No one could see him here. But it had been important for him to see, this time.

He'd made a new adjustment to the platform. The idea had been to test it out at the grocery store last night, to check it was working, but since the police had taken over the scene, he'd had to change his approach. This was a live test, instead. He wanted to watch to be sure it worked, because he wasn't going to get a chance to find out otherwise.

The news reports never really said how the victims died. They didn't go into enough detail. But he really did want them to be painless, and the fact that Veronica Rowse had been reported as having sustained 'other injuries' in one report he'd read had troubled him. He'd rigged the platform to fall quicker this time, to snap back and away with a little bounce upwards first. The idea was that it would throw the woman standing on it right now up into the air a bit, so when she fell, the rope snapped taut and broke her neck right away. That was all.

It was a risk, sitting here to watch her. He knew that. But it was an acceptable one. The police knew he liked abandoned places, and so he'd changed something there as well: found a location they wouldn't think of. Not a barn or a closed-down store or a remote gas station.

A basement.

The idea had come to him like divine inspiration, really. And he was almost completely confident there was no way anyone would trace him here – not unless they were literally following him, and he had been careful about that, too. Gone all around the houses, even with an unconscious woman in the back of his trunk. He'd examined every car behind him every time he stopped at lights, and he was pretty sure that this wasn't going to be the night he was caught. He'd done everything he could to be sure of it.

The house above his head wasn't abandoned – just vacant. It had had one elderly owner who'd died recently, and the house was up for sale. Tomorrow evening, there was going to be an open house. Perfect for someone to come in and discover the body. He figured he could set up tomorrow's platform in another vacant house he'd found, and the police wouldn't have time to adapt to this new kind of location in time.

162

After that, he'd figure it out. He had reams of research back at home, tons of ideas to use.

The woman on the platform was making a kind of desperate gasping noise, racking sobs that went through her whole body. Paul straightened slightly, wondering if she was going to end up hanging herself before the platform even went down. But the noose stayed in place, and she remained on the platform, upright. Just sobbing.

It was harsh, but it was necessary. She needed to die. She should have been grateful for the extra time that she'd had, not sad that it was ending. Some people just couldn't see what the universe was giving them.

To get all of that time for free, when she didn't even deserve it. It was disgusting, really. And now to act like she was having something taken away from her? Some people were so entitled.

Paul got up, checking his watch. She couldn't see him exactly, but maybe she sensed movement, because she struggled more wildly and tried to cry out against the gag. He ignored her, opening the door that led up and out of the basement and stepping outside. He'd been in there for long enough already. He had to check his phone, see if he had missed anything while he was down there without any signal.

He paused in the empty dining room of the property, a room at the back of the house where no one would see him from the windows that faced the street. His phone slowly blossomed back to life as he gained signal strength, up above ground once more: a number of notifications chimed one after the other, appearing on the screen.

A lot of missed calls from work. Paul swore under his breath. He should have checked earlier. If they needed him and he was just sitting down there waiting, he was letting everyone down.

There was a voicemail: he listened to it briefly, hearing the voice of his supervisor coming over the line.

"Paul, I don't know where you are today, but please come straight to the hospital when you get this. We've got an emergency situation, all hands on-deck. Big accident downtown. And please stop turning your phone off when you're on call. We need you here as soon as possible."

Paul ended the call as the voicemail's electronic voice chimed in, telling him which buttons to press if he wanted to save the message. He swore under his breath again, glancing around. He hadn't left any sign of himself behind, other than the woman in the basement. He'd been careful about that. If someone came in while he was out, they wouldn't be able to pin this on him.

Not unless she was still alive, of course. She'd recognized him. He'd seen it in her eyes as he approached with the needle. Seeing him in connection with medical items must have triggered her memory.

But, damnit, he was needed. He did take his job very seriously, and there were plenty of people who needed help or could be saved *before* their hearts stopped. People who weren't supposed to die today. Those people, he could save. *Should* save. He could get back here before the timer went off and the platform dropped, just to make sure it was all as fast as he wanted it to be.

He turned to leave the house through the back door, emerging into the cold but bright sunshine, taking the slightly longer route back to his car to avoid being seen – but walking fast.

CHAPTER THIRTY ONE

Laura sat in the small office reserved for the managers of the hospital's ambulance service, tapping her walkie talkie against her knee anxiously. She hated waiting like this. Not being able to do anything.

But she'd done everything she could, at least. All she had left was waiting. Waiting for Paul Payne to arrive for the fake emergency callout she'd organized with his supervisor.

"Anything yet?" she said, speaking into the walkie. She could see the main ambulance parking area through the windows of the office, but that was all. She couldn't see the road, or the employee parking lot. The idea was to wait here, out of sight, until Paul came inside to receive his assignment. He wouldn't be expecting an ambush. If anything, he'd probably be ready to eat humble pie at this stage and apologize for how late he was.

She hoped.

She was beginning to wonder if he was running so late because he'd figured out it was a trap and wasn't coming at all.

The radio crackled to life in her hands. "Nothing yet," came the response. One of the security guards at the employee parking lot entrance, who'd been fully briefed on the situation.

Laura had called Nate and filled him in already, and he was supposedly on the way with a small group of detectives from the precinct to make sure they would have enough manpower to take him down. She supposed she should be happy that Paul hadn't showed up yet, that she wasn't having to tackle him alone.

But she wasn't. She was wired instead. Wishing he would get here so that she could do her job and take him down.

Her cell phone buzzed in her pocket, and Laura checked it to see a message from Nate: *ETA five minutes*. The supervisor, who was still sitting at her desk and having to actually run the ambulances while also sharing the same nerves Laura felt, glanced at her in alarm. Laura just shook her head, and the woman, an older Hispanic EMT with short-cropped white hair who had done her time on the service already, dropped her tense shoulders by a single notch.

The radio crackled into life, making those shoulders shoot back up – and Laura's too. "Okay, I can see his car approaching now."

"Great. Let him into the parking lot as normal," Laura said. "Remember, don't let on that anything is different than normal."

There was no response from the radio – which, she hoped, meant that the security guard was staying quiet and doing what he was told as Paul pulled up to the barrier and showed his staff pass. Laura drummed her fingers on the seat, staying as still as she could otherwise. The inclination was to move forward, to go right and stand in the window and watch for his arrival. But she needed to stay out of sight now. She was right by the door, and as soon as he'd gotten himself inside the office fully, she would be able to move between him and the only exit and ensure he wasn't going to go anywhere.

She glanced at the supervisor. The woman seemed to be shaking slightly, her hand wavering as she reached for her mug of coffee and took a sip, perhaps to try and steady her nerves.

Laura tensed more as each moment passed, trying to imagine his progress. He would be pulling through the barriers, moving into the parking lot. Parking his car. Getting out. Would he spend a moment inside first, or would he race towards the office, thinking he was needed?

"Hey, Paul!" the voice was muffled by the door, but it made Laura stiffen, her spine going dead straight and her hand moving automatically to rest on her gun in its holster.

"Oh, hey, man. I just got called in."

"Really? Why?"

"What do you mean? For the big accident downtown."

"Big accident?" There was a short laugh. "First I'm hearing of it, if so. We've still got three ambulances in the bay waiting for call-outs."

"What?"

"Yeah. You sure you got your information right, buddy?"

Laura closed her eyes for a brief moment, praying that it wouldn't make a difference. That Paul would come to the office to see what was going on anyway. That he would still fall into their trap.

"Maybe not," Paul said. There was a new note in his voice now. Something… something like clarity. "You know what, I probably picked up an old message by mistake. I guess I'll head to the breakroom instead, get something to eat and then head back home."

"I'll walk with you."

Laura didn't hesitate to hear the rest of the conversation. She didn't need to. He was on the move, going in the opposite direction. It was too late. She needed to step out there now, stop him from getting back into his car. She leapt to her feet and threw open the door of the office to the cold air, getting him in her sights immediately.

He was standing only a few hundred yards away, facing her, talking to another EMT in uniform. Laura opened her mouth to say something, but he met her eyes in that moment and he knew. She saw so clearly that he knew.

He took off running before she even had time to get a handle on what to do.

Laura cursed and launched herself forward, practically flying out of the office door and after him. "Stop! FBI!" she shouted. "Paul Payne – stop!"

Of course, predictably, her words did nothing. He was shooting straight back towards the parking lot. Laura blasted past the confused coworker who was standing there nonplussed, only getting a glimpse of a puzzled facial expression and nothing more before he was far behind her. She kept Paul in her sights, but the EMT was young and fit, clearly full of stamina. More than that, he probably knew that he was running for his life – or, at least, his freedom. He was fast.

He ducked and wove between the first few rows of cars, leaving Laura double-guessing where he was going to be, making her lose precious time by trying to follow his unpredictable twists and turns, trying to get an angle that would put her on course to intercept him only for him to head in a different direction.

Laura's heart was already hammering rapidly in her chest, her lungs burning with the cold air as she tried to get enough of it to power her legs. He darted right at the last second in front of a huge SUV, disappearing behind it for a moment, blocked by the blacked-out windows. Laura lost sight of him as she fought to keep up, running around the same vehicle and floundering momentarily –

Until she spotted him, off to the far right this time, making his way straight down the row of cars and having to slam his hands onto the side of a car that almost ran into him to stop his own momentum.

Laura put on a fresh burst of speed, taking advantage of his enforced pause. The owner of the car he'd stopped was gesturing angrily, shouting something, but Paul dodged around the front end and carried on running. Laura adjusted her own trajectory, taking a wider sweep that brought her around the front of the vehicle without having to pause, success driving her on. She was closer now. Close enough that she felt like she was really going to catch him. Even without a vision, she could see where he was –

He darted right one more time unexpectedly, throwing himself down a gap between two of the hospital's buildings, making Laura skid against the tarmac to arrest her own motion and throw herself in the same direction.

He was… in a dead end?

Laura kept running as long as he did, her eyes scanning the area as much as she could while still keeping her sights firmly on him. He'd led her into little more than an alleyway, a place that held huge trash bins overflowing with waste from the hospital. She couldn't see any doors to either side. Where was he planning to escape? Did he know of some secret or hidden –

Laura didn't have time to stop herself when he did, spinning abruptly right in front of her. She barreled right into him, almost tripping over her own feet as her brain told herself she needed an immediate halt, her arms flying up to cushion the blow. But he was ready. He used his own arms to deflect her, doing little more than grabbing her and moving to the side, letting her own momentum do the rest. He hurled her towards the approaching wall, and without the support of her own feet anymore Laura stumbled, falling to the ground.

She couldn't stop it happening – couldn't manage anything other than to brace – almost not even that – and she rolled as she hit the ground, over and over until she was breathless. When she did stop, it was a moment before the world stopped spinning around her –

And then she saw him, filling her whole field of view, moving over her and then dropping. He sat his whole weight on her, pinning her arms, stopping her from reaching for her gun. Laura only had time to gasp out a breath before the blow landed, hitting her in the face, just above her right eye. It snapped her head to the side, leaving her even more dazed than the fall had, unable to process her next action.

Pain – that was all she could process for a moment – and the feeling of the cold floor under her, of how she couldn't move –

She managed to turn her head, opening her eyes again to a light that now seemed far too bright, looking up at him. He seemed like a giant over her now, his fist drawn back almost comically, like she was watching some far-fetched action movie. Her brain seemed to be moving too slow. She knew he was going to hit her again. She knew she didn't want that to happen. She just couldn't seem to do anything to stop it.

And then his hand dropped and instead he grabbed for something else – for something down beside her –

For her gun.

168

He pointed it at her head, and looked her right in the eye, and Laura knew. She was going to die.

"Freeze!"

The shout seemed to come from nowhere, from everywhere, echoing all around them and bouncing off the brickwork of the two buildings. Laura could barely take it in, couldn't understand why Paul would shout something like that, only it was him that was frozen, as if someone had suddenly turned him into a statue...

Until he swung around, pointing the gun in the other direction instead.

She let her head loll to the side, and she saw him. Nate. Standing there at the foot of the alleyway with his gun drawn and pointed at Paul, advancing slowly with a scattering of local cops behind him.

"Put your hands above your head, slowly," Nate ordered. He didn't take his eyes away from Paul. Reality was coming back to Laura, bleeding back into her head. Which hurt, incidentally.

"Put yours up," Paul replied. His voice wasn't shaking. He was steady. Firm. Laura blinked her eyes twice to bring his hands into focus, saw that they were firm too. His finger was on the trigger.

The safety was off.

He was ready to shoot.

Laura felt it in her gut. The wave of nausea, the shadow creeping across everything. The aura of death. She'd felt it so many times around Nate. She knew he was at risk. She knew he was going to die.

And she felt it in her gut that he was going to die now if she didn't do something.

"Come on, drop the gun," Nate was saying. "There are more of us. Be smart. You're not walking away from this."

"Then at least I'll take you with me," Paul replied. "And you'll never know why I did it. You want to know, don't you?"

Laura saw it. Saw Nate hesitate. He was going to do it, wasn't he? Put his gun down. Raise his hands. Ask Paul to come peacefully.

And Paul would start firing and wouldn't stop until they were all dead and he could run.

Laura's head lolled to the side, so heavy and slow, and she saw them. A pair of crutches, discarded in the trash for some reason. One of them was broken, she saw. But the other...

"Alright," Nate was saying. "Let's be calm and talk about this. If we just put the guns down..."

Laura reached for the crutch, the one that was whole.

And she swung.

She felt the impact along her whole arm, ricocheting into her skull, and for a moment she had no idea what she had managed to do, or not do. But then she blinked and saw Paul laying on the floor next to her, turned away so she couldn't see his face, and Nate rushing towards them to dive with his handcuffs.

"Laura? You alright?" he called out.

"Yeah," she managed, though it came out more as a groan, belying her answer.

Nate covered the last bit of ground rapidly and snapped a pair of handcuffs onto Paul's wrists. It was only then that he yanked the EMT to his feet, pulling him away from Laura. She groaned again, sitting up, feeling how the cold of the ground had seeped into her bones through her clothes. She was dirty, cold, and in pain, and still a little groggy.

"You're under arrest for assaulting a law enforcement officer. At the very least," Nate said, then to the other cops: "Take him in."

He turned back to Laura and offered her his hand, and for once she took it, even though the swirling black aura of death around him almost made her throw up before she was back on her feet – though this time, she could swear, it was a little lighter than it had been before.

But it was still there, even though it shouldn't have been.

She still hadn't saved his life.

CHAPTER THIRTY TWO

Laura glared at Paul across the interview room table, placing her own hands flat on the surface between them. She could feel Nate glancing at her every now and then, as if he wasn't entirely sure that she should be in the room. She'd reassured him as many times as she could bear that she was fine.

All she had was a bit of a black eye.

An eye that she was still able to use, albeit with a bit of a squint, to glare at Paul Payne and let him know that his presence was not appreciated.

"Alright," Nate said, clearly feeling that it was down to him to take charge of the situation. "There's something I want to ask you, Paul. I'm very curious. You're an EMT. You've trained to get to this position, dedicated years of your life to the service. You've saved so many lives. So, why start taking them?"

"Taking them back," Paul said, lifting his eyes from Laura's to respond directly to Nate.

"Excuse me?"

"You said taking them," Paul clarified. "I'm not just taking them. I'm taking them *back*."

Nate shifted in his chair. "So, you gave them their lives and you get to decide whether they get to keep them? Is that it? You felt they didn't deserve the lives they'd been living?"

"None of them deserve a second chance," Paul said, bitterly. "No one does. It's not about what you do with the time you get afterwards. It's not supposed to be yours. That's not the way any of this works."

"Why don't you tell us how it works, then?" Laura asked, lifting her chin. The challenge simmered barely under the surface of her words. *Tell us how it works, if you're so smart. If you've got this all figured out.*

Paul moved his hands loosely across the table. They were cuffed, a chain between them, clinking as he moved. "It's pretty simple. When you die, you die. That's it. You're not supposed to come back and get another chance. It's not fair on everyone else."

171

"Why not?" Laura asked. "We can't all just carry on living together? Isn't that the miracle of modern medicine, that people don't have to die unnecessarily?"

"But they were dead," Paul insisted darkly. "They were dead already. They *came back*. That's what's wrong with this whole thing. If they stayed dead like they were supposed to, I wouldn't have to do anything."

"Paul, you have to forgive me," Nate said. "I'm confused. Aren't you the one who actively brought them back to life in the first place? Why did you do that, if you don't think it's right?"

Paul studied his hands, like he couldn't bear to look up at their faces. "I was wrong back then," he said. "But it's part of my job, anyway. It's hard not to do it. Everyone's looking at you, waiting for you to make the call. And I don't want to stop being an EMT. I like helping people. Especially people who can be saved. Those people – they need me. I can't stop helping them just because there are some out there who... who cheated. Who used me to cheat."

"Where does this all come from?" Laura asked, hearing her own voice surprisingly soft. She had this sense of Paul like he was a wounded animal. A creature in pain. It was written throughout every note of his voice. There was a deep trauma in his words, a horrible conflict between the man who wanted to do good and the one who believed that some people needed to die. "When did you start thinking that these people needed to die – at your own hands?"

"The guilt got too much for me," he said, his face twisting a little involuntarily. He looked like he was holding back tears. It was a strangely tender look, for a man who had just killed three people and tried to beat her unconscious. "I couldn't take it anymore. I just kept thinking about those people, walking around out there with lives they weren't supposed to have. All the ripple effect from that. The people they could hurt, the ways they could cause other problems. It's like... it's like time travel."

"Time travel?" Nate asked. Laura blinked, hearing her own surprise reflected in Nate's voice.

"You ever watch one of those movies where they talk about how going back in time is so dangerous?" Paul asked. He tilted his head up to look at them both, his voice soft. He was a good talker. A storyteller. Laura found herself hanging on his next word, waiting for the revelation that would explain it all. "If you change just one thing, it could ripple out and change everything else. Like, if you step on a butterfly, then when you come back to your own time, you could find out the whole world has ended."

"What you feel is that the people you resuscitated could be changing the natural order of things, just by being alive?" Laura asked, choosing her words carefully to not make it sound like she was laughing at him. "That there's a set path the world should be on, and these people are throwing it off?"

"Right," Paul said, and again he had that way about him – it almost made her feel like she should be girlishly happy to have understood him, to have him praise her for it. "I couldn't let it go on. I had to put right the mistakes I made."

"Are you one of those mistakes yourself, Paul?" Nate asked, his voice quiet. When Paul stared at him for a moment, Nate shifted, opening the closed file he'd had sitting in front of him all this time. "We didn't find anything on your record in terms of criminal behavior. But I did find your medical records, and they're interesting, aren't they?"

Paul swallowed, looking down at the table as if ashamed. "You found out about the crash."

"I haven't seen this report," Laura said, which was a lie, but a convenient one. "Why don't you fill me in? Tell me about this crash."

Paul shifted, swallowing again. "It was when I was a kid," he said, his voice hoarse for a moment, like it was a lump in his throat he was trying to swallow down. "I was in the car with my mom."

"She was driving?" Laura said. It wasn't really a question, because obviously if he was a kid then he couldn't have been the one behind the wheel. But she said it to prompt him to talk. To fill in more details.

"She wasn't doing anything wrong," Paul said. There was a trace of the child in his voice, a kind of railing cry against the unfairness of the world. "She was just driving. This other car came out of nowhere and hit us. It wasn't her fault."

"What happened then?" Laura asked.

"She died." Paul said the two words with a kind of cut-off choking sob, like it was too hard to say more. Like he was going to carry on but couldn't. He was still stubbornly staring at his hands, or maybe the table beyond them. So many years had passed, and he was still carrying so much grief about it. Still struggling to bear it. Laura felt, somewhere in the back of her mind, a wrenching pain on his behalf. The pain of a child losing his mother – it almost didn't bear thinking about.

But for the rest of her, in the front of her mind, Laura knew what he'd done. The pain he had caused to other families. And no amount of sympathy would make up for that.

"What about you?" Nate asked, taking the top page out of the file and turning it around, placing it on the table in front of Paul. "What about your injuries?"

Paul nodded, but there was an almost mutinous look on his face. "You already know."

"Tell me," Laura said, still pretending she had no idea what he was about to reveal.

Paul made a grimace, moving his hands to his chest, like it was physically painful for him to talk about it. To admit the truth.

"I died," he said. "But they brought me back to life. They brought me back, and not her."

And there it was – the crux of it.

"You had all this extra time," Laura said, leaning forward in her chair. "Why shouldn't other people get the chance to have that, too? Why are you the only one who gets it?"

"I shouldn't have had it," Paul burst out, and when he looked up at them both again there were tears openly and silently streaming down his face. "It wasn't right! I should have died with her. And all I've done with that extra time is make it worse. I kept saving them and they shouldn't have survived either. It was Veronica who made me see. And then I saw how all of them were supposed to have died. Their time was up! You don't get more time! You don't!"

"You only went after your own patients," Nate said. "Why is that? Why not just look into the records and take out anyone who survived something like this? Why not go to a survivor's help group and plant a bomb? Why do it this way?"

"Because I was the one who made these mistakes, and I have to fix them," Paul said. His voice was raw with emotion, with utter conviction. It was clear to Laura that everything he was saying was as real to him as undisputable fact. "That was what I wanted to do. Fix every mistake I made, and then fix myself last. I was going to find them all. Start here and then go on the run, maybe. Track down the ones who left or moved. I didn't want to be cruel. I gave them time to think about it. To realize what was happening and deal with it. And then I set the platforms to break their necks. It… it was supposed to be fast. I know I messed up a couple of times, but – don't you see? It's because I'm wrong. I'm not meant to be here. Everything I do – it's always going to be wrong!"

Laura watched him, the war between compassion and hard-faced justice still ongoing inside her head. He was so damaged, so traumatized. Ever since he was a little boy, he had carried this awful guilt. Then he'd started saving people, doing something good with his life. And yet that trauma had twisted it, made it into something that caused him even more guilt. It wasn't totally his fault. He'd obviously needed mental health care, interventions that had never happened. He had grown up with a weight that had mutated and twisted everything around him.

But ultimately, he was still the one who had taken that decision to end someone else's life, even knowing what it was like to lose someone you loved. And no amount of trauma could ever condone that.

"How did you set up the platforms?" Laura asked. "They're fairly sophisticated, but I didn't see any hint of building work, or anything related in your work history."

"I learned it," he said, with just the tiniest inflection of pride. "I didn't have a clue how to do it, so I spent a lot of time online working it out. I had to make a lot of test runs before I knew they worked. I even set one up at home for a bit, not far off the ground, to see if it would work with my weight."

"What about the supplies?" Nate asked. "We've had a chance to look over your bank records briefly, but I didn't see any mention of a building supply company."

"I used false names," he said. "Paid in cash at the sites. I went to different places each time, gave them different fake IDs if they asked for them. I just picked up a bit here and there. Nothing to raise anyone's suspicion."

He'd been so careful, Laura thought. And he'd been caught anyway. She was proud of that herself, proud that they'd managed to put all of the pieces together and bring him in. It was good work.

But there was something nagging at her. He'd been so careful, and now he was just spilling everything like it was nothing to him. He was emotional, yes, but he wasn't even trying to hide any of it. It was pouring out of him so easily, without them having to force it.

Laura said nothing for a moment. She picked up a piece of paper and wrote something quickly on it: *stay quiet*. Passing it across to Nate without setting it at an angle where Paul would be able to read it, she then glanced at her watch and pretended to be studying the files she had set in front of herself before flipping the folder closed.

It was all for show. A test. She wanted to know if her theory was correct.

Nate did as he was told, even following her lead. He closed the file he had in front of him as well, placing the medical record back inside it. Then he glanced at her, not moving or saying anything else, like he was waiting for her to be finished.

And it worked.

"I had to be careful with buying the clocks, too," Paul said, unprompted. "I knew they were on sale here, but after I bought the first one in person, I found out they sold them online as well. Then I just had to use the fake IDs, put in different names and delivery addresses. I even had one delivered to the hospital."

"You're stalling us," Laura said, immediately.

Paul stared at her, his eyes blinking and his mouth moving in a kind of unspoken stutter before he found his voice again. "What?"

"You're stalling us." It was a clear statement, not a question. She already knew that she was right. "You have another victim on a platform somewhere right now, don't you?"

Paul continued to only stare at her, as if he was somehow shocked by what she was saying. Laura wasn't buying a single second of it. He was only trying to keep the delay going. Keep them in the room, so they weren't out there, investigating. Stopping his final victim from falling to their death.

"Where?" Laura snapped, leaning across the table towards him, her words harsh as a slap. "Where are they?"

Slowly, so slowly at first, she thought she might be imagining it, Paul's expression changed.

He wasn't crying any longer.

He was smiling.

"I'm not going to tell you," he said. "It doesn't matter what you to do me or what you threaten me with. Or what kind of deal you tell me I can get with a judge. I won't tell you where they are now."

"How much time do they have left?" Laura asked, even though she knew there was little hope he was going to answer it straight.

"I won't tell you," Paul said again, still smiling that odd smile, that little look of victory that he was still going to get one more of his 'mistakes' crossed off his list.

Laura slammed her hand on the table and stood, making a dash for the door of the interview room.

He wasn't going to tell them a thing – and if she didn't figure this out fast, one more person was going to die in spite of all their success.

She shouted out as she ran down the hall, calling for any detective available to follow her before it was too late.

CHAPTER THIRTY THREE

Laura rummaged through the evidence boxes on Paul Payne's kitchen counter frantically, trying to find something, anything, that would trigger a vision. She needed something pivotal – something that would be strong enough to tell her what she needed to know. It was as though the local cops going through Paul Payne's apartment had started just bagging up every single thing in sight without discrimination.

"Laura?" Nate asked, approaching her with a worried tone. She didn't look up to catch his expression. She had a feeling she knew what it would look like, anyway. Like she was being crazy. "What are you doing?"

"I need something," Laura said. She glanced across the room. The two locals who had been resting near the doorframe, watching her with equally concerned looks, suddenly realized they had something important to do in another room and disappeared, leaving her alone with Nate. "I told you. If I touch something, it can make the vision come on. I need to see."

"Are you still doing this?" Nate asked. He sighed. "Laura, we really need to figure this out. Maybe instead of just touching things we should actually be *looking* at them. You know, for clues."

"Here!" Laura said triumphantly, pulling out a slim laptop from the bottom of the box. The cops had evidently put it in to be taken to the lab and analyzed by their own techs. They didn't have time for that. By the time anyone even got access to it, it would probably be several days too late.

She opened the evidence bag, pulling the top seal apart with a flourish.

"Wait!" Nate said, reaching out and catching hold of her arm. Laura tensed, but it was fine. He'd grabbed the sleeve of her jacket. The aura of death didn't come out to choke her. "Don't touch that! You're not wearing gloves!"

"I know," Laura said. And it probably didn't make any difference anyway. Procedure was procedure, but she doubted they would need fingerprints to prove who this laptop belonged to or who had used it. Paul's login details, his own personal files, would be all over it.

She pulled her arm out of Nate's grasp and grabbed hold of the laptop, the one he must have used to make online purchases and perform searches and do so much related to his plans, and she felt a sickening but reassuring stab of pain in her head at the same time.

"Laura, what are-!"

Laura was looking at a woman, looking at her straight on. They were in a basement, she thought immediately. There was something about it. The bare wall behind her, the concrete floor underneath. The lightbulb that was unlit nearby, hanging from the ceiling without any kind of shade. And the darkness. It was dark there, so dim Laura could only just make out enough of the details to name them.

She was bound and gagged, just like the others. Her arms as well as her hands, like Lincoln Ware, so she couldn't struggle at all. She was weeping, eyes blackened by mascara. The timer on her chest was counting down.

Laura did the math quickly, taking in the time shown on the clock and how long was left on the timer. This woman was going to die at eight in the evening. She was heaving for breath, panicking, her eyes constantly moving like she was searching for some kind of hope.

There was none.

"You doing? You know you're breaking protocol! Come on!"

Laura looked at Nate, his words oddly disjointed in her memory now even though he must have said the whole sentence without pause. She fought to breathe for a moment, feeling it was over: she'd done it. At last, she'd managed to trigger a vision that actually helped.

But how much had it helped?

"I saw it," she said, dropping the laptop back into the evidence bag on the kitchen counter, almost stammering in her rush to get the words out. "I saw where she is."

"What?" Nate said, his eyes wide, huge. "Where?"

"A basement, I think," Laura said. She pressed her hand against her forehead. "Definitely a basement. Underground. It had that feeling to it. Bare brick walls and concrete floors. Maybe a bit of an older property, the kind that hasn't been refurbished and made pretty. And it was big, I think."

"A big, old basement," Nate said, looking at her like she was talking in tongues. Maybe, as far as he was concerned, she was.

"Just let me think," Laura said. She hesitated, then called out. "Hey! Local guys – are you still there?"

There was a few moments' pause before the two cops she had seen earlier reappeared in the doorway. They were both wearing gloves, and one of them was still putting a framed photograph into an evidence bag. They really were bagging up everything. They were young, maybe inexperienced.

"Ma'am?" one of them asked.

"How good is your local knowledge?" Laura asked.

"I don't know," the one who had already spoken said, glancing at his colleague. "Pretty good?"

"What about when it comes to real estate?"

They both shrugged. "There's a guy on our team whose brother is in real estate."

"Good," Laura said. "Call him, now, and hand the phone to me."

She said the words with such a snap to them that they both immediately complied, digging out their cell phones. The one who got there first quickly stretched out his hand, and Laura grabbed it as the dial tone rang out.

"Hey, Tony."

"Not Tony," Laura replied. The voice sounded somewhat familiar, though she couldn't quite place it. "This is FBI Agent Laura Frost. Your colleague just dialed you up for me. I need to speak to a real estate expert, and I'm told you're related to one."

"Yeah, my brother," the officer replied. "Do you want me to bring him to the precinct? He should be just finishing up at work, he's usually there late."

Laura checked her watch. It was almost seven. Damnit. All that time they'd spent on Paul – bringing him in, getting his history and details sent through, preparing an interview strategy. They'd been playing into his hands the whole time. They had hardly any time left to find her.

"We'll go to him," Laura said. "Wait – your voice. You were the one who knew where to find the barn, on the radio?"

"Yes, ma'am."

"Then get to thinking while I'm driving over to your brother's office. Call him and tell him to stay there, and to look up any properties he knows of either on the market or abandoned that would have a large basement space. Unfurnished, bare walls and concrete floor. Got that?"

"Yes, ma'am."

Laura hung up the phone, throwing it at the officer who had dialed for her, and cocked her head at Nate to indicate he should follow her as she dashed back outside to the car.

***

179

"We haven't got a choice," Laura said, grabbing one of the three pieces of paper off the table. "We have to go, and we have to go now."

"I still don't like splitting up," Nate growled, but his words were falling on deaf ears. He took one of the other pages reluctantly, which left just one behind.

"You'll have to cover the other one," Laura said, looking at the officer whose help had brought them this far. His nametag read McCoy. "Your partner is still in the car?"

"Yes, ma'am," he said, taking the last sheet smartly. "We'll get there as soon as we can."

"Make sure you do," Laura said, but then thought better of her brash instruction. "And be careful. We have the guy in custody, but that doesn't mean there won't be danger around – especially if this is an abandoned property. Who knows what kind of repair it might be in?"

"Right," he said, and then all three of them were heading for the door, leaving McCoy's brother to watch them go with a bemused look on his face.

The man had come through in a big way. He'd found them a list of properties by the time they arrived, and Laura had been able to use the photographs to narrow it down. But it wasn't clear enough. Basements with brick walls and concrete floors – they weren't exactly uncommon.

She thought she'd picked out the right one. But she wasn't sure enough to risk a woman's life. That was why she was getting into the car alone, speeding off towards the property she thought fit best while Nate requisitioned the realtor's car and McCoy went off in the other direction.

Three locations. Only three. And she had to hope to God that the realtor actually had the details of all the properties in Atlanta that did fit the bill, because if he didn't, they were probably on a wild goose chase.

It felt like an absolute lifetime and also no time at all before her heart-racing drive through the darkening streets had her pulling up at the address her GPS indicated. She didn't bother parking properly, simply slamming on the brakes and jumping out of the car. She saw the time on the car's display before she shut it off. There were only a handful of minutes before eight. She didn't have any time to lose.

She threw herself into the front door, hearing a groan of complaint from the wood. She didn't have the keys. The realtor hadn't been selling the property himself, just knew where to find the details online. They didn't have time to wait for the keys. It was now or never.

Laura stepped back from the door, nursing an aching shoulder already, and drew her gun. She fired at the lock, then again until the force of the blow coupled with the location made it move on its hinges, telling her she'd done it.

She pushed through, leaving this door open in her wake as well as she ran into the house.

It was old, and big, and very dark. There were no streetlights shining in further than the two front rooms of the house, and the rest was plunged into blackness. Laura fumbled to grab her flashlight, remembering the floor plan she'd seen on the records. She finally got it turned on just as she reached the basement door, down the hall where she'd expected, and wrenched it open.

She clattered down the stairs, then stopped. It was huge down here. There were two doors leading down, she remembered – one from outside, one from inside. And the whole footprint was bigger than her entire apartment plus room for another. There were stone columns spaced throughout, holding everything up, and old storage racks, and sheets hanging where someone had started renovating but never finished...

Laura could hear her own breath panting, her own blood pounding in her ears. She could only see where the beam of light from her flashlight hit. Where was she? Was Laura in the wrong place?

She darted around a storage rack only to see nothing promising ahead. To the left, though, a sheet hung. Laura caught her breath. She hated this. Hated the way this felt like a horror movie. Like something was about to jump out at her.

She heard something and froze.

It came again.

A sob. A woman's sob.

Laura ran in the direction of the sound, pushing the sheet out of her way. There, at the far end of the basement – there she was! She was standing on the platform, attached to the wall itself beside a stepladder, and the timer on her chest –

Sixty seconds.

Laura dropped her gun in her panic, knowing she needed a hand free. Nothing else mattered, not for the next minute – she had to get up there – she grabbed the stepladder, found it unstable, the legs not set out properly, not balanced.

Fifty seconds until the platform gave way. It wasn't enough. She couldn't get up there. Laura thought fast, dragging the stepladder away from the wall and moving it, repositioning it at the end of the platform. There was clearance between them.

Forty seconds. Laura kicked out the legs desperately, getting them to lock into place. There wasn't even time to test that it was set up properly. She climbed onto the first step, and it held her weight. Thirty seconds. The woman was sobbing desperately, making high-pitched sounds behind the gag, like she was trying to scream. Laura climbed the rest of the way to the top.

Twenty seconds. She was shorter than Paul Payne, couldn't reach as far as he could. The end of the platform was right in front of her body, the woman standing just a little way beyond. Fifteen. The platform would drop, and even though it would drop onto the stepladder, Laura didn't know if it was enough. There would still be a fall. Not enough to break her neck. Maybe enough to choke her.

Ten seconds. Laura had no more time to think. She lunged, throwing her body weight forward. She grabbed her by the legs, getting her own feet balanced on the wooden platform, standing –

The timer hit zero and there was a sickening lurch as the platform gave way –

Then another one as it hit the ladder, making Laura struggle to retain her balance, holding onto the woman desperately, and then…

She steadied herself and took a breath.

"Okay," she said. She didn't know whether she was trying to calm down the sobs of the woman she was holding in her arms, or trying to reassure herself, counteract the adrenaline making her feel like she was on fire. "Okay. Just hold still a moment. I'm going to cut the ropes, and we can climb down together."

CHAPTER THIRTY FOUR

Laura looked up, as if she'd sensed him coming somehow, just at the moment that Nate stepped into the basement. He had to duck his head to get through the doorway and hunched all the way down the stairs as if he was afraid of hitting his head. It was only when he joined her, standing next to the seat she had found on an upturned crate, that he straightened up.

And he said nothing.

Laura looked at him, watched his face as he took it all in. The basement. The ropes. The platform, which was still supported on the ladder, everything preserved as much as possible for scene of crime photography.

"It's…" he said. Then he stopped. There were only a few other people down here: the photographers had to finish their job before the other professionals could move in and start interacting with the environment, dusting things for prints, bagging up evidence, and all the rest. They were isolated enough in the space within the large basement that they could talk freely – but it seemed that he didn't want to.

"It's exactly how I described it?" Laura suggested, thinking he was having a problem with admitting it. Strangely, she felt calm. Calmer than she had in a long while. Maybe because this was it – the moment of truth. He couldn't avoid it any longer. He would have to see that she was serious about her abilities.

There was a long pause.

"Yeah," Nate said. There was a tone in his voice like he was still trying to figure out how she'd done that.

"That's because I saw it," she said. "I told you, Nate."

"Yeah." He didn't say anything else. He was still looking out at the scene, his hands on his hips, like he was having a hard time understanding it and needed to keep looking.

And then he looked at her at last, and Laura saw it in his eyes. He believed her. He did.

But there was something else, something she couldn't quite fully define.

Fear?

Mistrust?

Disgust?

Whatever it was, it wasn't positive.

He was looking at her like he was seeing her fully for the first time, and he couldn't believe he'd tolerated her for so long.

"Nate?" she said.

He shook his head. "I'll go finish up with the locals. Make sure Captain Blackford has everything he needs. We should be on a flight out of here within a few hours."

"Nate?" she said again, jumping up from her crate as he started to walk away. She felt a panic bubbling up inside her. Something wasn't right here. She couldn't let him go like this.

"We need to get home," he said. And he was leaving. Not looking at her.

She reached out in desperation and grabbed his arm, her bare hand connecting with his skin, even though she knew she'd feel it. The aura.

Part of her had hoped it would have gone away by now, that feeling it earlier had only been an afterglow, that he was safe now, but –

But there was a pain in her head that hadn't been there before and –

She saw him. The vision was him, only him, black space all around except for behind him – and behind him was only sky, gray and clouded, and it was like looking at the world upside down because it didn't make sense.

Only it did make sense. The worst kind of sense.

His mouth was open, screaming, his eyes wide in a way she had never seen them. Pure and utter terror. His arms and legs flailed in space like he was trying to grab onto something, but there was nothing, nothing at all.

He was falling.

He was falling to his death.

"I think the flights are pretty busy at this time of day," Nate said, shaking her off without meeting her eyes as she snapped back out of the vision. "We'll probably end up having to sit separately. It's fine, though, right? We can get some sleep. I'll let you know when the tickets are booked."

Laura watched him go, her voice failing in her throat, tears springing to her eyes.

He was drifting away from her. He believed, and it made no difference. The vision of death was stronger than ever, more immediate. More precise and real. And she knew what was going to happen to him now.

And he was walking away from her, and she couldn't stop it from happening.

CHAPTER THIRTY FIVE

"Mommy!"

"Hey, baby!" Laura exclaimed, throwing out her arms to catch Lacey as she ran towards her. Laura felt her knee hit the ground and was pretty sure she'd grazed it a little, but it didn't matter.

It felt so good.

She looked up and saw Marcus watching them from inside the car. He nodded slowly, then started the engine back up and pulled away, though she saw his eyes watching them in his mirror the whole while. Until she decided to stop watching him back, because there was something far more important right in front of her.

"Are you ready for our fun weekend?" Laura asked, unhooking the backpack from her little daughter's shoulders so she didn't have to keep carrying it.

"Yeah!" Lacey exclaimed. "Daddy says you're going to take me out for ice cream!"

"Does he?" Laura said. She glanced with a wry smile in the direction that Marcus had gone. He'd still had to do a little something to sabotage her, she supposed, even if it wasn't the serious kind of sabotage. "Are you sure you want ice cream? Even though it's winter?"

"Yeah!" Lacey yelled again, punching her tiny fist in the air. "I always want ice cream!"

Laura laughed a little, kissing her on the forehead before she stood up. "Alright. I'll make you a deal. Let's get inside and get you all set up and unpack your bag, and then we can go out for ice cream together. Okay?"

"Okay, Mommy!" Lacey replied happily, reaching up out of habit and grabbing Laura's hand.

As they walked into the apartment building, Laura felt something lodging inside her chest. Something that was sharp, but also just the right shape to fit there. Like a shard of her heart coming back home to rest. The feel of Lacey's hand inside her own, her daughter's happy chatter, the thought of a whole weekend together.

There was so much going on in her life right now. There was Nate, and the way he had looked at her when he responded to her call and saw the basement exactly as she had described it. Like he believed her, but not like that was a good thing.

And his death, which she now knew was still coming. And she knew how.

There were her visions, and the ways that they were changing. She still didn't understand why or how. She still hadn't found anyone else like herself, anyone who could help her understand it. Teach her the rules. She still felt like she was probably the only person in the world who could do this, and she was so alone with it that it terrified her.

And there was the bottle, always beckoning, just out of sight.

But as determined as she was to slay all of her demons, Laura wasn't going to think about that today. Not as they stepped into the elevator, not as she led Lacey inside her apartment for the first time, and not as she helped her get set up on the second-hand bed Laura had managed to find at a low price in time for the visit.

And definitely not as they headed to the ice cream parlor, smiling and laughing, not caring that it was entirely the wrong season for ice cream.

"What are we going to do tomorrow?" Lacey asked, when she was sitting happily with the spoon in her mouth, kicking her little legs in the air above the ground she couldn't reach from her chair.

"Hmm," Laura said, pretending to think. "How about making a new friend?"

"A new friend?" Lacey repeated, her eyes getting big with excitement. "Who?"

"Well," Laura said, reaching out with a napkin to wipe a drop of ice cream that had melted from Lacey's chin. "I know another little girl who is about your age. She's living with her uncle right now, and we thought the two of you might like to spend some time together. What do you think? A playdate?"

Lacey thought about it, already grinning. "Does she have a pony?"

Laura laughed. "I don't think she has a real pony. But I bet you can play with some toy ponies if you ask nicely."

"Okay," Lacey said, shrugging her tiny shoulders effortlessly. Laura smiled, brushing her blonde hair back over her shoulder before she managed to drip more ice cream onto it.

Tomorrow, she could kill two birds with one stone: spend time with Lacey, and also help Chris with Amy, make sure she was settling in fine. They had weekends, after all, now. Every weekend from now until forever, stretching out into the distance like beacons, showing Laura the way to keep her life on track and be happy again.

But for today, it was all about her daughter. Laura laughed at Lacey as she missed her mouth entirely with a spoonful of melted ice cream and dropped it on her dress, reaching over to clean it up.

"After this, let's go home," Laura said, and when Lacey nodded okay, a warmth settled into her heart that had been missing for far, far too long.

And even the thought of all the things that threatened to come and take it away couldn't chill it again – not today.

NOW AVAILABLE!

ALREADY DEAD
(A Laura Frost FBI Suspense Thriller—Book 5)

A new serial killer leaves a creepy signature at each crime scene: a burning candle. Psychic—and FBI Special Agent—Laura Frost must unearth why. But will her psychic vision lead her astray?

"A MASTERPIECE OF THRILLER AND MYSTERY. Blake Pierce did a magnificent job developing characters with a psychological side so well described that we feel inside their minds, follow their fears and cheer for their success. Full of twists, this book will keep you awake until the turn of the last page."
--Books and Movie Reviews, Roberto Mattos (re Once Gone)

ALREADY DEAD (A Laura Frost FBI Suspense Thriller) is book #5 in a long-anticipated new series by #1 bestseller and USA Today bestselling author Blake Pierce, whose bestseller Once Gone (a free download) has received over 1,000 five star reviews. The series begins with ALREADY GONE (Book #1).

FBI Special Agent and single mom Laura Frost, 35, is haunted by her talent: a psychic ability which she refuses to face and which she keeps secret from her colleagues. While Laura gets obscured glimpses of what the killer may do next, she must decide whether to trust her confusing gift—or her investigative work.

As a string of bodies turns up, abandoned in increasingly public places, the FBI notes that they all have something in common: a single, burning candle at the scene of the crime. Is he playing a sick game?

Laura must decode the riddle: what does the fire mean? What drives him? And, most importantly, who is next?

A page-turning and harrowing crime thriller featuring a brilliant and tortured FBI agent, the LAURA FROST series is a startlingly fresh mystery, rife with suspense, twists and turns, shocking revelations, and driven by a breakneck pace that will keep you flipping pages late into the night.

Book #6 (ALREADY TAKEN) is also available!

Blake Pierce

Blake Pierce is the USA Today bestselling author of the RILEY PAGE mystery series, which includes seventeen books. Blake Pierce is also the author of the MACKENZIE WHITE mystery series, comprising fourteen books; of the AVERY BLACK mystery series, comprising six books; of the KERI LOCKE mystery series, comprising five books; of the MAKING OF RILEY PAIGE mystery series, comprising six books; of the KATE WISE mystery series, comprising seven books; of the CHLOE FINE psychological suspense mystery, comprising six books; of the JESSIE HUNT psychological suspense thriller series, comprising nineteen books; of the AU PAIR psychological suspense thriller series, comprising three books; of the ZOE PRIME mystery series, comprising six books; of the ADELE SHARP mystery series, comprising thirteen books; of the EUROPEAN VOYAGE cozy mystery series, comprising six books (and counting); of the new LAURA FROST FBI suspense thriller, comprising four books (and counting); of the new ELLA DARK FBI suspense thriller, comprising six books (and counting); of the A YEAR IN EUROPE cozy mystery series, comprising nine books (and counting); of the AVA GOLD mystery series, comprising three books (and counting); and of the RACHEL GIFT mystery series, comprising three books (and counting).

An avid reader and lifelong fan of the mystery and thriller genres, Blake loves to hear from you, so please feel free to visit www.blakepierceauthor.com to learn more and stay in touch.

BOOKS BY BLAKE PIERCE

RACHEL GIFT MYSTERY SERIES
HER LAST WISH (Book #1)
HER LAST CHANCE (Book #2)
HER LAST HOPE (Book #3)

AVA GOLD MYSTERY SERIES
CITY OF PREY (Book #1)
CITY OF FEAR (Book #2)
CITY OF BONES (Book #3)

A YEAR IN EUROPE
A MURDER IN PARIS (Book #1)
DEATH IN FLORENCE (Book #2)
VENGEANCE IN VIENNA (Book #3)
A FATALITY IN SPAIN (Book #4)
SCANDAL IN LONDON (Book #5)
AN IMPOSTOR IN DUBLIN (Book #6)
SEDUCTION IN BORDEAUX (Book #7)
JEALOUSY IN SWITZERLAND (Book #8)
A DEBACLE IN PRAGUE (Book #9)

ELLA DARK FBI SUSPENSE THRILLER
GIRL, ALONE (Book #1)
GIRL, TAKEN (Book #2)
GIRL, HUNTED (Book #3)
GIRL, SILENCED (Book #4)
GIRL, VANISHED (Book 5)
GIRL ERASED (Book #6)

LAURA FROST FBI SUSPENSE THRILLER
ALREADY GONE (Book #1)
ALREADY SEEN (Book #2)
ALREADY TRAPPED (Book #3)
ALREADY MISSING (Book #4)

EUROPEAN VOYAGE COZY MYSTERY SERIES
MURDER (AND BAKLAVA) (Book #1)
DEATH (AND APPLE STRUDEL) (Book #2)

CRIME (AND LAGER) (Book #3)
MISFORTUNE (AND GOUDA) (Book #4)
CALAMITY (AND A DANISH) (Book #5)
MAYHEM (AND HERRING) (Book #6)

ADELE SHARP MYSTERY SERIES
LEFT TO DIE (Book #1)
LEFT TO RUN (Book #2)
LEFT TO HIDE (Book #3)
LEFT TO KILL (Book #4)
LEFT TO MURDER (Book #5)
LEFT TO ENVY (Book #6)
LEFT TO LAPSE (Book #7)
LEFT TO VANISH (Book #8)
LEFT TO HUNT (Book #9)
LEFT TO FEAR (Book #10)
LEFT TO PREY (Book #11)
LEFT TO LURE (Book #12)
LEFT TO CRAVE (Book #13)

THE AU PAIR SERIES
ALMOST GONE (Book#1)
ALMOST LOST (Book #2)
ALMOST DEAD (Book #3)

ZOE PRIME MYSTERY SERIES
FACE OF DEATH (Book#1)
FACE OF MURDER (Book #2)
FACE OF FEAR (Book #3)
FACE OF MADNESS (Book #4)
FACE OF FURY (Book #5)
FACE OF DARKNESS (Book #6)

A JESSIE HUNT PSYCHOLOGICAL SUSPENSE SERIES
THE PERFECT WIFE (Book #1)
THE PERFECT BLOCK (Book #2)
THE PERFECT HOUSE (Book #3)
THE PERFECT SMILE (Book #4)
THE PERFECT LIE (Book #5)
THE PERFECT LOOK (Book #6)

THE PERFECT AFFAIR (Book #7)
THE PERFECT ALIBI (Book #8)
THE PERFECT NEIGHBOR (Book #9)
THE PERFECT DISGUISE (Book #10)
THE PERFECT SECRET (Book #11)
THE PERFECT FAÇADE (Book #12)
THE PERFECT IMPRESSION (Book #13)
THE PERFECT DECEIT (Book #14)
THE PERFECT MISTRESS (Book #15)
THE PERFECT IMAGE (Book #16)
THE PERFECT VEIL (Book #17)
THE PERFECT INDISCRETION (Book #18)
THE PERFECT RUMOR (Book #19)

CHLOE FINE PSYCHOLOGICAL SUSPENSE SERIES
NEXT DOOR (Book #1)
A NEIGHBOR'S LIE (Book #2)
CUL DE SAC (Book #3)
SILENT NEIGHBOR (Book #4)
HOMECOMING (Book #5)
TINTED WINDOWS (Book #6)

KATE WISE MYSTERY SERIES
IF SHE KNEW (Book #1)
IF SHE SAW (Book #2)
IF SHE RAN (Book #3)
IF SHE HID (Book #4)
IF SHE FLED (Book #5)
IF SHE FEARED (Book #6)
IF SHE HEARD (Book #7)

THE MAKING OF RILEY PAIGE SERIES
WATCHING (Book #1)
WAITING (Book #2)
LURING (Book #3)
TAKING (Book #4)
STALKING (Book #5)
KILLING (Book #6)

RILEY PAIGE MYSTERY SERIES

ONCE GONE (Book #1)
ONCE TAKEN (Book #2)
ONCE CRAVED (Book #3)
ONCE LURED (Book #4)
ONCE HUNTED (Book #5)
ONCE PINED (Book #6)
ONCE FORSAKEN (Book #7)
ONCE COLD (Book #8)
ONCE STALKED (Book #9)
ONCE LOST (Book #10)
ONCE BURIED (Book #11)
ONCE BOUND (Book #12)
ONCE TRAPPED (Book #13)
ONCE DORMANT (Book #14)
ONCE SHUNNED (Book #15)
ONCE MISSED (Book #16)
ONCE CHOSEN (Book #17)

MACKENZIE WHITE MYSTERY SERIES
BEFORE HE KILLS (Book #1)
BEFORE HE SEES (Book #2)
BEFORE HE COVETS (Book #3)
BEFORE HE TAKES (Book #4)
BEFORE HE NEEDS (Book #5)
BEFORE HE FEELS (Book #6)
BEFORE HE SINS (Book #7)
BEFORE HE HUNTS (Book #8)
BEFORE HE PREYS (Book #9)
BEFORE HE LONGS (Book #10)
BEFORE HE LAPSES (Book #11)
BEFORE HE ENVIES (Book #12)
BEFORE HE STALKS (Book #13)
BEFORE HE HARMS (Book #14)

AVERY BLACK MYSTERY SERIES
CAUSE TO KILL (Book #1)
CAUSE TO RUN (Book #2)
CAUSE TO HIDE (Book #3)
CAUSE TO FEAR (Book #4)
CAUSE TO SAVE (Book #5)

CAUSE TO DREAD (Book #6)

KERI LOCKE MYSTERY SERIES
A TRACE OF DEATH (Book #1)
A TRACE OF MUDER (Book #2)
A TRACE OF VICE (Book #3)
A TRACE OF CRIME (Book #4)
A TRACE OF HOPE (Book #5)

Made in United States
North Haven, CT
29 August 2022

23437830R00114